Storm Tossed Moon

Maggie Craig

ISBN 978-1-7392757-1-6

Cover design by Cathy Helms of Avalon Graphics.

For Ria and Alexander,
with much love,
and thanks for all their kindnesses,
(especially the writing nook, the mounting block – and Savannah.)

Acknowledgements

My grateful thanks to the following people:

my editor, Eleanor Leese, for much appreciated brainstorming and editorial input. Eleanor is both an editor and an author, writing as Ellie Darkins.

Inverness Outlanders, not forgetting Hamish, for their warm friendship and generous support.

Highlanders 4 Hire, for putting on a display of sword-fighting on a gloriously warm and sunny March day and helpfully answering my follow-up questions.

Steven Kerr, Librarian of the Royal College of Surgeons of Edinburgh and Dr Jacqueline Cahif, College Archivist, for fascinating and inspiring information held in the College Library.

The Open University, for creating and teaching their course A218,
Medicine and Society in Europe, 1500-1930.

Storm over Scotland

Storm Tossed Moon is the third in the *Storm over Scotland* series. If you would like to read from the very first moment when the two very different worlds of Miss Christian Rankeillor and Captain Robert Catto collided or just want to refresh your memory, here is a brief summary of the first two books.

Gathering Storm

Edinburgh, Yuletide 1743: Redcoat officer Robert Catto would rather be anywhere else on earth than Scotland. Seconded back from the wars in Europe to captain the city's Town Guard, he fears his covert mission to assess the strength of the Jacobite threat will force him to confront the past he tries so hard to forget. Christian Rankeillor and her surgeon-apothecary father are hiding a Jacobite agent with a price on his head in Edinburgh Royal Infirmary: a hanging offence.

As they pick their way through a labyrinth of intrigue, Robert Catto and Christian Rankeillor are increasingly drawn to each other and increasingly forced to question their own deeply-held political beliefs and convictions: and danger lurks in the flickering shadows around every comer.

Dance to the Storm

In a snow-swept Edinburgh, Robert Catto and Christian Rankeillor face each other across a divide no bridge can cross. She's in deadly danger: not least from him. His investigations have turned up compelling evidence of a real threat posed to the House of Hanover by a plan to restore the House of Stuart to the British throne.

Robert Catto always does his duty. It's all he's ever had to hold on to: but he's in danger too. Forced to confront his difficult past and a family connection which could call his loyalty to the crown into question, he could be risking the ruin of his military career. Then there's runaway Geordie Smart, his sister Alice and young African boy Joshua. All three have been cruelly treated by bored and vicious members of the local gentry. Robert Catto and Christian Rankeillor stand ready to help all three young people but the law is not on their side.

How is Robert Catto to reconcile doing his duty with his feelings for Christian Rankeillor? How is she to balance her commitment to her father, their friends and the Stuart Cause with her feelings for Robert Catto? Especially when each day that passes sees them falling ever more deeply in love with each other.

The story continues in *Storm Tossed Moon* and will be concluded in *On the Wings of the Storm.*

Chapter 1

Geordie's Smart's eyelids were fluttering. 'Any moment now,' Christian Rankeillor said softly. 'Stand by, Joshua.'

The African boy nodded. 'At the ready, miss.'

She was kneeling beside Geordie's head, where he lay on his front on the mattress Betty had helped her lay in front of the library fire yesterday evening. That seemed like a long time ago now. So much had happened since.

Joshua was sitting on a footstool on the other side of the mattress, poised to move when Christian gave the word. She had told him she expected Geordie would want to ease nature once he came round from the sleeping draught she had given him last night. She'd already been through to the shop, chilly in the late December morning, to fetch the screen behind which she and her father examined their patients who needed more than to simply buy physic. Betty had brought in a chamber pot and placed it behind the screen.

Christian had laid out some other things on the seat of one of the armchairs which flanked the fire. A china cup holding ground willow bark mixed with water. A wooden bowl with a little porridge in it, milk and salt already added. A spoon to eat it with. She hoped Geordie was going to be hungry. Joshua had already had his porridge, sitting with the rest of the household at the kitchen table.

She had laid an old, well-laundered nightshirt over the arm of the chair. She'd found it at the back of the linen press. It had been Jamie's as a boy, when he had often stayed overnight here in Infirmary Street. *Och, Jamie ... why did you do what you did? Why, Jamie?* She squared her shoulders. She could not think about that now, the dreadful thing Jamie had done.

She glanced across at the fire. Banked in overnight, it was still giving off some warmth, enough light too as the coals and the dross dwindled down to the nest of the grate. 'Although it'll need redding up and reviving soon,' she said, thinking aloud. 'But it'll keep for a wee while.'

Joshua nodded. 'Aye. No' until Geordie's awake. We dinna want to disturb him until we've got him settled again. Then I'll can do the fire for you, miss.'

She threw him a smile across the still not quite awake Geordie. 'Maybe not while you're wearing those fine clothes.'

Joshua looked down at himself. He was wearing dark blue velvet breeches and a fine white linen shirt and neckcloth. The full ruffled cuffs of the shirt spilled over his hands. He made an expression of disgust deep in his throat and tugged at them, as though he wanted to tear them off.

'These are the plainest clothes I have. Miss Charlotte likes to dress me up.'

Studying his bent head with its tight black curls, Christian's breath caught in her throat. He had spoken in a very flat tone of voice but there was a wealth of pain in his words. Like his friend, it seemed he too had suffered some sort of an ordeal at the hands of Charlotte and Cosmo Liddell out at Eastfield in East Lothian yesterday.

Unlike Geordie, Joshua hadn't been flogged. Although Christian was pretty sure something brutal had happened to him too. Something humiliating. She could tell by the way he was finding it difficult to look her in the eye.

Her generous mouth tightened. Damn the Liddells, their arrogance, overweening sense of self-importance and the careless cruelty they had meted out to these two boys. It made her so bloody angry! Made her want to assure Joshua he was never going back to Eastfield. Only she knew she couldn't.

Earlier this morning, in this same room, Robert Catto had held out a spar of hope. *Slaves and indentured servants can be freed.* He had tempered that statement even before he had made it. *Promises made and not kept are worse than promises not made at all.*

Christian settled now for different words, laying a comforting hand on Joshua's arm. 'You got away. You brought Geordie with you. That was such a brave thing to do.'

She saw him bite his lip. He knew better than anyone how precarious his position was, how short-lived his new-found freedom might be. Geordie and his sister Alice were in a very similar position. Born into a coal mining family, they were trapped in perpetual servitude, bound for life to the Liddell family. The prospect of any of them being forced back to Eastfield was unthinkable. Except that it might have to be thought about.

Christian felt a shudder run through her as she thought of what Charlotte Liddell's brother Cosmo and his friends had done to Alice. Those fiends should have to answer for their brutal assault on an innocent young girl. Only they never would. One law for the rich. One law for the poor.

'Twas worse even than that. In this profoundly unfair world, the Liddells had the law on their side when it came to the three young people currently finding shelter in Infirmary Street: and the law was a powerful foe.

It stood now ranged against Christian's father Patrick, herself and their friends. All thanks to Robert Catto, the man who always did his duty. How were they to help Joshua, Geordie and Alice when they might not be able to help themselves?

'Oh,' Joshua said, bursting in with welcome eagerness on her troubled thoughts, 'I think that's Geordie awake now.'

Awake and turning his head from one side to the other, his abundance of golden-haired waves glinting in the dull gleam cast by the fire. 'Joshua,' he said. 'Miss Kirsty.'

'Good morning, Geordie. Are you fit for some breakfast?'

He blinked at her like a solemn owl. 'You've brought me ma breakfast?'

'I have. Do you think you can sit up to eat it?'

She could see the dilemma on the pale young face. He didn't much feel like eating – or moving, probably – but she had brought him his breakfast. Until yesterday he had been the cook boy at the guard-house, serving Robert Catto and any members of the Town Guard on duty with the meals he made for them. Now she was serving him. Overawed he might be but good manners dictated he do as she suggested.

He raised himself up on his hands and arms – and froze midway, gasping with pain. The flogging had lacerated his back, breaking the skin where the cruel leather knots had hit. As one, Christian and Joshua laid gentle hands on his skinny shoulders.

'Take your time,' she said. 'Give yourself a moment.'

'Aye,' Joshua said. 'There's no hurry, Geordie. Gin ye need tae relieve yourself, I'll help you behind the screen. Miss Kirsty will promise tae look away. Tae spare your blushes, like. Is that not right, miss?'

She played along, lifting one hand in front of her eyes, heartened beyond measure by that flash of humour from Joshua. Laughter. Care. Kindness. That was how they would get through all this.

For somehow they had to.

Chapter 2

A few miles away, Charlotte Liddell was also waking up. Stretching, she pushed her legs down the bed. With a piercing shriek, she drew them up again. Her linen sheets were as cold as ice. She was wideawake now, catapulted into the painful awareness that her mouth was dry, her stomach sour and her head aching. Everyone at Eastfield House had drunk themselves into a stupor last night. Both above and below stairs. It wasn't an uncommon occurrence.

She and her brother Cosmo really shouldn't tolerate it from the servants. She'd bawl them out about it today. Just as soon as her head hurt less than it did right now. She reached out one hand to the other side of the big high bed. The sheets were cold there too. She couldn't quite remember if she'd had a bedfellow last night, had only a confused recollection of slurred words and thrashing limbs.

Propping herself up on her elbows, she screeched out a name. 'Joshua!' The young African boy acted as her personal footman. The glorified cupboard which was his bedroom was a few yards along the corridor from her own grand one.

'Where are you, you damned little black slug? Go down to the kitchen right now and get one of those bloody lazy good-for-nothings to come up here immediately. My fire has gone out overnight. Am I to freeze to death?'

Silence. No hurried young footsteps approaching her bedroom door. Nothing.

It took her a minute or two to sit up and prepare to slide her feet and legs down onto the floor. Waiting for her swimming head to settle, she spat out a few filthy words. 'Where are you?' she yelled again. 'I want you in here. Right now! Do you want more of what you got yesterday?'

She smiled, reliving how the boy had been tormented. Seeing again how they had forced him to watch his friend being flogged. All done on her orders. The Smart boy was a runaway from the Eastfield coal mine. He'd got no more than he'd deserved.

Pulling on her wrapper, she stumbled along the corridor to Joshua's bedroom, shrieking for her lady's maid as she went. She stood for a moment blinking at the pallet on the floor which was the boy's bed before the young woman came up behind her. Whirling round, Charlotte slapped her hard across the face. 'Where is he?' she demanded. 'Where has he gone?'

'How should I ken?' the girl asked. 'Were we no' all blootered last night?'

That earned her another slap. 'Ow!' she yelped, rubbing her cheek and casting Charlotte a baleful look.

'Stop whining! Go and get everyone out of their beds! I want this house searched from top to bottom!'

Once the search had established Joshua was indeed gone, Charlotte stood at the open front door of Eastfield House and shrieked some more.

'Bloody hell, Charlotte,' drawled Cosmo, 'give it a rest. My head aches enough as it is.'

'Mine too,' said his friend Arthur Menzies of Edmonstone. In their nightshirts and banyans, both men lay stretched out on two luxurious red velvet sofas. Trimmed with gilded wood, those were set at right angles to each other in the grand entrance lobby of the house. The two men had taken no part in the search for Joshua, leaving that to the servants.

Charlotte had sent one of the footmen to order the chief overseer of the mine to check the outbuilding where the Smart brat had been thrown yesterday afternoon after he'd been flogged. Both men were walking back to the house now. Behind them stood the pithead and the two rows of miners' cottages which faced each other across it. The footman slid off towards the side of the house, heading for the kitchen door. The overseer stopped at the foot of the wide front steps.

'Gone,' he said. 'Nae sign o' him. Ah dinna think he could

have got away on his own. He was gey puggled after he was flogged.'

'Of course he didn't get away on his own!' snapped Charlotte. 'The little black slug must have helped him. Go and look for them!'

'Where?' the overseer demanded. Powerfully built, he folded his beefy arms across his chest and gave Charlotte back look for look. Hostile. Challenging. Knowing. Having the impertinence to come to the front door. All of which led Edmonstone to an inescapable conclusion. She must have coupled with the brute, which surprised him not at all. She had the morals of a farm cat.

She had chosen this man to administer the flogging yesterday. He'd organized the young black's punishment too, stripping the boy naked before bucket after bucket of freezing cold water was flung over him until he was shivering, trembling and distraught. Not that Edmonstone cared. Some were born to suffer.

'They're no' here. So where should I look, mistress?'

'Wherever they've gone, you dolt! Follow their trail! Ask people if they saw them.' She laughed. An unpleasant sound. 'Hard not to notice Joshua.'

Arthur Menzies came upright, swinging his legs over the front of the sofa. 'Charlotte…'

She ignored him, narrowing her eyes. Good God, she must be trying some thinking. Not her strong suit. 'Twas as though an idea was hovering but her claret and brandy clouded brain was struggling to bring it into focus. Didn't stop her from rattling out an order. 'Find out if they went through Musselburgh. You'd better take a horse from the stables.'

Another leer from the man standing at the foot of the front steps. The stables. That must be where he and Charlotte met. Edmonstone could imagine them there, rutting like animals on top of a horse blanket laid on a pile of straw. Rutting like an animal was always Charlotte's preferred style.

Her intimacy with this man clearly entitled him to damn all in her eyes. Certainly not to look at or speak to her the way he was doing now. Only her rage at the dual escape could have prompted her to offer the use of one of the horses to pursue the runaways. An idea Arthur Menzies had to nip in the bud right now. The overseer pre-empted him.

'It was dark when they left. Wha would hae seen them in Musselburgh? How dae ye ken they went there?'

'Don't answer me back! Or I'll have you flogged too!'

The leer gave way to scornful disbelief. It would be a brave man who would agree to flog this man. Or a very foolish one. Everyone at Eastfield feared him: and his vicious fists and feet.

'Charlotte,' Arthur Menzies said again. 'Have you forgotten that we are confined to the house till further notice by the orders of Captain Catto? With no one else allowed to leave the estate? While I'm at it, I believe you were supposed to go to Lady Bruce's house at Leith yesterday. Also on his orders, which you chose to disobey.'

She whirled round to him. 'Disobey?' she repeated, her voice shrill with disbelief. 'His orders? Pray tell, Arthur, from where does the bloody man derive his authority? Who exactly is Captain Robert Catto to command the Liddells?' she demanded, pronouncing each part of that name with vicious sarcasm. Her venom towards the man who bore it was palpable. Clearly Catto had not been tempted by Charlotte's charms. No doubt doubly galling when she'd probably had a wee fancy for him. Anyone in breeches.

He has the authority. From two sources. A confusing idea in many ways. Edmonstone too was struggling to focus his thoughts. Especially about that conundrum. It didn't help that Charlotte was still screaming her head off. Damn the bloody bitch. She was hard work.

'Charlotte,' he said, 'think about this. How would we know where to look for them?'

'Yes, Charlotte,' Cosmo asked. He sat up, looking pleased with himself, 'how would we know that?' He seldom had an original thought in his primped and pampered head but he was quick to parrot someone else's.

Struggling to hold on to his temper, Arthur Menzies walked over to her. 'Why don't we close this door and go through and have some breakfast?' He swung the door shut, paying no heed to the man standing at the foot of the steps. 'Cosmo?'

'Yes. That's the thing to do. Nothing else we can do. Have to bide here for the time being.' He stood up, snapping his fingers at the waiting footman. 'Breakfast. See to it.'

Charlotte's contemptuous gaze washed over her brother and her lover. One of her many lovers, Arthur thought sourly.

'So we should drink coffee and eat eggs and meekly accept that our property has been stolen from us?' She pointed towards herself. 'Some of which property I took it upon myself to reclaim before I was forced to leave Edinburgh. Wrote to Charles Paterson, our damn fool of a lawyer. Told him Robert Catto had been harbouring the Smart girl and her brother. Making him not a fit and proper person to command the Town Guard.'

Arthur Menzies sucked in a breath. 'You did what?'

She hadn't heard him. Instead, she repeated a few of the words she had just uttered. 'The Smart girl and her brother.' The most unpleasant of smiles spread across her face. 'Of course. Where else would they have gone?'

'Charlotte—'

She ignored him. 'I'll have even more to tell Provost Coutts now.'

'What do you mean – *more* to tell him?'

'I wrote to him too,' she said, her face glowing with triumph. 'About Robert Catto. Requiring the bloody man to be immediately dismissed from his post. He ought to be cashiered. Turned out onto the street without a penny.'

On the point of firing back an angry rebuke, Edmonstone stopped short. The stupid little bitch had no idea what was really going on here. Yet somehow her words had struck a chord, made him think twice. About several things.

He had taken Robert Catto at his own valuation after the disaster of Daft Friday when the man had arrested him, Cosmo and the Jacobite agent in the private supper room at the Assembly Rooms in Edinburgh. Moments before, he had watched in disbelief as it instantly became clear the agent and Robert Catto were father and son. Long and bitterly estranged on Catto's side, that too had been crystal clear.

So why had he had taken Catto's word for it that he had subsequently allowed the Jacobite agent to escape, along with Jamie Buchan? That their hostile encounter at the Assembly

Rooms had been mere play-acting? Dragging himself out of the alcohol-induced fog in which he'd spent the last few days, Arthur Menzies saw now how that didn't make sense.

Something else made no bloody sense either. For God's sake, Jamie Buchan had picked up a cushion and told Edmonstone and Cosmo to help him smother Catto, squeeze the last breath out of the man. It had been the Jacobite agent who had stopped them, aided by the surgeon-apothecary's daughter. After which Robert Catto had ordered his brute of a sergeant to give him and Cosmo a kicking, in the place where it hurt most. Even the memory of it brought tears to Edmonstone's eyes.

Why the fuck would Robert Catto then offer him an alliance, as long as he and Cosmo laid low at Eastfield for a while? Had the Town Guard captain played him for a fool? Smarting at the thought – by God, had he not endured enough humiliation on Daft Friday? – he followed Charlotte and Cosmo through to take breakfast.

Shutting out their inane bickering, he made a silent resolution. Stuck though he was here at Eastfield, somehow he would find out where Robert Catto's loyalties truly lay.

'Are you sure, Geordie?' Her arms folded, Christian looked down at him. 'There's no problem about you staying here in the library.'

'I'm sure, Miss Kirsty.' The boy was very pale but she could not miss the look of determination on his face. With Joshua's help, she'd managed to get him into one of the armchairs, two soft pillows behind his back. Joshua had previously helped him into the old nightshirt, also discreetly, behind the screen. Geordie had eaten his porridge, although he'd refused a second helping.

Sitting perched on the edge of the other armchair, Joshua looked anxiously at his friend. 'I'm thinking you should let yourself be advised by Miss Rankeillor, Geordie.'

Geordie closed his eyes for a moment. 'I want to go upstairs.'

Christian and Joshua exchanged a look. However slowly they took the stairs, this was going to hurt. Perhaps she'd made a mistake in telling him there was a hurly bed in the room where his sister Alice was still sleeping. Her plan had been to fetch her down to the library to be reunited with her wee brother and for Geordie to move up to the hurly bed tomorrow or the next day.

'I want to go upstairs,' he said again. He opened his eyes and looked at her where she stood gazing down at him. 'Please, miss.'

Christian unfolded her arms. 'Well, I suppose we'd better get you up there then. Joshua?'

Chapter 3

Christian Rankeillor was opening the door of her house in Infirmary Street in the way Robert Catto had come to expect. Cautiously, as he had impressed on her she must, her slender but capable fingers curled around the edge of the solid wood. The smile which curved her mouth when she saw him was also cautious. Yet it was intimate too. Holding a promise.

That little smile made his heart leap. Made him think of recent pleasures and anticipate future delights. Those much greater delights they had promised each other only this morning. That little smile also made him instantly regret not having scrawled a message and sending it on ahead. *I'll be at the front door this afternoon and I won't be alone. I'll have your father with me. We must be careful not to give anything away.* Despite everything jostling for position inside Catto's head, the secret she and he shared had to remain exactly that.

Over the past weeks he had also grown used to entering this house by its kitchen door and the large physic garden which lay behind it. There was much less chance of being noticed that way, although such an approach did involve vaulting over a few waist-high and chest-high walls. It hadn't seemed appropriate to ask a university professor to do the same. Even if the said professor looked a lot less daunting in a neat tie-wig rather than the tumbling grey curls of the full-bottomed one he'd been wearing the first time he and Catto had met.

His prisoner was an obviously vigorous man in his mid-forties. Patrick Rankeillor had spent the last two days riding back from Glasgow to Edinburgh through the freezing fogs and bone-chilling days of late December. 'Twas not a journey or means of travel to be undertaken by the faint-hearted, nor anyone not in the prime of life.

Over Rankeillor's protests that he had no need of a sedan chair, Catto had ordered one up anyway. Not only to keep the professor's return to his home in Infirmary Street as quiet as possible. Also because he wasn't sure he himself was capable of being civil to the bloody man. Walking with him from one side of Edinburgh to the other, of necessity by a discreet and circuitous route, would have tried his patience to the limit.

He'd needed that brisk walk down closes, through back courts, across gardens and the scramble over the rough stone walls which separated them. He'd had to scale one more to get here to the front of the house. No matter. The physical activity had allowed him to expend some of his pounding frustration and crackling energy. Or so he had to hope. Of all things, what he needed now was a clear head. For Kirsty Rankeillor's sake as much as his own. And her damn father.

It must now be approaching four of the clock, the short winter's day rapidly giving way to the long winter's night. He had delayed long enough after interviewing Rankeillor to allow that to happen, as he had delayed scaling the final wall until the last possible moment. He'd kept watch over it until he spotted the chair and its two caddies approaching along the man-made cavern of Infirmary Street. Grateful for small mercies, he saw he'd timed it right. Few lanterns above doors and to the sides of closes were yet lit, rendering this journey as covert as he could possibly make it.

He had reason to believe the Jacobite plotters were still in disarray after the dramatic events of Daft Friday. Yet in a city with houses and tall tenement lands as tightly packed as they were here in Edinburgh you never knew who might be watching, lurking in the shadows.

Seeing who else was standing on the doorstep, the professor's daughter flung the door wide, her face lighting up with joy. Catto hoped to God her father hadn't noticed the first private little smile directed at the man who had arrested him at the West Port an hour and more before.

'Och, Father, you're home at last! We were afraid you weren't going to make it in time to see in the New Year with us!'

'Into the house,' Catto growled, pre-empting Christian Rankeillor's clear intention of throwing her arms around her father's neck. 'Without delay.' He swung round, taking the black leather valise he was being handed up over the semi-circular stone entrance steps by one of the two caddies who had carried the sedan chair.

'Anything more we can do for ye, Captain?'

'No. After you have stowed the chair away, you may stand down. Not a word to anyone about any of this. Understood?'

He returned their nods of agreement with an inclination of his own head in thanks and dismissal. He was as sure as he could be that the now departing caddies would keep quiet. He had paid them in advance for this hire, adding a florin each to their fee. 'Twas not the silver only which would ensure their silence. They were members of the Edinburgh Town Guard of which he was the acting captain. He might have doubts about the loyalties of some of the guards, but not these two.

Both were foot soldiers in another force, Lord President Duncan Forbes of Culloden's Scotland-wide network of spies, informers and undercover agents. As was Catto's correspondent through in Glasgow. As he was himself. Although he was rather more than a foot soldier.

Patrick Rankeillor responded to his command. 'Of course, young sir. Into the house. Lead the way, Kirsty lass.'

That bloody adjective again. Too many people in Edinburgh used it when they addressed him. *Young sir. Young Captain Catto.* If any of the offenders knew an *Old Captain Catto* he was a Dutchman. He was almost twenty-five years old, for God's sake, his birthday only a few days away, and a battle-hardened veteran of the European Wars.

The detestable adjective also seemed to call his authority here in Edinburgh into question. He could not afford for that to happen. Not when he was walking the bloody tightrope he'd been balancing on since he'd first arrived here a month ago. Not when the situation had grown even more complex. In more ways than one.

Before Christmas, Lord President Duncan Forbes of Culloden had seconded Catto back to Scotland from the wars in Europe, made him acting Captain of Edinburgh's Town Guard. As such, his role was to keep the city's peace and apprehend wrongdoers. His real role was to play the part of a covert Jacobite.

Rumours of armed rebellion in the name of the exiled House of Stuart were beginning to circulate again. Catto's mission was to flush out those who really did hold such seditious views, deluded though he believed all Jacobites to be. Yesterday's men.

So while making sure Edinburgh's peace was kept and the city's gates well guarded, he had subtly presented himself as someone who might be willing to turn a blind eye to political manoeuvrings. He had spent time in the taverns, open but enigmatic. He had raised an eyebrow here, made a brief observation there, and he had listened more than he had spoken.

Discovering the threat might well be real had not been part of his plan. Nor had he expected to fall in love with one of those deluded Jacobites.

Perversely even more irritated by Rankeillor's good manners, he ushered the man into the house and closed the front door behind him. Standing on the black and white chequered floor of the front lobby, father and daughter embraced. Rankeillor's valise in one hand, Catto leant back against the door and waited. He had to allow them this moment of greeting.

The professor still wore his full-skirted riding coat. His daughter wore the practical dark blue dress she'd been wearing early this morning, a freshly laundered white kerchief tucked modestly into the square neck of her bodice. She'd discarded her neat white workaday cap in favour of wearing her hair loose, a few strands pulled back and secured high on the back of her head by a narrow white satin ribbon tied in a bow.

The gleaming waves of her glorious dark hair framed her lovely face and tumbled over her shoulders. She looked as she always did. Fresh and pretty and innocent. Watching them, Catto saw they both had tears in their eyes.

Without warning, an unwanted vision careered onto the stage of the private playhouse in his brain. He was seeing the Rankeillors not greeting but parting – and in the most final parting of all, the one at the foot of the scaffold. There would be tears a-plenty then. Unless he could pull the irons out of the fire and save them from their own folly. Right at this moment, after his interrogation of Rankeillor at the West Port, that seemed an impossible task.

Father and daughter turned as Betty Gilchrist the housekeeper came bustling through from the kitchen, wiping her hands on her apron. Her face too lit up with pleasure when she saw Rankeillor. Must be nice to receive so warm a welcome. Kirsty Rankeillor aside, 'twas not an experience to which Robert Catto was accustomed. Despite what the two of them had become to each other over this Yuletide, he knew her welcome to him was not without its reservations.

Which was vastly to understate the case. The two of them stood on opposite sides of a yawning and ever-widening chasm. How it could ever be bridged he did not know.

'Where is everybody?' he asked, walking forward to set Rankeillor's valise under the high and narrow table set against the back wall of the lobby. Its curved walnut top was polished to a dazzling gleam.

'They're all upstairs,' Christian Rankeillor replied, stepping back from her father to face Catto as he straightened up and turned towards her.

'Including Geordie?'

'Aye.'

Catto frowned. 'He managed the stairs?'

'With help from Joshua and myself.'

Patrick Rankeillor frowned in puzzlement. 'And wha micht Geordie and Joshua be, if you please? And why would this Geordie no' manage the stairs?'

'Your daughter will tell you the whole story later, Professor,' Catto said shortly. 'For now, I require the two of you to accompany me to the library. Madam?' he queried.

'Of course, sir—'

The housekeeper interrupted. 'The maister must hae something tae eat first! There's plenty o' soup left in the pot frae dinner time.'

Catto swung round, looking down his long nose at the little woman. She was more than a foot shorter than him. Thus far neither his height nor his air of command had served to intimidate her. Or get her to hold her tongue. Damn her eyes. 'The soup can wait. I cannot. I have other pressing matters to attend to before the day is over.' He turned back to Rankeillor. 'I require only a few more moments of your time, Professor. For now.'

The housekeeper put her hands on her skinny hips, squaring up to him. 'He's been oot in the cauld for twa days, riding hame fae Glasgow! He's needing fed!'

'Professor?' Catto said, raising one eyebrow in exasperated inquiry.

'Do you go back through to the kitchen, Betty,' Rankeillor urged. 'I took my meridian at an inn in Corstorphine no more than three hours since. I'll no' starve in the meantime.'

The housekeeper cast Catto a hostile look. So much for Christian Rankeillor claiming the wee witch was coming round to him. 'I'll tak your coat,' she said to the head of the household. 'Then at least you'll be a wee bittie mair comfortable. You should tak your riding boots aff too.'

'Later,' Patrick Rankeillor said, unfastening his riding coat and allowing her to slide it off his shoulders.

In one deft movement the housekeeper shook out the heavy bluey-grey woollen coat, swirled it round to fall into folds and laid it over the crook of her elbow. 'Does the library fire need coal, Miss Kirsty?'

'It's fine, Betty. I've not long put a few lumps on.' She smiled at the woman. 'A gey cheerful blaze. Perhaps you could take Captain Catto's coat also?'

Another ferocious look. 'He'd hae tae undo the buttons.'

It was hardly worth him taking his own tan leather horseman's coat off. He did not intend to tarry here. He'd already got plenty of information out of Patrick Rankeillor back at the West Port. More than enough. So he was not quite sure why he decided to comply with Christian Rankeillor's gently-worded suggestion. Perhaps to maintain the veneer of civilized behaviour. Perhaps, in so doing, to keep the dark thoughts at bay.

He undid the buttons of his coat, shrugging out of it so he could hand it over to the housekeeper without her yanking it off him and half strangling him in the process. He wouldn't put it past her. Bloody hell, that had been a foolish thought.

Strangling. Throttling. Hanging. What Rankeillor had already told him – or had been unable to conceal from him – was enough to hang the man. What his daughter had done, hiding a man with a price on his head, giving aid and succour to an enemy of the king, was enough to hang her. Christ, he didn't need those pictures in his head either.

The housekeeper took his coat from him, making some indeterminate noise of disapproval before heading off to the kitchen carrying both garments. Patrick Rankeillor followed her departure with a fond smile before transferring his gaze to Catto. 'She is very loyal to the Rankeillor family. And to this household.'

She's also a royal pain in the arse. And you're a fool, standing there smiling. Can't you see how serious this all is? Can't you see that your life and your house and your sodding household could all come crashing down, sweeping you and your daughter away with it?

Somehow he had to knock all that into Rankeillor's thick skull. Somehow he had to keep the despair and terror of it all out of his own head. He wouldn't be able to function otherwise.

For the moment, he merely indicated that father and daughter should walk ahead of him into the library. Not long since, Christian Rankeillor had flung an impassioned question at him. How were they to get through all of this? He'd told her the only way he knew how. By putting one foot in front of the other and keeping going until they did.

Chapter 4

Robert Catto stayed in the library only long enough to inform Patrick Rankeillor that, like his daughter, he was now under arrest on suspicion of giving aid and succour to a known rebel and enemy of the king. He added a sentence or two on the restrictions that arrest imposed.

'Professor Rankeillor,' he said. 'You understand the position?'

'You've made it very clear, laddie. My daughter and I are to remain in this hoose until you deem otherwise. Every member o' our household too.'

'Then I shall take my leave of Miss Rankeillor and yourself and call again tomorrow afternoon. When I shall require you to provide me with a written statement dictated by me to you on the basis of what you told me earlier. I presume I don't need to bring paper, ink and quills with me.'

A written statement. The words were innocuous enough. What they implied sent shivers up and down Christian's spine. Once everything was committed to paper there would be no denying her father's involvement with Jacobite politics and plots. She could not let him stand alone. Words tumbled out of her mouth. 'Won't you require a written statement from me too?'

Robert Catto answered her without looking at her. 'Absolutely not. Which is something else we shall discuss tomorrow.'

'Ah canna say we shall look forward to your visit wi' unalloyed joy,' Patrick said wryly, although he returned their gaoler's rather stiff bow of the head all the same. 'Show young Captain Catto out, lass.'

'By the kitchen door if you please, madam,' he said, swinging round to her.

'Of course, sir,' she replied, leading the way out into the

lobby. After closing the double doors of the library behind them, she took a quick little breath and turned to face him. Would they kiss? Steal an intimate and joyful little moment from the gravity of the situation?

The lobby and the corridor linking it to the kitchen and the back of house were growing shadowy, the sconces not yet lit. She could see his face well enough by the light still being afforded by the tall narrow windows which flanked the front door. No smile curved his mouth, no sparkle lit up his grey eyes.

She glanced at the staircase rising above their heads into the gloom of the upstairs landing. 'Do you want to see Geordie before you go?'

Following her gaze, he looked up the stairs. 'How is he?'

'Very stiff and sore.' She grimaced. 'As expected after what was done to him yesterday at Eastfield. But I'm sure he'd like to see you. Although I'd be loath to ask him to tackle the stairs again. And,' she said, as much to herself as to him, 'Betty might well have apoplexy if I take you up there.'

'Tell him I'll see him when he's fit to move more easily,' came the gruff response. His voice sharpened. 'Surely to God he could have stayed downstairs today. Every step must have hurt him more.'

'Every step was agony for him.'

'Then why make him do it?' he demanded.

'I didn't. He insisted. Once Joshua and I had helped him halfway there didn't seem much point in not going on up. When we reached the landing and he'd got his breath back, do you know what he said to me?'

'How *could* I know?' he snapped.

She took a moment, allowing her own temper to flare and fade. 'He told me he didn't want me to have to sleep in a chair for another night, watching over him. Now he was upstairs, his sister could help keep an eye on him. "You've done so much for me already, miss." That's what he said, Robert. "I know you must have lots of other things to do. You'd done so much for all three of us. You and the Captain. Sergeant Livingstone too. Mrs Betty as well."

When Robert Catto said nothing in response, she laid a

tentative hand on the sleeve of his white linen shirt and the strong arm beneath it. He was not wearing his red Town Guard uniform today, more soberly clad in black breeches and a plain blue waistcoat. Those were the clothes he'd been wearing yesterday and had slept in last night. Although his full-sleeved linen shirt and uncreased neckcloth looked as though they'd been put on fresh this morning.

He raised a hand to his head, as though to run his fingers through his hair. As she had observed over these last weeks, it was a characteristic gesture. Even when his gleaming chestnut waves were neatly tied back and confined by a black satin ribbon, as they were now. The ribbon too looked fresh and uncrumpled.

Early this morning, sitting at the table in the library with her, his hair had tumbled loose over his shoulders. Only a few hours ago. When he had allowed the mask to slip, the one he customarily wore to hide his feelings behind the austere military persona and his ferociously neat outward appearance.

'What's wrong, Robert?'

'Kirsty. For God's sake... What the Devil do you think is wrong?'

'I ken that well enough,' she said gravely. 'What I mean is what is wrong between you and me?'

'Everything,' he said, his voice bleak. 'This bloody mess.' Finally lowering his eyes from the staircase, he looked over her head to where there was nothing to see but the empty corridor. She had to call him back from whichever dark place he was heading for. From his terrible soldier's memories.

He had shared one truly awful one with her on Christmas Eve, trying to frighten her as to what the bloody consequences of armed rebellion might be. Told her the story of a farmhouse in Saxony he and his comrades had come across. The dreadful consequences to the family who had lived there as fighting spilled over into their previously peaceful lives.

Sparing her none of the details, the story had poured out of him after he had caught her trying to send a warning letter to her father while Patrick Rankeillor was still through in Glasgow. Trying to turn her from the path she and her father were on. Or had been on.

Relief. Startling and unsettling, the word and the emotion slid into her head. Seeking reassurance, however illogical it might be to look for that from Robert Catto, implacable enemy of the Stuart Cause, she tugged on his arm.

'This morning,' she began, pointing towards the library doors. 'In there.'

'What of it?'

'You and I stood up from the big table, stepped into each other's arms and made a promise, one to the other.'

That brought his gaze back to her face, his voice softening. 'Aye. That we did.'

'You also said you wanted us to stop seeing each other as enemies. That if there is a storm rushing towards us, we should do our best to weather it together. Side by side. Do you no longer want that?'

His eyes flashed. 'Of course I want that! How can you doubt it?'

She flexed her fingers, taking a firmer grip on his arm. 'Help me not to doubt it, Robert.'

'Not here,' he muttered, taking her by the hand. 'Come on.'

A few hurried steps brought them through the corridor to the closed door into the kitchen. He gripped her arm above the elbow, bringing her round to face him. 'At the West Port,' he said, the words blurted out. 'Your father did not deny anything I put to him. Not one single thing! Bloody hell, Kirsty, why are the two of you so unable to dissemble, so blind to the consequences of your actions? You're as bad as each other! And how you expect me to sort out this bloody mess – so much of it of your own making – I do not know!'

She bit her lip, then chose to answer him with gentleness. 'It's surely not so strange that my father and I are very alike in some ways. The apple does not fall far from the tree.'

He shook his head. With enough force to make the ends of his hair ribbon flutter. 'It doesn't necessarily follow. I'm nothing at all like … *him*.'

Him. John Roy Stuart, high-ranking Jacobite plotter and Robert Catto's estranged father. The father he claimed to hate with all his heart.

'You cannot even say his name,' she said sadly. 'Och, Robert. Does it hurt so very much, then?'

'We're talking about you, Kirsty,' he said tersely. 'Not me. A kiss,' he added. 'If you please.'

'Och, that was somewhat perfunctory, sir! What if I don't please?' Trying desperately to lighten the mood, she smiled up at him. Despite the frown between his russet brows, dare she hope she saw in his face that he had returned from one of those dark places he had been seeing in his mind's eye?

'Don't play games,' he said in his deep voice. 'Not today.'

She raised one hand to his face, dancing her fingertips over his cheek and down the line of his strong jaw. She could feel stubble beginning to form. 'No games,' she agreed, her voice a whisper in the increasing gloom. 'The time is long past for those.'

'You finally appreciate how serious all this is?' The words were rattled out. Here, in the depths of the corridor, 'twas difficult to read the expression on his face but his voice betrayed him. He sounded like a man in pain. His palpable distress was an arrow to her heart.

'Och Robert, I realized that long since! And you arresting my father today has brought it home to me a thousand times over! Made it all so much more real!'

He whirled her round so her back was to the kitchen door, seized one hand and sought the other. Interlacing his fingers with hers, he raised both their hands to rest against the door to either side of her head and dipped his head to kiss her. Hard. She responded with equal fervour, her lips parting under his urgent mouth. One sharp tug on her hands drew her closer to his tall body. As close as it was possible to be.

Growing darkness around them. Fire flaring up between them. His firm chest against her soft breasts. His hands releasing hers so he could slide his arms around her waist. Her arms reaching up to coil around his neck, under his tied-back hair. His long, strong legs pressed against her own. His growing arousal calling forth a response from the most intimate part of her own body. Sensation building upon sensation. Desire mounting.

Yet there was something despairing about this passionate embrace. She thought – no, she knew – that he felt the same.

That had to be why they both drew back from the kiss at the same time.

'We cannot do this,' she said, her breath coming fast and shallow.

'No,' he agreed. 'We cannot. Not here. Not now.'

'Maybe not ever. Fate is against us.'

'I do not want either of us to think like that.' He leant forward, resting his forehead against hers. *'I do not want that!'*

For a moment neither of them spoke. It was Christian who broke the silence. 'Step back, will you? I'm a wee bit hot.'

'I'm not surprised,' he said. 'I'm a wee bit hot myself.' The hint of amusement in his voice came and went. 'I have to do my duty, Kirsty. However much I might sometimes regret the necessity.'

'I know that. I understand that. Let us go into the kitchen.'

'Give me a moment,' he said, taking a few more steps back, putting some distance between them.

Her eyes flickered downwards before hastening back up to his face. 'Oh,' she said, hot all over again as she realized why he needed that moment. Her embarrassment did not stop her from asking a question. A very indiscreet one at that. Or maybe 'twas her very embarrassment which made her blurt it out, waving a hand in the vague direction of the crotch of his breeches. 'How do you persuade it to subside?'

'Persuade it to subside?' he repeated. He looked at her for a moment before amusement returned, stronger than before. He let out a bark of laughter, clapping one hand over his mouth to silence himself.

And in that moment, 'twas as though the floor beneath their feet shifted and moved and the clouds of despair surrounding them began to lift.

Chapter 5

She narrowed her eyes at him. 'What's so funny?'

He took his hand from his mouth. 'Y-you are,' he spluttered. The things you say. The way you say them. This frankness about … eh … bodily functions. I suppose that's what comes of being the daughter of a medical man. Of being a lady apothecary and anatomical artist yourself. Who sketches and paints the naked cadavers of men as well as women.' There was no mistaking the sparkle in his eyes now. 'Twas a flash of devilish glee.

'Not much point in drawing subjects with their clothes on,' she countered. Feeling her body too reacting to their embrace, she folded her arms across her betraying breasts.

'I suppose not. To answer your question – because I know you like to learn new things – I usually try thinking horrible thoughts. Fortunately,' he said, 'which may very well not be the right word, I have a plentiful supply of those in here.' He tapped his index finger against his temple. 'Right now I'm thinking about running the gauntlet of the fire-breathing dragon on the other side of this door.' He nodded towards it. 'The venomous looks the wee witch gives me could shrivel any man's ardour.'

'Robert Catto!' But she was laughing now too, even if their shared amusement perplexed her. 'Right now,' she said, mirroring what he had just said, 'I'm wondering how we can be finding any of this funny.'

'Because we have to.'

'There is that,' she said, remembering what Joshua had said this morning about sparing Geordie's blushes. She told Catto the story, adding the words which had leapt into her head at the time.

'Laughter. Care. Kindness. And I thought that if we can hold on to those, they can carry us through whatever lies ahead of us.

Whether the danger comes from the Liddells or … elsewhere. Does that make me impossibly naïve? Or disordered in my wits?' She wrinkled her nose, thinking about that.

'Moonstruck?' he suggested. 'That makes two of us. We might add two other words. Love. Hope. A very wise young woman recently told me hope can move mountains.' He stretched out a hand and drew his index finger lightly down her nose, still wrinkled in perplexity. 'I love it when you do this. Although we need straight faces now. We mustn't arouse the dragon's suspicions.'

'As though we're going to our executions— Oh. That is a prodigious unfortunate metaphor, is it not?'

'Let's try for serious but composed. Do you think we can manage that?'

Walking into the kitchen, Christian did her best to look serious but composed. He was absolutely right. They could not afford to look like a man and woman who had emerged from a passionate and mutually arousing embrace only moments before. Betty Gilchrist had sharp eyes, especially when it came to her young mistress. She was standing at the range stirring the big soup pot which bubbled and simmered on it most days. With two large brass lanterns set on high shelves on opposite walls, the room was well-lit.

Turning at their entry, the housekeeper's attention went straight to Robert Catto. She was directing another ferocious glower at him.

Irritated though she was by that, Christian adopted a pleasant tone of voice. 'Where did you put the Captain's coat, Betty?'

'I hung it up at the back door. Where else would I hae put it?'

'Is the lantern through in the wee lobby lit?'

'Aye.' Betty's glower hadn't faded. 'Seeing as how I assumed this one wouldna be staying here long.' Unforgiving eyes flickered from Robert Catto back to Christian. 'I've heated up the broth. I'll tak a plate through tae your faither.'

'I'm sure he'll appreciate that. I'll show the Captain out.'

The only answer she got was another of Betty's grunts of disapproval.

Chapter 6

'Why the Devil do you and your father put up with her?'

They were in the back lobby, a safe distance away from the kitchen and concealed by a sharp corner from anyone who might come into it. A selection of tartan plaids, cloaks and coats, including his own, hung from hooks on the back door. A glass lantern, smaller than those in the kitchen, sat on the deep windowsill to the right of the door. The candle flame was steady, bathing the small white-washed space in warm yellow light. It was striking glints off the little brass bowl which sat next to it, as well as the shining brass of the curved tops of the well-polished coat hooks.

'I sometimes wonder. Och,' she added, raising her arms and fisting her hands in a gesture of exasperation, 'I'm so annoyed with her for being like that with you today! I really thought she had seen your worth.'

'My worth?' he queried, his voice grown very dry. 'I have that, do I?'

'Yes! You showed your worth yesterday evening when you and Mr Livingstone rescued Geordie and Joshua. Betty admires you for that, I know she does!'

'Really?' Catto drawled. 'I doubt she admires anything about me. Not one little thing.'

Christian Rankeillor frowned. 'She did spread that blanket over you last night. After you had fallen asleep in front of the library fire. She also got up early this morning to put the porridge on, so you could have a bowl before you left the house.'

He shrugged. 'A temporary cessation of hostilities only. She sees me as a danger to your reputation. Which I am. Don't stand in front of the window.' Reinforcing the command, he took her by the elbow and pulled her back from the glass.

Her eyes widened. 'You think someone might be watching us from out in the Physic Garden?'

'I'm being careful. That's all.'

'What about when you go out there? In the dark?'

'I can look after myself. Besides which, watchers watch. They seldom do more.'

She shivered. Damn. Somehow he knew she was thinking about the watcher who had done more. Or failed to. On Daft Friday, undoubtedly coerced into it, medical student Murdo Robertson had not had the stomach to dispatch Catto. She had been a witness to that event. It had scared her, of course it had. She had not lived a life like his, with danger lying in wait round every corner, liable at any moment to explode into violence. Dear God, he was so much more than a danger to her reputation.

'Interesting times, Kirsty.' Once again he raised one hand to her face, drawing his fingertips down the side of it, keeping his touch as soft as thistledown. 'We are living in interesting times.'

She raised her own hand, circling her fingers around his wrist, under the narrow ruffle of his shirt cuff. 'I wish you and I had met each other in very dull times. The most uneventful times imaginable!'

'So do I, Kirsty. So do I. Not have to navigate our way through this bloody mess in which we find ourselves.' Wondering how it was possible to feel so happy and so sad – and so desperately worried for her – all at the same time, a previous conversation sprang to mind. 'Stumbled upon each other in a garden full of sunflowers.'

'Och, Robert…' she breathed. They kissed, gently this time. Then, unable to keep his hands off her, he stroked the gleaming fall of her hair.

'I take it you've had a busy day.'

'You might say that. Betty and I had to get everyone settled. What's happened has upset Mary and Tibby too,' she said, naming the two young maidservants who normally helped keep the Rankeillor household running smoothly. 'We had our work cut out, making sure everyone was calm and comforted. Not to mention fed and watered.'

The wryly amused expression became a frown. 'Even though Geordie had to be persuaded to eat anything.'

'Give him time,' Catto said. 'Speaking of which, how long have we got?'

'Until Betty comes through? She's going to be fussing over my father for at least the next ten minutes.'

'So taken up with him she's forgotten her self-appointed task of guarding your virtue?'

She put her hands on her hips and looked at him as though he was a halfwit. 'You're hardly likely to ravish me up against the back door.'

'Och, I don't know. The idea does have a certain appeal.'

When she gave a quick little gasp, his eyes dropped to her lovely mouth. Her delicate pink lips were slightly parted. Desire. She felt it as much as he did. He raised his eyes again and saw the confirmation of that in her own.

His pulse quickened. Bugger. He might have to try thinking those horrible thoughts again. Or he could consider the other emotions chasing themselves across her so expressive face. Shyness. Nervousness. Embarrassment at his words. Her bravado had been replaced by a deep rosy blush.

'Sorry,' he offered. 'Not something a gentleman should say to a young lady.'

She came out fighting. 'Where's the gentleman?' she asked, pretending to look past him and around the lobby. 'I can't see one.'

'You've done it again!' he said, his voice an amused growl.

'Done what?'

'Made me laugh! Made me *like* you!'

She tilted her head back, giving him an appraising look. 'That's bad, is it? Liking me?'

'It's almost worse than the loving.' Abruptly serious again, he lifted one of her hands and pressed a kiss on the back of it. 'Kirsty. Let us not waste any of these ten minutes. The Lord President returns to Edinburgh sometime in the middle of January—'

'Will you have incurred his wrath by what you did last night?'

'Very possibly,' he said, doing his best to sound unconcerned, even flippant.

She was having none of it. 'You broke the law, did you not? And you are an officer of the law.'

'A clever lawyer might be able to dispute that I broke the law. I did not actually take the boys away from Eastfield.'

'Will it make a difference to the Lord President that you found them on the bridge at Musselburgh? You had gone out looking for Geordie. You had every intention of taking him from Eastfield if you had to. You have compounded the offence by also bringing Joshua back with you.'

'I wasn't going to leave him there!'

'Of course you weren't. You're not made that way. What I mean is that the Liddells' grievance against you is now even stronger than it was. The letter Charlotte sent to Mr Paterson the lawyer, accusing you of not being a fit and proper person to command the Town Guard—'

'Which letter your friend the aforementioned clever lawyer flung into the fire.'

'Which will not stop her from repeating her accusations to the Lord President once he returns to Edinburgh.'

'At the moment I have her, her brother and their friend Mr Menzies of Edmonstone at a considerable disadvantage. Let me worry about that nest of vipers. Further oblige me by thinking about yourself for a change. Once I have given the Lord President the intelligence I have gathered, matters will be out of my hands. Much may depend on how I present my findings and Culloden does prefer striking bargains to—'

'Throwing people into the Tolbooth?' she suggested. 'Hanging them?'

He rolled his eyes, once again trying to treat those words as something to be dismissed. Not quite succeeding. 'Aye. But even a man as powerful as Duncan Forbes of Culloden is answerable to others.'

'The Duke of Argyll,' she supplied. 'The Marquis of Tweeddale.' She pulled a face when she said that name. 'Whose Edinburgh home is no distance from here. Over the Cowgate and up off the Canongate.' She inclined her head, indicating the direction in which Tweeddale Court lay. 'Not that he spends much time there. A Secretary of State for Scotland,' she added with studied contempt, 'who prefers London to Edinburgh.'

'Yes. Those two. Not to mention King George himself.' He squeezed the hands he held. 'And don't tell me he's the Elector of Hanover. Calling him that can get people into trouble. I'm going to do my damnedest to keep you out of this but you've got to help me. We must both tread carefully. As I've also already told you. On Yule Day, in case you've forgotten.'

'I haven't forgotten.'

'Then why did you say you expected I would want a written statement from you as well as your father?'

Her defiant chin went up. One of the first things he had noticed about her. That and her eyes. Green as a summer meadow. So clear. So honest. Too damn honest.

'The words slipped out of my mouth before I could stop them. Nor am I sorry for saying them, Robert.'

'That's what worries me. Also that more words might slip out of your mouth. In front of the Lord President and anyone else who might closely question you. Does Culloden know you are a gifted artist?'

'You will show him the map I drew?'

'Of course I will. I cannot *not* show it to him. But I'd rather not tell him you were the cartographer. I repeat. Does he know of your artistic talent?'

She shrugged, as though to deny the praise. 'He knows I draw and paint. Which is not so unusual. Several of my friends also do so.'

'This is no time for false modesty, Kirsty!'

'Robert…' She looked past him once again, this time in the direction of the kitchen. 'Betty will be here soon.'

'So look me in the eye and answer the question before she gets here.' He tugged on her hands and her focus returned to his face.

'Yes. He knows. He has complimented me on my drawings and paintings several times. I think he also suspects I do the anatomical drawings for my father.'

Catto groaned. 'Then we must make it abundantly clear to the Lord President and any other interested parties that you drew the map whilst being ignorant of its true purpose. Which you were, were you not?'

Yes.' She moistened her lips.

'As we must also make abundantly clear you had nothing to do with the Jacobite agent. Did not even know he was here in Edinburgh. Or that he was being hidden in the Royal Infirmary. If the Lord President wants to speak to you directly, that is what you must tell him. Agreed?'

She did not immediately respond, only continued to look at him out of those too honest eyes.

'Answer me, Kirsty.'

'I think I can hear Betty coming.'

'I can't. So answer me. Now.'

Leaning against the old cloaks and coats, she listened to the sound of his footsteps as he walked away, straining her ears to hear them for as long as possible. Which was not long at all. She had to check an instinctive move closer to the window, in the hope of seeing his tall figure depart.

She glanced at the lantern on the windowsill. She could stretch out her arm, lift it, open the glass door and blow out the candle. Then she could look out of the window without fear of being seen. But any watcher hiding out there in the shadows of the physic garden might see the movement of her arm and hand. *Interesting times*. The words made her shiver.

She waited a moment longer, all the same. Were Robert Catto to look back, he would see the lit window. A flickering flame in the darkness pressing in all around them.

As she walked from the lobby back into the kitchen, the knob of the door through to the rest of the house turned. Carrying a wooden tray topped by an empty soup plate and spoon, Betty backed into the room. Christian set down the lantern she had carried through from the back lobby and hurried round the kitchen table to swing the door wide for the housekeeper.

'Yon one's gone, then?' she asked, indicating the back lobby with a lift of her chin.

'Captain Catto has left, yes.' Now it was she who was on the receiving end of one of Betty's glowers. The older woman turned and headed for the pantry with her burden. Christian could still feel the disapproval.

'I hear he's coming back the morn.'

'He is. Betty, did you say anything to my father about the Captain?'

She regretted the words the moment they were out of her mouth. The tray still in her hands, the housekeeper swung round to look at her. The glower had been replaced by a look which combined anxiety with concern.

'Is there anything I need to say to your faither? Anything he should ken about yon one wha's just left? About him and you, lass?'

Care. She really cares about me. That's why she's asking. That's why she looks so worried. Care. Kindness. Love, on both sides. It's not going too far to say that. And there's always been laughter. Lots of laughter. Hope too. God knows, we all need that. Especially now.

She looked back at Betty Gilchrist and wondered how she could even be contemplating lying to her. This woman who was the nearest she'd ever had to a mother. This woman who had looked after her throughout her life. This woman who had comforted her when she was upset and shared her joys when she was happy.

'No, Betty,' she said, giving the housekeeper the only possible answer. It might even be the honest one. Now her father was home, the chances of her and Robert Catto having the opportunity to meet up in private was more unlikely than ever. Vanishingly small. 'There's nothing you need to say to my father about Captain Catto and me. Nothing at all.'

Chapter 7

Striking out for the far wall of the physic garden, Catto was walking with a measured step, not moving too quickly. He remained very aware of the sound of his shoes crunching on the gravel path beneath his feet, although he did not think anyone was lurking in the shadows. His years of soldiering had given him a sixth sense about such things. Or maybe it came from a certain feyness he had inherited from his Buchan and Highland forebears. Not that he would ever admit that, not to another living soul.

He continued to assess his surroundings as he always did, alert to any possible danger. Most definitely a soldier's habit. He glanced over towards the pagoda-shaped summer house. Painted white, the wooden boards of its walls were a dull gleam against the encroaching night. The little wooden building stood in the centre of the garden, where all the neatly laid out paths converged.

As he had previously observed, the vegetable and herb beds within the grid of paths were dormant. Naturally enough, this being December. They would burst into life in the Spring, ready for the Rankeillors and other apothecaries to pick them for their lotions and potions. Spring. Three months away. What might have happened by then?

The unwanted pictures flashed once more across his mind. Not only Patrick Rankeillor on the scaffold but his daughter too. Not for the first time, Catto tried telling himself that while they might hang women, they didn't hang ladies. Not these days.

A shudder ran through him, stopping him in his tracks. Oh God, but if this Jacobite threat really was a serious one, there could be no doubt it would provoke the harshest of responses, from

Duncan Forbes as much as anyone else. The mailed fist would emerge from the velvet glove. Reprisals would be brutal and no respecter of class or gender. All that beauty and intelligence could be destroyed, wiped out in a matter of moments, her life and talents and kindness scattered to the four winds.

For a moment the hideous pictures in his head threatened to unman him, made him want to bend forward and retch out the fear and despair. Until he raised his shoulders in a great shaky breath and made a silent promise to himself. *Not if I have anything to do with it. Please God. Help me do this. Help me save her. From herself, if I have to.*

Nor was that the only danger she might face. He had told her to let him deal with the Liddells and Arthur Menzies of Edmonstone but he remained all-too-aware Eastfield House was both a precarious and an untenable prison. It was too far out into the country for him to order regular patrols. He didn't have the manpower. Besides which, he didn't want to draw attention to the place.

Eastfield would hold only if Edmonstone continued to believe Catto was on the Jacobite side. He still couldn't quite understand why the man had been gullible enough to believe that in the first place, hoped to God he wasn't smart enough to work out the truth of the matter.

He started walking again, continuing to edge his way around the dark and deserted Physic Garden. He was taking a careful route along the path which ran along its back wall before it met the corner of the garden and turned sharply right. Twenty paces along this wall brought him to the spot he'd previously chosen as his best crossing point on his discreet route back to the High Street some way east of the guard-house.

He hoisted himself up onto the wall. It was almost as tall as he was. Straddling it, he brought each leg in turn over the topmost stones, bracing himself with the heels of his hands on the rough masonry. He leapt down onto hard-packed earth – and drew his breath in again, this time on a hiss of pain. Bugger. Every so often the wound left by the musket ball he had taken in his thigh at Dettingen back in May issued a vicious reminder it had not yet fully healed.

Muttering a string of curses, he bent forward. Pushing the front flap of his leather coat out of the way, he slid his hand down his thigh over his breeches to cover the site of the wound. Trying to give his aching flesh some comfort, willing the stabbing pains to recede and allow him to catch his breath, coming too ragged and too loud. Bloody hell… *Bloody hell*. The pain was refusing to lessen, bringing quick tears to his eyes. He lifted his spare hand to dash the moisture away.

He longed to feel Kirsty Rankeillor's healing touch. Her cool, capable hands, resting gently on his leg. His naked leg, no barrier between her fingers and his bare skin. Or she could kiss it better. The private playhouse in his brain offered him a picture of her doing that, her lips moving up the inside of his thigh … and he could not quite suppress a moan of longing and desire.

He wondered if she knew what lovers did when they were alone in bed together. She knew the human body, yes. She would know the fundamentals of how men and women joined together. He doubted she knew all the pleasures a man and woman might share. She was a virgin. How could she know?

Another little moan floated out between his cold lips, his breath white in the chilly darkness, desire beginning to defeat pain. How he would love to introduce her to all those different pleasures. Lovingly and with patience. Only ever with her consent. Although he hoped she would be amenable to some coaxing and cajoling. He'd enjoy that too.

And maybe he had somehow left these freezing dark spaces in Edinburgh behind and magically decamped for a few foolish moments to Cloud Cuckoo Land. How the Devil were they to find a time and a place to be alone together on even one occasion? Especially now her father was home. Let alone what might be going to happen after the Lord President came back to Edinburgh next month.

He had first met Duncan Forbes in his childhood, during those brief, happy months when his mother had brought her children home to Scotland. Culloden had taken an interest in Mary Catto's son and his subsequent military career ever since, keeping in touch with the occasional letter. He had offered him this assignment in Edinburgh in exchange for military advancement.

Poisoned chalice though it was. Yet if the Lord President had not summoned him back, he would never have met Christian Rankeillor.

Cautiously, Catto straightened up, arching his back against the wall behind him. There was a small lump of something between the masonry and him. He slid his hand into his deep coat pocket, his fingers finding the book which was in there. *The Life and Adventures of Robinson Crusoe.* He'd completely forgotten about it. The plan had been for him to return to Infirmary Street this afternoon and read some of it aloud to Geordie and any of the other orphans of the storm currently in residence at the Rankeillor house who wanted to hear it. Those amongst them who weren't scared of him, at any rate.

He'd asked Kirsty Rankeillor if she could feed him afterwards. *In exchange for your kind thought?* That was what she had asked. No chance of that now. Neither the reading, the feeding, nor the chance for her and him to somehow find a few more moments alone together away from the suspicious surveillance of her housekeeper. He might not want either of them to think fate was against them but facts had to be faced. Damn each and every one of those facts to hell.

Once again he tried a cautious step or two forward. Sore but no longer a stabbing pain, more a dull ache. He had a few more walls to scramble over on his secret journey through the gardens and closes of Edinburgh but he took them slowly, counting them down in his head.

One more to go. He climbed over it, lowering his feet with some care onto what felt like frosted grass. A low growl froze him to the spot.

In Edinburgh Royal Infirmary Lady Governess Agnes Moncur and medical student Murdo Robertson were deep in conversation. Sitting in the apothecary's shop off the lofty and echoing main lobby of the hospital, they were keeping their voices low. A single wax candle in a pewter candlestick flickered on the small table at which they sat.

Murdo was looking miserably at Agnes. 'You surely cannot believe Kirsty has betrayed us?'

'I don't want to, Mr Robertson.' Her face was troubled. 'I really do not want to. But why did she go out of her way not to see us when she delivered the last batch of physic here on Christmas Eve? Choosing to come while we were all occupied on the ward round and not even leaving a note? Nor do I think we can take what the Town Guard captain said to you at face value. He might have been trying to pull the wool over your eyes. You saw him escorting Kirsty home after the Daft Friday ball, did you not?'

'He might equally have been arresting her. And now has her in his power, able to insist she did indeed go out of her way not to see us on Yule E'en.'

'So you're not sure he's on our side either? Even though he appeared to hint he is sympathetic to the Cause? And failed to arrest *you* after he had found the evidence of Mr Fox's stay in the hospital?'

'I don't know what to think about him.' Which was not exactly true. Jamie Buchan had been absolutely sure Robert Catto was no Jacobite. Only now Jamie was gone and Murdo could not seek his advice or quiz him further, which was a bleak thought.

'We need to know one way or the other,' Agnes said. 'Both about the Town Guard captain and Kirsty. The snow has delayed us long enough as it is.' She grimaced. 'Along with the confusion following the events of Daft Friday. Thank God our visitor got away safely!'

'Aye,' Murdo agreed, hearing the emotion in her voice. 'Thank God.'

'You did good service to the Cause there, Mr Robertson.'

'I was glad to be able to do what I could. Very glad.' He dipped his head, embarrassed by the praise. Feeling unworthy of it. He might have helped Mr Fox – that being the *nom-de-guerre* of the Jacobite agent - escape from Edinburgh but he had failed to shoot Robert Catto dead. Och, but he could not be sorry about that! That he had allowed Jamie Buchan to talk him into even attempting cold blooded murder was a source of aching regret.

Yet his failure to act had undoubtedly allowed Robert Catto to pass on information to whoever that terrifying man reported to. Information which might hang Professor Rankeillor – oh, and dear God in Heaven, even his daughter too. Two people who had always been so kind to a shy country boy after he had come to Edinburgh from his home in Perthshire to study at the university.

'But Mrs Moncur,' he burst out, 'how are we to know? You cannot go about Edinburgh asking questions. You are too well-kent. As the resident, I'm not supposed to leave the hospital.' He grimaced. 'Even though I did on Daft Friday.'

Agnes Moncur nodded her head in agreement 'Aye, you're in enough trouble with Professor Monro as it is for having exchanged residency duties with Mr Buchan of Balnamoon. Apart from which, if you were to pay even a hasty visit to Kirsty at Infirmary Street, we couldn't know who might be watching you.'

'So what are we to do?'

'We are not without friends, Mr Robertson. People who can move about Edinburgh without drawing attention to themselves.'

Murdo continued to look at her, torn between loyalty to the Cause and loyalty to the Rankeillors. 'But how will it help us to know? If Captain Catto is working against us, he will already have passed the information to his superiors and the damage will have been done. They will know we are planning something.'

Agnes raised an admonishing finger. 'Knowledge is always useful, Mr Robertson. Whether it can be used immediately or at a later date. Given mutual trust, knowledge can be passed on to others who might well be able to act upon it. To the detriment of those who are playing a deep game. Making sure such people get their just deserts.'

Something about the way she said that made Murdo suppress a shiver. He could almost feel sorry for the Town Guard captain.

Chapter 8

'Good boy,' Catto said softly. The dog approached, tail wagging. He didn't so much see that as feel it through the stirring of the air around both man and beast. A small dog with a white coat, the colour discernible by its dull gleam in the darkness. He'd known a wee dog like this once, a playmate of his boyhood.

'Good boy,' he said again, bending forward and extending his fingers for the dog to sniff. A door opened, a shaft of light streaming out into the blackness of the garden.

'Bobby,' called a female voice. She sounded like an older woman. 'Come in now. Your supper's ready.'

'Come in Bobby,' trilled a much younger voice in imitation of the older one. 'Your supper's ready. Do as granny says.'

Bobby the dog licked Catto's fingers. 'On you go, namesake,' he whispered. 'You heard them. Your food's waiting for you.'

He watched as the dog ran to the house, a blur of movement in the dark. Animal and child greeted each other as though they'd been apart for a year. Granny laughed. A cheerful tableau on the back doorstep. Until they all went back inside, the woman closing the door behind them and leaving him alone in the darkness.

Unseen hands grabbed Catto's heart. The ache of loneliness, of forever being shut out, hurt every bit as much as his leg had a few moments before. Standing in the lee of the wall, he tilted his head back against it, silently asking himself a question which had become a familiar one over the past weeks. What the fuck was he doing here in Edinburgh in the dying days of December, skulking around like a thief in the night?

All around him, people would be settling in for the long winter's evening. Putting more coal on the fire. Laying a bowl of food on the kitchen floor for the dog or the cat, preparing their own evening meal. Talking and laughing and telling stories. Keeping each other company. Turning their backs on the darkness and chill of the outside world.

They'd be doing the same in the Rankeillor household too. Not that anyone there was without worries. To put it mildly. Yet he knew Kirsty Rankeillor and her father would be putting a brave face on it. *Keeping everyone's spirits up.* He had to grudgingly admit Betty Gilchrist the housekeeper would be too.

It was so long since he had been part of that world, sure of his own place in a loving family. He might pretend to Kirsty Rankeillor the encounter with the man he refused to think of as his father had not disturbed him in any way. Painful honesty compelled him to admit, if only to himself, that it had shaken him to the core. All those *might have beens and what ifs*. Useless to dwell on those. He couldn't change his past.

He gazed up at the darkening sky above his head, watching the grey ribbons of smoke curling up from Edinburgh's abundance of chimneys. They hid the moon. Yet he knew it was there. How else could he be moonstruck?

Sitting with Kirsty Rankeillor at Infirmary Street early this morning, he had floated an astounding idea. She had previously described him as *racketing about Europe in the service of the Elector of Hanover*. He'd quoted those words back to her. To his own amazement, he'd suggested he might be capable of choosing a different path, decide to settle down somewhere.

Marry me. Those were the words he had wanted to say to her. She had stopped him by placing her fingertips against his lips, given him back his own words, told him not to make promises he'd never be able to keep.

She was right – and he really must have lost his wits. Sod it, what was the etiquette for asking one of your prisoners for the hand of the other in marriage? Did he really think Patrick Rankeillor would give his blessing to such a match or be in any position to say yea or nay? Or that she would be either?

It wasn't only fate which stood against them. It was his hatred of the Jacobite Cause and her devotion to it.

None of this stopped him from wanting her: and for so much

more than a passionate but short-lived affair. He wanted to go to bed with her every night and wake up with her every morning. He wanted her enough to make him forget the military ambitions which had seemed so important to him a few short weeks ago.

He wanted to be with her when the spring and summer came and they could stroll around the physic garden enjoying little breezes wafting up the scent of the herbs and flowers. He could see them there, her in a pretty summer gown and a straw hat, crouching down to harvest what she needed to make physic, him standing by holding her basket.

Want doesn't always get. He knew that only too well. As he couldn't change the past, he'd have to be more of a poor bloody fool than he already was to think he could change the future. If there was a ferocious storm rushing towards them, he couldn't draw his sword or raise his musket, shove the people he cared about behind him and fight it off. It would roar up like a tempest at sea, gathering its strength, howling its fury and crashing onto whichever rocks and shores it pleased, sweeping away whoever it chose.

The people he cared about.

Her, of course. Now there were others too.

Anger flared up inside him at the thought of those bastards out at Eastfield having Geordie flogged yesterday. He was pretty sure they had ill-treated young Joshua too. What they had to done to Alice Smart was cruel beyond measure, vile and depraved. Catto swore. Comprehensively and violently. They should pay for all of it. By God, they should pay for what they had done!

He'd made Cosmo Liddell and Arthur Menzies write and sign statements admitting they and their friend Hector Grant of Soutra had brutally raped Alice Smart. Turning Catto's stomach, it had been all too clear how much they had relished the task. Revelling in the pain and degradation they had inflicted on an innocent young girl.

They thought they were untouchable. Above the law. Protected by the Byzantine intertwined relationships of the Scottish aristocracy and gentry. They might well be right when it came to Alice, Geordie and Joshua. Although he doubted if being well connected would allow them to slither out from under an accusation of treason. Especially when there was a lot more to Arthur Menzies of Edmonstone than met the eye.

He presented himself of as much of an empty-headed fop as his friend Cosmo Liddell. After a low-voiced conversation in an Edinburgh tavern, Catto knew that for the pretence it was. He was pretty damn sure Edmonstone was a member – or at the very least a messenger – of *The Association.* Also known as *The Concert of Gentlemen*, this shadowy organization was dedicated to the restoration of the House of Stuart to the throne of Britain.

Not quite so shadowy now. Catto had established Patrick Rankeillor was one of its members. His fists clenched. God damn the bloody fool for putting himself and his daughter into so much fucking danger! Where did it come from, this slavish adoration of the Stuarts? Why were people prepared to risk life, limb, family and future for that sodding family?

For a moment, the anger threatened to consume him, until he forced himself to take a deep breath: and then another one. Right now he needed a plan, needed to work out a strategy.

Liddell and Edmonstone couldn't care less about Alice Smart but he was damn sure they wouldn't want the story of how they had ill-used her to circulate in polite society. Oh, some of the young bucks they ran with also saw maidservants and other young girls far below them in social status as fair game. The mothers of the well-off girls they hoped to marry might take a different view.

One weapon which could be used against them. He should start forging it without delay, before the Lord President came back to Edinburgh. The plan was already forming in his head. It came with a risk, of course. Didn't everything?

It would be worth it if he could change the future for Alice, Geordie and Joshua, do his damnedest to set them on the right course. For now they were safe at Infirmary Street. Warm, well-fed, clean and well-cared for. He thought of the grandmother and grandchild he had seen calling in Bobby the dog and wished with all his heart for a permanent happy home for all three orphans of the storm.

Not only for them. For him and Kirsty Rankeillor too.

The rising moon glided out from behind a cloud and the ribbons of smoke drifting up from Edinburgh's chimneys. Standing there in the chilly darkness, gazing up at the pale-yellow orb, Robert Catto dared to hope and dared to dream.

Chapter 9

Father?'

Patrick Rankeillor turned his head away from his prolonged contemplation of the fire burning in the library grate and gave his daughter an unconvincing attempt at a reassuring smile. 'I'm all right, lass.'

They both knew he was very far from being all right. How could he be after what she had just told him? The hardest part had been telling him about Jamie Buchan of Balnamoon, Patrick's surgical apprentice and the nearest he'd ever had to a son. There had been no way of softening that blow. The blood had drained from her father's face as Christian had recounted how Jamie had murdered a young woman in cold blood.

He'd got Jeannie Carmichael drunk and then smothered her, dumping her body round the side of the Royal Infirmary so he could pretend to find the corpse the following morning, with Christian at his side. Knowing he must have waited for her to arrive at the hospital to be a witness to this supposedly unexpected and shocking discovery was a bitter pill to swallow.

Jamie had silenced the young prostitute so she could not carry out her threat to tell Robert Catto what she knew. The girl had seen Jamie and Patrick Rankeillor bundling John Roy Stuart into the Royal Infirmary. She could have had no idea who or what he was, only that something illicit was going on. Already a wanted man for his support of the Stuart Cause, John Roy had lain low in the hospital for nigh on a week, incapacitated by a badly sprained ankle. He'd sustained the injury during the pell-mell escape from Surgeons' Hall, when word had reached them the Town Guard was on its way to mount a raid.

Christian had taken the fugitive food and given him medical

attention where he was concealed in one of the row of cells at the back of the Infirmary. Those were designed to safely contain patients whose wounds were not physical or visible, specifically those who might pose a danger to themselves or others. Some called those patients lunatics. Kinder people used the word Robert Catto had used of himself and her. Moonstruck.

'But our visitor got away safely?' Patrick asked now. *Our visitor*. Names of Jacobite agents were said out loud as seldom as possible. Jamie had given John Roy Stuart one *nom-de-guerre*: Mr Fox, taking that description from his red hair. The son who refused to acknowledge him as his father had inherited that colouring as chestnut.

'Aye,' Christian replied and then, swallowing the lump in her throat, 'and Jamie with him.'

'What a price to pay. A young lass dead and Jamie...' His face working painfully, Patrick left the sentence unfinished.

Jamie turning himself into a murderer. Those were the words her father had been unable to say. Jamie, a man who had dedicated his life to healing the sick, had ended a life. It went against every tenet of the medical creed. *First, do no harm.* Those words came right at the beginning of the Hippocratic oath doctors swore to obey.

Yet Jamie had done the worst harm one person can do to another. Robbed Jeannie Carmichael of her life. All for the sake of the Cause. All to help the Stuarts regain the throne. One life sacrificed. How many more sacrifices might be to come?

Robert Catto had quoted Machiavelli to Christian on that subject, asking her if she believed the end justified the means. Where and under what circumstances the question had been posed was one of several strands she had left out of her story. For she had not told her father everything, not by a Highland mile.

Patrick Rankeillor did not need to know Jamie had been prepared to take another life, handing her a pistol and telling her to shoot Robert Catto. Nor had she told him Robert Catto was the long-estranged son of John Roy Stuart. The two men had come face-to-face at the Assembly Rooms on the night of the Daft Friday ball.

She didn't know if she believed the end justified the means.

Especially after the death of Jeannie Carmichael and the near-death of Robert Catto. All her life she had been a passionate supporter of the Jacobite Cause, believing the restoration had to happen. She believed too it would not only give Scotland her lost independence back but bring about all manner of improvements in the lives of Scotland's citizens, be they highborn or humble.

She still believed that. Heart and soul, she still believed it! But she could not deny the question which had crept into her head as to whether the longed-for restoration was worth war and bloodshed.

Since Jamie had done what he had done. Since Robert Catto had marched into her life, carrying the smoke and carnage of the battlefield of Europe with him, forcing her to face reality. He had all but called her a fool for believing there could be a peaceful transition, a *coup d'état* with no blood spilled. *Those who hold the reins of power do not easily relinquish them.*

Her father lifted the brandy glass at his elbow, took a sip and set it down again. 'Are *you* all right, lass?'

'I'm fine,' she assured him. 'I've had plenty to occupy me. It's been a wee bit busy here this past week or so.'

'So it would seem. The young man who has just left the house,' he went on, 'this Captain Robert Catto.'

'What about him?' she asked, shifting on the smooth brocade of the green and gold armchair.

'It strikes me as somewhat incongruous that he has placed baith you and me under arrest. Yet has also rescued these two laddies and brought them here for safety. Asking you tae hide them frae the Liddells. No' tae mention the lassie, wha you tell me was here already. Alice, is it?'

Christian nodded. 'This was the obvious place for them to come. Especially Geordie, who needed medical attention. Which I was able to give.'

Patrick's face darkened. 'Aye. Whit barbarous folk the Liddells are, tae order the flogging o' a boy who's little mair than a bairn. As for what Cosmo Liddell and his friends did to young Alice...' He raised his hands in frustration, unable to find the words to express his disgust.

'Barbarous,' Christian echoed. 'Nor does Alice have any hope of redress in law.' Her mouth settled into a tight line. 'The same law that allowed Geordie to be flogged. Because he took his courage in both hands and ran away from Eastfield.'

'Aye,' Patrick agreed, equally grim. 'The perpetual servitude endured by the colliers and the brutal punishments meted out to those who try to escape is a grave injustice. The enslavement of folk like the young African boy is an affront to our common humanity.' He sighed. 'Although we know there are those among us who profit from this vile trade.'

'Joshua,' she supplied. 'That is his name.'

Patrick nodded, taking in the information. 'But both Joshua and Geordie are subject to the law. Which means young Captain Catto is running a gey big risk by breaking that law. Something which might well damage his military career.'

'He's running a huge risk,' Christian agreed, a few more sentences running silently through her head. *Because he is a good man. There's a very kind heart beating under that arrogant exterior. Now, to our mutual astonishment, he and I have discovered we love each other and I've promised to give myself to him. Without marriage, without any guarantees, without any hope we might have a future together.*

She knew only too well why she hadn't passed on the information that Robert Catto was John Roy Stuart's son: because it would be a betrayal of her lover. The word leapt into her head. Despite everything, despite the near impossibility they could ever truly become lovers, it sent a thrill fizzing and tumbling through her veins.

Pulling off his tie-wig and setting it aside, Patrick Rankeillor tugged at his neckcloth. Aside from allowing Betty to help him out of his riding coat, he was still dressed for the road.

'Shall I run upstairs and fetch your banyan and slippers?' Christian asked as he eased his feet out of his riding boots. 'Then you could relax a little.' She pulled a face. 'As much as you can after having been arrested. Was it a hard ride back from Glasgow?'

'Nothing to speak of.'

Waiting until he raised his head again, she looked him in the eye. 'So you have proved to yourself you can withstand the rigour of long rides.'

'Christian,' Patrick said, a warning note in his voice. 'Not now.'

She had guessed that was why he had chosen to travel to and from Glasgow on horseback rather than take the mail coach as he normally did. Before he had left Edinburgh she had expressed her shock that he would consider joining any Jacobite army not only as a surgeon but also as a soldier, sword and pistols at the ready. He had told her he could not ask other men to do what he would not.

Which was something she did not want to think about now. Or ever. Another deeply troubling thought.

He smiled at her, softening the rebuke, before glancing over at the brocade bell-pull which hung to one side of the fireplace. It was fashioned out of the same green and gold material which covered the armchairs. 'I'll ring for one o' the lassies in a moment and ask her to fetch my dishabilly.' He set his riding boots neatly together beside the armchair before loosening his neckcloth, sliding it off and putting it with his wig. 'I understand from Betty young Mr Catto has been a regular caller here at Infirmary Street since he arrested you on Daft Friday.'

'Yes,' Christian said, sending up a silent prayer Betty had told him no more than that. Certainly nothing about how she had invited Robert Catto and Geordie to eat their Yule Day Dinner here in Infirmary Street. How could she explain that away?

'I trust the young man has behaved with propriety at all times. That at no point has he threatened you. In any way.'

'He has not.' Which was not exactly true. He had threatened her with the terrible consequences armed uprising might bring. Not a subject she was going to raise now. And if Robert Catto had not behaved with propriety at all times, neither had she.

'That is not how he goes about things. From what I have seen of him,' she added hastily. More honest words tripped off her tongue. 'Yet I fear I have told him too much, Father. I did not mean to but he has a way of getting answers out of you.' She clasped her hands together on her lap. 'It is more that he deduced the answers from what I said or did not say. Or how I looked when he posed certain questions.'

Patrick sighed. 'Aye. I found the same thing when he questioned me at the West Port. Although it likely wasna too difficult for him tae deduce the answers, Kirsty. There are only so mony possibilities efter all.'

'That's what he said.' She regretted those words as soon as they had left her mouth. They gave too much away. Normally the shrewdest of men, her father did not seem to notice. Nor had he asked how Alice had come to be at Infirmary Street. Both omissions had be a sign of how distressed he was about Jamie.

'This has been a gey difficult time for you, lass. I'm sorry you've had tae deal wi' it all on your own.'

'But now you are home, Father. And I am very glad of it.' Which she was, despite knowing his return was going to make any assignation with Robert Catto so much more difficult to accomplish.

'I fear what may be going to happen next,' she said, thinking she was speaking nothing but the truth. About several things.

'We shall cross our bridges when we come tae them, my dear. Now, before Betty comes back in tae fuss over me again, tell me more about the three new members o' our household.'

'Betty can help us with that,' Christian said, feeling a rush of relief as the conversation moved onto safer ground. 'She has taken them all to her bosom. Being the mother hen. As she also is with Mary and Tibby.'

'Yourself too, lass. She's aye been that to you.'

Christian nodded. 'Indeed, Father. Shall we go through and allow her to fuss over you again and you can hear her version of the story? Although,' she added, 'we should leave Alice's ordeal to one side while she is present.' A pang of compassion seized her. 'I fear she relives it over and over again as it is.'

Patrick rose to his feet, meeting Christian in the middle of the brightly-coloured hearthrug as she too stood up. He laid a reassuring hand on her shoulder. 'The human mind, like the human body, is capable o' healing its wounds. Far more than we give it credit for. Time and gentle treatment will help.'

Christian followed him through to the kitchen, watching and listening as he smiled at Tibby and asked her to fetch his banyan and slippers from upstairs. He would keep his feelings well hidden, she knew. Privately, he would struggle to come to terms with what Jamie had done. How could he not? A little voice in her head told her how much distress she too could cause him if she and Robert Catto did somehow manage to become lovers in more than name.

Despite her discomfort and unease, one emotion held sway inside her head and inside her heart. Over this most turbulent Yuletide, Robert Catto had escaped all the harm which might have befallen him, emerged unscathed from every threat. He was safe and sound – and he was hers, as she was his. Whatever might lie before them, they had found each other, in this place and this time.

God help them both.

Chapter 10

It was the following morning and Robert Catto was sitting in the warm house of Mr Charles Paterson, on the first floor of a tenement land where the Cowgate opened out into the Grassmarket. Made a nice change from the guard-house up on the Lawnmarket, a chilly place without Geordie there to tend to the fires. He'd have to ask one of the guards to remedy the situation.

The lawyer was pouring him a second cup of coffee. 'I'm glad your mission was successful, Captain.'

Catto took the dainty little porcelain cup from him with a word of thanks. 'So am I. Although I regret not being able to save the boys from ill-usage at the hands of the Liddells and Arthur Menzies of Edmonstone.'

'All three of them my clients,' Paterson said, his distaste obvious. Returning to his chair, he raised his own refilled cup of coffee to his lips. 'I should probably be pressing you to allow me to visit them. Unpleasant though the prospect always is.' He grimaced. 'Hard to fathom such deliberate cruelty. Especially towards blameless innocents.'

'Indeed,' Catto said, allowing himself a moment to savour the aroma wafting up on fragrant ribbons of steam from his cup to his nose. You took your pleasures where you found them. 'This really is excellent coffee, Mr Paterson.'

The lawyer inclined his head. An alert and watchful man, he put Catto in mind of a heron, standing motionless at the side of a burn ready to spear a fish on its beak. Catto did not intend to be the unfortunate fish. Quite the reverse. Yet he was about to take a big risk here. He could only hope it was a calculated one. Also that he was imagining the smell of burning boats.

'How does your wife, sir?' He had seen Elspeth Paterson, big with child, on his previous visit to this house. She had not been in evidence this morning.

Paterson's face softened. 'She is well. In full bloom, you might say. Near her time.'

'And I'm sure you very naturally do not want to be far from home as she draws ever closer to it. I'm sure therefore you are not contemplating a visit to Eastfield to see your clients for a while yet. Certainly not – let us say – over the next fortnight. Perhaps a little longer.'

The resemblance to a sharp-eyed heron was back again. 'Is that a warning, Captain?'

Catto turned his free hand over, spreading his long fingers in a gesture of invitation. 'Let us call it a recommendation.'

'Which I should follow if I know what's good for me?'

'I should strongly advise it. I think,' he went on, aware of the steady thump of his heart, 'now might be the time for me to lay my cards on the table.'

Paterson inclined his head to one side, taking his measure. 'I cannot imagine you often do such a thing, Mr Catto.'

'In our current circumstances it seems the best way forward.'

'Our current circumstances?'

'You know what I mean, Mr Paterson. The dangerous business in which I believe you are involved. Along with Mr Arthur Menzies of Edmonstone and the Honourable Cosmo Liddell. Although I believe the latter's involvement to be peripheral, your Cause's interest in him purely to do with his wealth.'

'Ah,' said the lawyer. 'So definitely not *your* Cause. I had wondered.'

Catto drained his coffee in one long swallow and set his cup down on the high table at his elbow. 'Most definitely not my Cause.'

'You *have* been playing a deep game, Mr Catto. At the behest of our esteemed Lord President, perhaps? I believe he is due to return here from Inverness in around a fortnight's time, perhaps a little longer.'

Catto left the question and the repetition of his own timescale unanswered. 'I cannot strike any sort of a bargain with you. I do not have that power.'

'You've already told me that. Before you rode to the rescue of the two boys.'

'They still need rescuing. Legally. Your assistance in this endeavour would give me the ammunition with which to approach the person who can strike bargains with you.'

'Ah,' Paterson said again.

He came out of the close where the Patersons lived and walked the few steps along to the Grassmarket. It was a rare open space in this crowded city, a long, wide rectangle which seemed always to be bustling and busy. The taverns on the ground floors of the tall tenements on either side catered to thirsty farmers on market days, shop keepers and their customers every day.

Hawkers set up their stalls in the wide space between the two rows of buildings, selling all manners of goods. Vegetables. Eggs. Loaves of bread. Ribbons and pins and other female fripperies. Sweets for children. Women with wicker baskets over the crooks of their arms went about their shopping. A hot chestnut brazier was firing up for midday. A gaggle of barefoot urchins stood grinning in front of it, warming their grubby hands.

A cutler sat behind his round whetstone, working the treadle which supported it to spin the stone and sharpen a knife for the man standing in front of him. There was no way of shielding your ears from the screeching as metal met stone, although the customer was taking the occasional sidestep to avoid the sparks flying out from the process. Both men were well happed up. The day was cold but crisp and sunny, with a blue sky overhead.

Life being lived. Yet this was a place of death too. So many Covenanters, men and women, had died here for their unswerving religious convictions, condemned for their refusal to accept any earthly king as head of the church. Those bloody years some sixty or seventy years ago had acquired the chilling name of the Killing Times.

Public hangings were still held here. Big though the Grassmarket was, Sergeant Crichton of the Town Guard had told Catto you could hardly find a place to stand on these occasions. Not his idea of entertainment. Unless he was watching Cosmo

Liddell, Arthur Menzies and Hector Grant twisting in the wind.

His eyes drifted over to the other side of the marketplace. Jeannie Carmichael, the young prostitute murdered by Jamie Buchan of Balnamoon, had lived in a dilapidated lodging house over there. Funny how the poor like her and the comfortably-off like the Patersons lived so close to each other in Edinburgh, cheek by jowl. There were plans for the city to expand to the north in an elegant new town. Doubtless the well-off would decamp there, leaving old Edinburgh to the poor. Although 'twas not something which was going to happen overnight.

He allowed his thoughts to dwell for a moment on Jeannie Carmichael, regretting how callously he had used her. That Balnamoon had pushed her into his path did not excuse him. He could still hear the lass giggle as he had bodily lifted her up over pools of piss, shite and rotting cabbage leaves and vegetable peelings, placing her against the wall of that dark close where he had fucked her. A barefoot girl, whose name he only knew because Kirsty Rankeillor had asked him to find it out, according her and her brief existence on this Earth some small shred of dignity.

He turned his head to the opposite side of the Grassmarket, where Candlemaker Row straggled down the brae, following a high wall running around the lower edge of Greyfriars' Kirkyard. Jeannie Carmichael was buried there. A fortnight since, early on a chilly morning peppered with showers of hailstones, Catto had watched her pitifully small, rough-hewn coffin being lowered into the ground. Maybe he could arrange for a grave marker to be put there, her initials at least carved into a small stone block, as he'd seen in other burial grounds.

His attention was caught by a quick movement, so slight he might have imagined it. Had the man strolling over there beneath the graveyard wall been looking at him, turning his head away a few seconds too late? If Edinburgh's Jacobite plotters had recovered enough from the disarray of Daft Friday to put a watch on him again, that was all to the good.

Charles Paterson's politics were well known. Being observed paying the lawyer a visit would burnish Catto's own credentials as a secret Jacobite sympathizer, allow him to keep up the pretence. For the next fortnight at least, or whenever the Lord President returned to Edinburgh. Paterson now knew how far that was from the truth, of course, but Catto was confident the arrangement he'd reached with the man would hold. He had to be.

He'd asked the lawyer to draw up the necessary documents to give Joshua his freedom and release Geordie and Alice Smart from perpetual servitude. He would present the paperwork to the Lord President on his return, ready to be signed, sealed and delivered.

If he played his cards right, Culloden would heed his advice, part of the bargain he hoped he would seek to strike over Liddell's and Edmonstone's involvement in the Jacobite plot. As the legal representative for the Eastfield estate, Charles Paterson was empowered to sign documents on their behalf. All that would then be required would be for the Lord President – Scotland's senior law officer – to countersign them.

He had asked Charles Paterson to keep his own counsel about all of this. For the sake of three young people who deserved better lives than they'd had up till now. Without it being overtly stated, for the sake of the lawyer's own future and that of his beloved wife and the impending and, as Catto suspected, long-awaited, arrival. Fixing him with his intelligent gaze, Paterson had observed that despite what Catto had said, it seemed 'twas not only the Lord President who was adept at striking bargains.

Catto remained uneasily aware he could not guarantee the Lord President would take his advice, nor how he might react when he was presented with the papers Paterson had agreed to draw up. He might think Catto had jumped the gun, exceeded his authority as temporary Captain of Edinburgh's Town Guard.

Culloden might well not be too happy either about how Catto had dealt with Cosmo Liddell, his unpleasant sister Charlotte and Arthur Menzies of Edmonstone. His orders had been to watch them but to treat them with kid gloves. The Liddells and their wider family were not only well-connected but also powerful, wielding considerable influence in many spheres. Including the army.

Catto smiled grimly to himself as he stood there surveying

the Grassmarket. He'd had Sergeant Livingstone – *no orders needed, Captain* - kick them both in the balls as some small revenge for their rape of Alice Smart. Subsequently he had put the fear of God into Edmonstone as to what hideous and brutal punishments the British state meted out to those it deemed guilty of treason. Not exactly handling them with kid gloves.

Would he do it all again? Damn right he would.

His eye was caught by a dyer's pole, projecting several feet out over the cobblestones from the first floor of a building. A man pushing a wheeled barrow full of waxed paper packages – by the looks of it, meat to be delivered – stopped in front of him. 'Aye. That's the one.' He spoke with some relish. 'That's where we strung up Captain Porteous.'

Catto cocked one eyebrow. *'We?'* he queried.

'Well,' his informant told him, grinning broadly, 'ah didna dae ony o' the stringing up but ah was cheering on them that did!' His teeth reminded Catto of Davie Rintoul. Mouth like a badly-kept graveyard. A member of the Town Guard, Rintoul had allowed the escape through the Netherbow Port on Daft Friday. *Tell the Captain I'm sorry!* That's what he had called to Geordie before following the Jacobite agent and Jamie Buchan out into the swirling snow.

Musing on the different strands within this particular memory, Catto offered a vague response. 'How terribly fascinating.'

'Eh?'

'Never mind.' He turned on his heel, heading for the West Bow.

The man called after him. 'That showed the Toon Guard whit we thocht o' them!'

Catto swung round. 'And if you don't go about your lawful business forthwith, I'll show you what I think of you.'

The man folded his arms across his beefy chest, leant to one side and spat on the causeway. 'Oh, aye? And who the fuck are you?'

'I'm the captain of the Town Guard, that's who. Now bugger off or you'll see the inside of the Tolbooth.'

As he strode up the steep curving slope of the West Bow, Catto spared a thought for Captain Porteous, his unfortunate forerunner as head of the Town Guard. Various oblique comments had piqued his curiosity as to what had befallen the man but no one had seemed to want to tell him exactly what. It had been Arthur Menzies of Edmonstone who had finally told him the story.

Playing the drunk, Catto had accepted Menzies' offer of seeing him safely home to the guard-house. Pretending to slur his words as they walked together over the cobblestones, he'd asked what had happened to Captain Porteous.

The mob hanged him.

Catto had asked why.

He crossed them and they took their revenge. Hanged him from a dyer's pole in the Grassmarket. A man in his position can't be too careful, sir. Your position too, eh?

Halfway up the West Bow, a girl was standing in a doorway, her arms folded. 'You in a big hurry, sir?' she asked with a smile. 'Ah could put some joy into your morning if you have a wee whilie tae spare.'

He turned a laughing face to her, amused by how she had phrased her pitch. 'You're starting early today.' His eyes fell to the breasts swelling over the top of her bodice. A man could look, couldn't he? No harm in looking. Especially when there was no modest kerchief tucked in there. Although it was a bit cold for her to be displaying her charms. The goose bumps on her pale skin told that tale.

'A girl has to earn her bread.'

'Aye, but I'm spoken for, sweetheart.'

A cynical look crossed her face, followed by a wistful one. 'She's a lucky girl.'

He laughed again. 'Not sure she would agree with you.' Digging into the purse in his coat pocket, he found a sixpence. 'Here,' he said, tossing it to her. 'Away down to the Grassmarket and buy some hot chestnuts. Or a ribbon to match your bonnie blue eyes.'

Catching the coin and closing her fingers over it, she gave him a dazzling smile in response.

Chapter 11

'Are these all right for you, Father?'

Christian and Patrick were in the library. He was sitting at the spectacularly untidy dining table which served as his desk and she was standing beside him. He'd been looking through her latest anatomical drawings. She had made larger scale copies of earlier sketches she had drawn after two dissections carried out in November and early December.

'Much more than all right,' he assured her. 'Excellent as your drawings always are.' He used them as an aid to teaching his students at the Old College. That she was the anatomical artist was a well-kept secret. The ladies who set the rules by which society in Edinburgh was governed would he horrified to learn a young unmarried girl drew the naked cadavers of both men and women. Or they would pretend to be.

'Excellent,' Patrick said again, holding the drawings in his two hands. 'Now, where shall we put these until they're needed?' He grimaced. 'If I havena been clapped in irons afore classes start again.'

'Of course they'll be needed!' To her own ears her supposed confidence sounded as flat as a cracked bell. Smiling up at her, wigless as he usually was at home, his own fair hair cut short, Patrick seemed to be taking strength from it.

She was feeling anything but strong this morning, worn out after a restless night. Tossing and turning. Thinking and worrying. Falling into a fitful sleep only to wake up from a succession of terrible nightmares. Nightmares whose details evaporated as soon as she woke up but left her with the fear. Her heart pounding and her mouth dry. Knowing she'd been dreaming about dreadful things happening to everyone she loved and cared about.

Her father. Betty, Mary and Tibby. Alice, Geordie and Joshua. Her friends. Robert Catto.

'Are you all right, lass? You're looking a wee bittie tired.'

She blinked, bringing herself back to the here and now, and took the drawings from him. 'I'll keep these safe in a folio until your classes start up again. After I've put them away I'm going through to the shop to check we have enough physic. You know how people save their ailments up over the Daft Days.' She was already heading towards her own smaller and infinitely tidier desk and the cabinet which sat beside it.

'Indeed,' Patrick said, 'only tae present themselves in a steady stream o' misery in the first few days o' the New Year. Shall I come through and help you, my dear?'

'Och no, it won't take me long. Besides, you said you had some other papers to go through before we eat.'

She was glad she had her back to him. For in the midst of her troubled night an idea had come to her. She knew where she and Robert Catto could meet in private.

Once she had cleaned and put away the pestle and mortar and the little brass scales, she replaced the last two newly filled blue and white pottery apothecary's jars on the wooden shelves behind the counter. Those were painted apple-green. 'Blue and green should never be seen,' she muttered to herself. 'And you're havering, Kirsty Rankeillor. Get on with it. He'll be here soon.'

She was not thinking of her father. As she had not really needed to check their stocks of physic. Always well prepared, she had done so a week ago, so there had been very little to do. What she had wanted was to be in the shop on her own, knowing her father was busy behind the closed double doors which led from the shop into the library while Betty and everyone else was either in the kitchen or upstairs.

Nobody could see her from the street, either. The shop door was closed, a blind of stiff cream-coloured paper drawn down over the window in the top of it. The window shutters were also closed, although the breaks between the panels of wood which formed them allowed plenty of light to spill into the shop. It looked like it was a really sunny day out there now.

Leaning back against the solid wood of the shop counter, she tapped her thumb nail against her teeth. *He'll be here soon.* Her eyes fluttered shut. In her mind's eye she could see Robert Catto striding towards her through the streets of Edinburgh. Or leaping over the garden walls which lay between the guard-house and Infirmary Street, the skirts of his long leather coat flying out as he walked. As eager to reach her as she was for him to arrive.

She wanted him so much, with a physical desire she had never before experienced. She longed to feel his kiss again, longed to feel his arms about her. Holding her close. Caressing her. One hand rising to cup her breast. She lowered her own hand, spreading her fingers out over her clothes to still the flutters inside her stomach.

Her eyes snapped open. How could she even be contemplating lying with Robert Catto? *How could she?* This thought too had troubled her throughout the night. He was the enemy, hostile to everything she held dear. Implacably opposed to the Stuart Cause, a danger to her father, their friends and herself. Determined to do his duty to German Geordie and the House of Hanover. Fooling those friends he shared their Jacobite loyalties with the sole aim of enticing them ever further into the trap he had been laying since he had arrived in Edinburgh.

She should have told Agnes Moncur and Murdo Robertson Robert Catto was not what he seemed. Instead, on Christmas Eve, she had timed the delivery of her last batch of physic to the hospital knowing both would be busy on the ward round. She could still have given them a warning, tucked a wee note inside one of the two wicker baskets which held the physic.

He is not on our side. That was all she would have needed to write.

Only she hadn't. Because she had fallen in love with him. Because she feared the consequences to him if he was unmasked. She had chosen Robert Catto over the Cause. Flooded with guilt, she bent forward and buried her face in her hands.

Behind her, one of the double doors from the lobby into the shop creaked open. Head snapping up, Christian whirled round. 'B-Betty?' she stuttered.

With a little trill, Lucy the cat, more white than black, leapt in one lithe movement up onto the shop counter, calling forth a fierce whisper of reproach from her mistress, using the cat's full Sunday name. 'Och, Lucrezia Borgia, what a fright you gave me!'

Only once her heartbeat had begun to slow down to its normal rate did she address the cat again, speaking this time in a soft murmur. 'That was a guilty conscience talking, was it not? You're not supposed to be up here, puss,' she added, though she made no move to lift the cat down onto the floor.

Instead, she watched as Lucy set about washing herself, tiny pink tongue darting in and out of her mouth. The frantic activity stopped as abruptly as it had started. 'That was a quick wash. A lick and promise, is it? Och, dinna look at me like that!' she implored, as the cat surveyed her out of bright and all-knowing eyes.

She tickled the top of the furry head with her fingers, murmuring soft words, hardly knowing what she was saying. 'He likes you, you know. Appropriate for a man called Catto, don't you think?'

The voice of the man called Catto rang round her head. *No turning back. Agreed?*

Yesterday morning he'd asked her to cup her hands, wrapped his own around them, told her he was placing his heart there for safe-keeping, told her his home would be in her hands. She had promised she would keep his heart safe. As he had promised he would do his best for her father and their friends.

Still she stood there, tormented by indecision. Even if she took this next step, how would it be possible for them to meet? What if they did manage to and Betty and her father found out? He would be so disappointed in her. Betty would be distraught.

No turning back. Agreed?

She *had* agreed, made him a promise. Because when she'd been waiting for him to return after rescuing Geordie and Joshua from Eastfield she had thought how it would be if he didn't come back. How she would spend the rest of her life longing for the touch of his hand and the sound of his voice. How she would spend the rest of her life wishing they had made love to each other.

Christian lifted her chin. Feeling she was stepping over an invisible line taking her from safety into danger, she selected one of the household keys which hung on a steel ring and chain at her waist. It opened a locked cupboard in the row which ran along the wall behind the counter. There were a few keys inside there too, seldom used but kept safe for whenever they might be needed. She lifted two sturdy ones off their hooks.

Locking the cupboard again, she stood up straight and took a breath, deep enough to slacken her grip. The keys slipped out of her fingers and fell with a clatter onto the wooden floor. Sinking into a crouch, she covered them with one hand to stop the noise, her heart once again racing. Springing to her feet, she slipped the keys into the quilted pocket she wore under her gown, tied around her waist by a narrow linen tape.

Left ajar by Lucy, one of the doors out into the lobby creaked again.

Chapter 12

'Letter for you, Captain.' The post office clerk swung round to the wall of wooden pigeon-holes behind him and back again to proffer it across the wooden counter. 'Glasgow mail coach has just come in. This the one you were hoping for yesterday?'

Ignoring the question, Catto reached out and found he had to tug. The man seemed reluctant to let the little folded packet go.

'Something important, I'm thinking?'

'Tell you what,' Catto growled. 'You mind your own business and I'll mind mine.'

His mood plummeting, he walked the short distance to the guard-house with the letter burning a hole in his pocket. Like a lit fuse snaking its way towards a barrel of gunpowder. He had a bad feeling about what he was going to find in here. He had recognized the neat handwriting as belonging to the woman who acted as the Lord President's eyes and ears in Glasgow.

Catto had written to her after Daft Friday, asking her to 'redouble your efforts in the matters previously discussed.' You had to be careful about letters going through the public mails. You could use code or a cipher, of course, but in so doing you ran the risk of signalling to any interested parties you had something to hide.

The two guards on duty stood up when he entered the guard-house, Sergeant Crichton giving him a passably decent salute. That was progress. He couldn't expect them to follow full military discipline. Most were tradesmen. Some, like Crichton and Livingstone, ran their own businesses. Like Livingstone, many were Highlanders, with the sometimes prickly pride of their race. You couldn't order them about like raw recruits.

In any case, he'd always believed in mutual respect between

private men and officers. As he had always thought the brutal floggings meted out to private men guilty of misdemeanours were a mistake. He knew the previous Captain of the Town Guard had ordered some harsh punishments here in Edinburgh too, as humiliating as they were brutal.

A guard who had been disciplined was forced to sit for an extended period astride a wooden horse, no wider than the narrow edge of a plank, outside the guard-house. As discomfort became pain and pain became agony, he would also be subjected to name-calling – and sometimes worse – from disgruntled citizens. Many called the Town Guard the Town Rats. This was not a popular brigade.

Catto had no intention of ordering such punishments. Bad for morale as much as anything else. His approach seemed to be working as far the men were concerned. Despite the too frequent and deeply irritating prefacing of *Young* before his name, he thought he was beginning to earn their respect. Though right at this moment that observation was not lifting his mood by one iota.

'Anything to report?'

Sergeant Crichton shook his head. 'Not a thing, sir. Very quiet. It'll likely be different on Old Year's Night. Can be as rowdy as Daft Friday.'

'So I understand, Sergeant. I've drawn up the rosters. We'll have a full complement on duty. Here and at the posts around the city.'

'Where's young Geordie got to, young Captain Catto?' asked the second guard. 'He's usually got our dinner ready at this hour.'

'He had to go home for a while. Someone ill.' The lie tripped easily off his tongue. He was impatient to read the letter. While at the same time dreading what he was going to find in there. He glanced at the guard-room fire, which was burning brightly. Whatever was going on in your head, there was always time for a word of appreciation and encouragement.

'That's a welcome sight on a chilly morning.'

'Fire in your bedchamber not lit?' asked the second guard. 'I'll soon sort it out.'

'It would be grand if you could do it sometime this afternoon.

I have to go back out again shortly.'

'What about your meridian?' Crichton asked.

'Going to take it down at *The White Horse.* Can you bespeak some victuals for the two of you and I'll reimburse you later?'

'I'm about to go off duty, Mr Catto. Just waiting on my relief. I'll order something on my way home and ask for it to be delivered.' A stout man himself, Sergeant Crichton patted the stomach of the other guard. He was well-built but nowhere near his own girth. 'We dinna want this one tae fade away through lack o' nourishment.'

'That's mair likely tae happen tae your relief,' came the reply. 'He's a right skinny-malinky-long-legs.'

Their laughter followed Catto as he left the guard-room. A few moments later, still wearing his leather coat, he was sitting at his desk in his bedchamber at the opposite end of the building, reading through the letter from the informant for the second time. Two names he didn't recognize. Two he did. Making a fist, he thumped it on his desk, muttering a few obscenities.

Andrew Wood, shoemaker in the High Street of Glasgow. The informant had seen Patrick Rankeillor paying an evening visit to his workshop, where the two other people mentioned in the letter had joined him, one after the other. Rankeillor had stayed for an hour before all three had left – again separately – allowing a few moments between each departure. Shortly after the last of the three had departed, the shoemaker had walked the few yards from his workshop to his nearby house. The inference was clear. The meeting had been a covert one.

A shoemaker. Armies were always in want of shoes. They wore out quickly when foot soldiers were on the march. So this could be yet more evidence of a rising being in the planning. Catto cursed louder this time, raising his head from the letter and speaking the words into the chill of his bedchamber.

'Fucking hell. Fucking bloody hell. What a crowd of sodding bloody fools they are. Ready to risk not only their own lives and safety but those of their families too. All for the sake of the sodding Stuarts and their sodding bloody Cause, dead but it won't lie down, kept alive by dreamers and fools like Patrick Rankeillor and Andrew Wood and God knows how many others.'

Andrew Wood who just happened to be the brother of Meg Wood, one of Kirsty Rankeillor's closest friends. Not so close now. Catto had contributed to the fracturing of that friendship. A distressed Meg Wood had blurted out her brother's name, demanding to know if Kirsty Rankeillor didn't care about him and into what danger he might be led by a new rising in support of the Stuarts.

Of course I care! You cannot think I do not care about your brother! And you've just given him another name, Meg! Kirsty Rankeillor had said those words, pointing a shaking finger at Catto. Both girls had looked at him, their faces pale and stricken. He had looked back, outwardly impassive, knowing he could not say he would forget that name. His duty demanded he take a note of it and pass it on. Once again, he spoke out loud.

'Damn all Jacobites to hell.'

Except for one. Elbows propped on his desk, he leant forward and put his head in his hands.

There was a knock at the door of his bedchamber.

Christian leapt to her feet. Relief swept through her when she saw Joshua standing there at the door with his fingers wrapped around the edge of it.

'It's all r-right,' she stuttered. 'You can come in. No one can see you with the shutters closed.'

'I'm no' usually such a scaredy-cat,' he offered, pushing the door wider and taking a couple of steps into the room.

'I dinna think you are. Not at all,' Christian responded, pulling herself together. 'Especially not after what you did the night before last.'

The night before last, when he had summoned up his courage to take himself and Geordie away from Eastfield.

He gave her an uncertain look and began stroking the cat, who was still sitting placidly on the counter. 'I was real feart the whole time, miss.'

'That's what being brave is. Being feart but still doing what you know you have to do.'

He cocked his head to one side, considering. 'Maybe, miss. Maybe. Mrs Betty sent me to find you and tell you we're nearly ready to eat.'

He stopped looking at Christian in favour of looking around the shop, the blue and white pottery jars on the shelves, the small wooden drawers of physic with their Latin names written on black and gilt-edged labels, the pestle and mortar and the little brass weighing scales on the surface below them.

'I like those,' he said, using the hand which wasn't stroking Lucrezia Borgia to point towards the scales and the different sized weights neatly stacked beside them.

'Oh, so do I! For some reason it's very satisfying to measure out the physic on such dainty scales. Would you like me to show you how to do it sometime?'

His eyes shot back to her face. 'I'd like that fine, miss. I really would.'

'We'll do that, then,' she said, warmed by his interest. Touched too. 'But not right now or we'll be in trouble with Mrs Betty.'

'I'll take the wee cat,' Joshua said, picking Lucy up to hold her secure in his arms. Standing there looking at them, Christian found a string of thoughts and emotions trailing through her head. About being scared. About being brave. About being subjected for the whole of your young life to the whims of a cruel mistress but still finding the courage to help a friend despite what it might cost you. About not knowing what the future might hold but still being ready and willing to learn new things.

She was scared too. Of what might be going to happen when the Lord President returned to Edinburgh. The possible consequences to her father, herself and their friends of what they had done were terrifying. So terrifying she was doing her utmost not to think about them. As she now knew, there was a major flaw in her strategy. Shutting it all out during a busy day was just about possible – only for the nightmares to ambush you at night.

An even more immediate fear was that Cosmo and Charlotte Liddell would somehow find out where Joshua, Geordie and Alice were. Robert Catto had said he had the Liddells at a considerable disadvantage, presumably because he now had them too under house arrest. But what was to stop them from sending some of the brutes who worked for them to overpower the young people and carry them back to Eastfield?

If they tried to force entry to this house, would she and her father be able to stop them? If the three young people were taken back to Eastfield, the law would say they had to stay there, trapped once again in the miserable lives they thought they had escaped. Mired in back-breaking work, the ever-present threat of kicks, blows, floggings and Charlotte Liddell's cruel and capricious whims. Without freedom and without hope. Which would be even worse after they had tasted both.

Too many men, women and children led such miserable lives. Christian wished she could free them all from slavery and servitude, give them hope for a brighter and better future. Her heart grew heavy knowing she could not.

'Are you alright, Miss Kirsty?'

She blinked, and gave herself a shake. 'Just away in a dwam, Joshua. Let us go through.'

She could not save the world. As she could not know what lay in store for her father, their friends and herself. She could not know if she could help the orphans of the storm to a better life. What she could do was try. Joshua had set her an example, walking towards the future and not allowing fear to stop him.

There was something else she could do. However short-lived her love affair with Robert Catto might be, she would seize the chance of it with both hands. As she would choose to protect Betty and her father from what they didn't need to know. As she would – somehow – come to terms with her conscience about lying with a man who despised the Cause and was actively working against it. As she would not betray him to her friends and his enemies.

She followed boy and cat through, the big solid keys snug against her hip.

Chapter 13

Hastily raising his head, Catto turned, swung one arm over the back of his chair and called out the command to come in.

Archie Liddell stepped into the room. Skinny-malinky-long-legs. He should have guessed who Sergeant Crichton and the other guard had been talking about. Like Alice Smart and the young maids at Infirmary Street, someone else who was scared of him. From the look on his face, determined all the same to beard the lion in his den. He waited as Liddell's gaze swept over him, a frown settling between the younger man's dark brows. 'Are you all right, Mr Catto?'

'Not entirely,' he replied, caught off-guard both by the question and the concern evident in Liddell's expression.

'Can I do anything for you?'

Catto stood up. 'You can come into the room and close the door behind you. Here. Sit down on the chair and I'll take the bed. I expect you'd like to know what happened the night before last. How much did Mr Charles Paterson the lawyer tell you when he came here looking for me?'

'Enough,' Archie said, his mouth tightening. He lowered his lanky body into the chair Catto had turned to face the room. 'Just when I think my cousins can't behave any more badly than they already do, they prove me wrong.'

'It gets worse, Lieutenant,' Catto said wearily, sitting down on the edge of his bed. 'Sure you want to know?'

'I'm sure, Captain.'

Ten minutes later, the expression on Archie Liddell's face was one of disgust. 'What Cosmo and Arthur did to Geordie's sister was wicked,' he said, his voice not quite steady. 'Cruel in the extreme—' He broke off, swallowing hard.

'It's all right, Lieutenant. Give yourself a moment.'

Liddell drew in a deep breath. 'I'm fine, Captain. As for flogging Geordie—' Words once again failing him, he shot Catto a look from under his brows. 'You do know I would have come with you and Sergeant Livingstone to rescue them from Eastfield?'

'Aye. But I did not want to make life any more difficult for you. Or anyone else. As it stands, 'tis only I who has broken the law.'

'And Sergeant Livingstone.'

'I'm going to leave him out of it.'

'He may not let you.'

'We'll see about that.' Catto leant forward, waiting for the next question.

'How is Geordie?'

'In good hands.'

'What of Miss Rankeillor, Captain? Her situation?'

'I'm going to do my utmost to protect her from any consequences of her much to be regretted actions.' Catto pulled a face. 'If she'll let me.'

'Aye, Kirsty can be real stubborn.'

'You know her well?'

'She and I have been friends since childhood. Jamie, too.' His face clouded. 'I can scarce believe what he did to that other girl.'

'Men with a cause, Liddell. It makes them hold not only their own lives cheap but also the lives of everyone around them.'

The younger man shook his head. 'I cannot believe that of Professor Rankeillor, Captain. You're sure he was involved in the plot to get the Jacobite agent out of Edinburgh?'

'I'm sure.'

'What will you do when the professor returns to Edinburgh?'

'He's already here. Got back yesterday. That's why I'm sure he was involved. I've conducted a preliminary interrogation and now have him under house arrest at Infirmary Street.'

'Geordie is there too, I would jalouse.'

'Would you indeed?' Catto laid his hands on his knees under

the leather coat, readying himself to stand up. Liddell had something else to say. Judging by the steely look in his eyes, he was as determined on saying it as he had been to have this conversation.

'He must have been in want of medical care after what was done to him. Kirsty would have been all too ready to supply it. Hers will be the good hands you mentioned. I expect Geordie's sister is also at Infirmary Street. And young Joshua.'

'You seem to know all my secrets, Liddell.'

'I'm sure I don't. And as I've told you before, you can rely on my discretion about any I do know. You can rely absolutely on that, Captain.'

They looked at each other, both knowing which particular secret Liddell meant. He had been at the Assembly Rooms when Catto and John Roy Stuart had come face to face with each other. However much Catto might seek to deny the relationship, there had been no room for doubt the two were father and son.

'Thank you, Lieutenant,' he said gravely. 'I appreciate your discretion. I hope I may ask for your help too.'

'Anything I can do, sir.' The lieutenant laid his hand on his heart. 'Anything at all.'

'One is in your own field, as a student of the law. I believe Mr Charles Paterson would appreciate your assistance with some papers he is drawing up.'

He explained what those papers were, told Liddell he had discussed with Paterson the possibility of Liddell acting as his confidential clerk. 'Mr Paterson tells me he's had his eye on you for some time, would be very happy for you to take articles with him after you graduate from the university.'

Archie Liddell's face lit up in an expression of pure joy. 'That would be wonderful, my mother would be so happy!'

'You too, Liddell, I hope.'

'Oh aye, Captain, especially after what Charlotte said on Daft Friday—' He stopped short.

'I know what Miss Liddell said. Sergeant Livingstone told me. How she threatened to ruin your legal career before it had even started. What did you do to deserve such detestable relatives, Lieutenant?'

'According to Charlotte, it's because my father was stupid enough to marry a poor woman for love.' His voice was very flat. Then, in a lower voice but one filled with emotion. 'My parents were so happy together, Captain. So very happy. We all were, just the three of us, in our wee cottage out at Colinton.'

'Your father's dead?'

Liddell nodded. 'Five years ago. It's been a struggle for my mother, Captain. I'd love to be able to repay all the sacrifices she's made for me.'

'Well,' Catto said briskly, rising to his feet, 'working for Mr Charles Paterson will be an excellent start. Who already knew enough about your detestable cousins which was not to their credit. He knows even more now. So he'll be calling the tune, not them. I shall also give you a letter, telling him he can trust you implicitly.'

Flushed with pleasure, Liddell too stood up. 'Is there aught else I can do for you, Captain?'

'You know Edinburgh better than I do. Can you think where we might find a different hiding place for our three charges? Their current one is too easily guessed. As you have just done. I'm sure Sergeant Livingstone and his wife would be only too willing to help but the nature of their business precludes it.'

Liddell nodded. 'Too many eyes to see and too many ears to hear at *The White Horse*.'

'Exactly. It needs to be somewhere quiet. Where few would notice the arrival of three young people. Even though Joshua is rather noticeable. Also well-known from people having seen him escort Miss Liddell around Edinburgh.'

'He is that. A weel-kent face as well as a distinctive one.'

'Therefore we're looking for a place where people say little to outsiders and are disinclined to gossip about their neighbours. Yet not too far from Edinburgh so we might continue to keep a close eye on them until their position is safely and happily resolved.' He pulled a face. 'A tall order, I think.'

Archie Liddell was looking thoughtful. 'I might just have a suggestion for you, Captain.'

Chapter 14

Catto was in *The White Horse*, the coaching inn at the foot of the Canongate which Sergeant Livingstone ran with his young wife Marjorie. Despite her cheerful flirting with the customers, everyone knew she was as devoted to her husband as he was to her. They'd given Catto a warm welcome and a hearty dinner.

In exchange, he was now telling them how Geordie was. He made sure to speak in a low voice, standing at the bar a safe distance from the other customers and the booths in which they were eating. Those were wooden backed like church pews, only higher. Privacy for those with confidential matters to discuss over their dinner was further assured by framed opaque glass roundels at head height and above. They were in different colours, the bright winter sun striking red, green and blue glints from them.

Catto repeated the story Kirsty Rankeillor had told him about Geordie insisting on going upstairs at Infirmary Street so as not to be too much trouble to her.

Marjorie lifted a corner of her apron to dab her eyes. 'He's a grand laddie,' she managed, her voice trembling on the words. 'I'm hoping he'll soon be back down here, saying hello to the horses in our stable and making friends with our bairns, like he did afore.'

'Let's hope so,' Catto said, thinking how many difficulties had to be overcome before that could happen. 'For now, not a word to anyone, Mistress Livingstone. Including your bairns.'

'Not a word,' she assured him. 'They'll learn sometime, nae doot, although ah'd rather they didna ever hear what was done tae their friend. Such wickedness.'

Donnie Livingstone put his hand over hers where it lay on the bar. 'Aye. Wickedness is the word.'

Marjorie picked up the damp cloth with which she'd been wiping down the bar, put it on a round wooden tray and lifted her head in acknowledgement of the customer who had leant out of his booth and was calling over to her.

'One moment, Mistress Livingstone, if I may. Geordie and Joshua are both in need of clothes. I wonder if I might enlist your help in finding some.'

Kirsty Rankeillor had mentioned this before he had left Infirmary Street yesterday. Joshua only had what he stood up in. Geordie had nothing other than his borrowed nightshirt. As she had told Catto, she had disposed of the filthy and ragged breeches and tattered shirt which had been thrown to him at Eastfield after he had been flogged. They were bundled up now in a corner of the coal bunker outside the back door, to be tossed with similar contempt onto a bonfire when the physic garden was cleared of twigs and winter debris before being tidied up for the spring.

'Nothing fancy,' Catto said, remembering what she had said about Joshua clearly hating how the horrible Charlotte Liddell liked to dress him up in velvet and lace. 'Don't have to be new. A serviceable pair of breeches and a waistcoat each. Maybe three shirts apiece and some small clothes. It might excite interest were I to go about buying such items. I was wondering too if there might be some clothes your older boy has grown out of. I think he is perhaps a little taller than Geordie and Joshua.'

'I swear our Michael shoots up a bittie more every time I turn my back. He's all arms and legs!'

'My mother used to say that about me,' Catto confided, thinking what a nice woman she was. There were good people in this world and Marjorie and Donald John Livingstone were two of the best.

'I'm sure I can find you what's needed, Mr Catto.'

As his hand went to his pocket, she raised her own in a gesture of refusal. 'No need for payment now. If there's any reckoning to be paid, I'll let you know. I'll leave you to it, gentlemen.'

She was also leaving Catto to the piercing blue gaze of her husband.

Chapter 15

Livingstone was a fine figure of a man, with a mane of white hair sweeping back from his brow. From the moment Catto had first met him, he had thought the sergeant looked not unlike a kindly God. Albeit, with those shrewd blue eyes, one who gave you the distinct feeling he could see deep into your heart, knew the secrets of your very soul.

He and Livingstone had had a very strange conversation on their way towards Eastfield, when they had stopped for a few moments to allow the horses to drink from a burn. Waiting for their mounts to slake their thirst, they had sat looking out over the moonlit German ocean: and talked about love.

'What now, young sir?'

'In what sense do you mean, Sergeant?'

Please don't ask me the question you asked the night before last. The question the father of a daughter would ask. Are my intentions towards Kirsty Rankeillor honourable? Not right at this moment, they're not. They cannot be. So what gives me the right to take advantage of her, to take advantage of the situation? Where all the power is on my side?

'In whichever sense you are willing to share your thoughts with me.' Livingstone inclined his impressive head. 'In the hope I might perhaps be of some service to you.'

'You could tell me more of Captain Porteous' story.'

Livingstone raised his eyebrows. Like his hair, they were white and luxuriant. 'Not sure there's much more to tell.'

After Catto had found out that Porteous had been hanged by the mob, Livingstone had given him some details of the event, although with obvious reluctance. It had been eight years back, at one of those public hangings in the Grassmarket. Two local men, notorious smugglers, were to be executed. The huge crowd gathered to watch had been sympathetic to the condemned men and hostile to the Town Guard, on duty to ensure the sentence of the court was carried out.

'There were fears of a rescue attempt?' Catto asked now.

'Aye. Smugglers can be gey popular,' Livingstone said in his lilting West Highland accent. 'With all manner of folk, rich and poor.'

Catto nodded. 'The free-trading gentlemen who supply you with brandy, tea or lace without you having to pay duty on it. Cocking a snook at the law while they do it.'

'Exactly, Mr Catto. There was a lot of shouting. Insults being thrown at us. Foul language. The crowd jostling and moving like an angry sea.'

'Which threatened to come rushing in and overwhelm the men of the Town Guard?'

'Aye. I do not blame Captain Porteous for ordering us to fire warning shots over the heads of the crowd. I made sure to aim left or right. Up or down the Grassmarket and into empty space at either end. I do not believe others deliberately aimed at anyone.'

Livingstone's face was troubled. 'There are some as say Captain Porteous did, killing one man in the crowd standing not too far away from him. If he did, I did not see it.'

'You think some of the guards panicked and hardly knew in which direction they were firing?'

'Indeed. Hitting some folk watching from windows overlooking the Grassmarket.'

'Six dead, I think you said. And thirty wounded.'

'Aye. A bad day for Edinburgh and for the Town Guard. Captain Porteous was held responsible, arrested, charged with murder and sentenced to be hanged.'

'But pardoned.'

Livingstone nodded. 'By Queen Caroline. She was acting as regent while her man was back in Hanover.'

'She took a personal interest in the case?' Catto asked, puzzled.

'I do not think so. She would have been advised to sign the pardon, I'm thinking.'

'Because her advisers would not tolerate an officer of the law being arrested and tried?'

'That. Which did not sit well with the good folk of Edinburgh. The town was still in mourning. Growing angrier by the day, forbye. The pardon was seen as unwarranted interference by London in the affairs of Scotland.'

'It became a political matter?'

They were straying onto unsafe ground here. He would trust Livingstone with his life, especially after their rescue mission of two nights before What the man's politics were in this Scotland of dangerous and shifting loyalties was another matter entirely.

'It was a political matter from the beginning,' Livingstone said. 'There are those who say the leaders of the mob which broke into the Tolbooth to drag the captain out of it held views of a Jacobite nature.'

'There was evidence for that?'

'Some of the mob leaders appeared to be women. But women who were tall of stature, broad of shoulder and deep of voice.'

Catto cast him a doubtful look over the almost empty tankard of ale he'd just raised to his mouth. 'That doesn't necessarily make them Jacobites. Might have been trying to conceal their identities with the aim of evading punishment afterwards.'

'Aye,' Livingstone said. 'But they might also have been people well-kent in Edinburgh and of higher rank.'

'Why do you say that, Sergeant?'

'Two things. There are stories of ladies in sedan chairs being stopped and courteously advised to turn around and go home because there was likely to be trouble in the town that night. Those who gave the warnings might have been dressed like working men but it seemed they were gently bred, with gentle manners.'

Catto nodded, acknowledging the logic of those statements.

'Another wee detail has stayed lodged in my mind. After the mob forced entry to the Tolbooth, they carried Captain Porteous down to the Grassmarket. Where they broke into a ropemaker's to steal a length of rope. The next morning the ropemaker found a guinea on his counter.'

Catto whistled. 'A lot of money to pay for a length of rope.'

'Aye. Even if 'twas meant also to pay for the repair of the lock they smashed with a hammer to get into the shop.'

'Implying whoever put the coin on the counter was not a poor man?'

'Also that in hanging Captain Porteous the leaders of the mob were acting perfectly legally. According to the laws of Scotland, that is. Not those of England. Which many do not believe should hold sway here. Perhaps the gold coin also had a symbolic significance. There are those who say that in the Union of the Parliaments of 1707 Scots were bought and sold for English gold.'

'When some of the gentry and aristocracy took bribes to vote in favour of the Union.' Catto didn't care for that fact but he knew it to be a true one.

Livingstone nodded. 'Enough of them to sign the death warrant of the ancient kingdom.'

Aware of movement behind him, Catto turned and saw two customers heading for the door out into the street, bidding a cheerful goodbye to Marjorie Livingstone as they went, followed by a wave to her husband.

Swinging back round, Catto saw Livingstone raise his own hand in response. Then the eyes of the two men met.

The death warrant of the ancient kingdom. After an uncomfortable pause, Catto offered another phrase.

'The end of an old song.'

Livingstone held his gaze. 'It was indeed.'

The end o' an auld sang. The Lord President had quoted those words to him. They'd been said originally by Andrew Fletcher of Saltoun, one member of the Scottish parliament who had passionately opposed the political union with England. The Lord President was convinced the union was Scotland's best hope for peace and prosperity. Yet Catto had heard regret in Culloden's voice. That regret had spoken to something within himself. Unsettled, he veiled his thoughts behind a flippant comment.

'I can only hope I don't suffer the same fate as Captain Porteous.'

'I do not think you need worry on that score, Mr Catto. Captain Porteous was – well, there's no two ways about it – not a popular man. Sought favour with his superiors but was harsh and overbearing to those he saw as his inferiors. Who were equally the poor of Edinburgh and ourselves, as members of the Town Guard.'

Catto took a last swig of ale, setting the tankard down on the bar. 'Hardly think I'm a popular man cither, Livingstone. Don't know the Captain of the Town Guard ever can be. Think of the mob on Daft Friday.'

'Which you faced down, young Captain Catto.' The corners of Livingstone's mouth lifted. 'I hear you raised your musket and asked which one of them you should shoot first.'

'Even more reason for them to hate me.'

'No. They'll respect you for your strength. I've already heard folk speak admiringly of how you took control of the situation. You can be stern, Mr Catto, but you're always fair. Should I understand,' he went on, 'that you're thinking of making this temporary posting a permanent one?'

'Not my decision, Sergeant.'

'But one you would wish to take? All personal considerations aside,' Livingstone said carefully, 'I'm thinking you would make a grand job of it. You've already worked wonders.'

Catto inclined his head to one side, acknowledging the compliment. Warmed by it. He would play Devil's Advocate all the same. Old habits died hard.

'Not sure me taking permanent command of the Town Guard would ever be on the cards, Sergeant. Especially after what I chose to do two nights ago.'

Livingstone squared his powerful shoulders. 'I chose to do it with you, young Captain Catto. As I'll stand with you if there are any repercussions.'

Catto shot him a wry look. 'Archie Liddell said you would. But I cannot allow you to do so.' He raised a hand to stop Livingstone's protest. 'Besides which, there might be another reason against me being given permanent command. A reason of which you are very well-aware.'

Although he wasn't entirely sure of the validity of this particular argument. Wasn't his parentage and his deeply-regretted Jacobite connections exactly why the Lord President had thought he might find a use for him here in Edinburgh?

Livingstone fixed him with his steady blue gaze and gave him the same answer Archie Liddell had. 'A reason which stays between you and me, Captain. As does anything else you may have told me when we were on our way to Musselburgh. You can be sure of that. As you can be sure of finding me by your side if there is trouble about bringing the lads from Musselburgh to Infirmary Street.'

'You're a stubborn man, Livingstone.'

The sergeant laughed. 'Aye. Marjorie would agree with you there.' His face grew serious again. 'You really think there might be trouble heading towards us?'

'It's looking increasingly like it.'

'More evidence than the meeting which was taking place at the Assembly Rooms on Daft Friday?'

'Aye. Adding to that evidence.'

Livingstone drew in a breath. 'In case you're wondering, young Captain Catto, trouble such as we're talking about is not something I would welcome.'

'No?' Catto gave him back look for look.

'No,' the sergeant said firmly. 'A man may have his beliefs and opinions but may also have had a bellyful of war and bloodshed.'

'And not want to see it in his own backyard?'

'Exactly, young Captain Catto. Exactly.'

Chapter 16

Catto left *The White Horse* and walked up the Canongate. Crossing over the causeway, he headed off through a close which would lead him to the Cowgate Port. Even though he was approaching Infirmary Street from a different direction than usual, it seemed a good idea to also take a less than direct route. He'd made it his business as soon as he'd arrived in Edinburgh back in November to explore as many shortcuts and alternative ways of getting from one place to another as he could find.

He'd grown to like this one, taking him as it did past one of the town's bowling greens and between two long narrow vegetable gardens, where the tall tenements stretching back from the Canongate gave way to more open views. He could feel a greater freshness in the air, his nose telling him these gardens had not received a delivery in the early hours of this morning of what were sarcastically termed the flowers o' Edinburgh.

If you were lucky, the citizens of the Scottish capital waited a decent interval after the town gates were shut at 10 o'clock at night before shouting 'Gardyloo!', sticking their arms out of the windows of their tenement lands and upending their chamber pots onto the street below. However many storeys down that might be. The night soil scavengers had the unenviable overnight task of collecting the mixture of human waste, ashes and vegetable peelings and putting it all in carts to be taken away to nourish nursery gardens and farmers' fields.

Pausing for a moment, Catto raised his face to drink in the cleaner air and the expanded vista. Above the rooftops of the Palace of Holyroodhouse, the old residence of the Stuart kings and queens, the sloping ridge of Salisbury Crags rose up into the winter blue sky. Soaring behind and above was the rugged mountain they called Arthur's Seat. A volcano in ancient times, so he'd been told. Countless thousands of years ago, he supposed, when the world was young. Much farther back even than the legendary King Arthur and the Knights of the Round Table.

The world was old now, and tired. Human beings kept making the same mistakes, over and over again. Kept hurting their fellow men and women, over and over again. As he and Kirsty Rankeillor seemed destined to hurt each other. In the situation in which they found themselves, how could it be otherwise?

Last night as he had vaulted his way over the walls on his way back from Infirmary Street and dared to dream, the idea he had already tentatively mentioned to her had taken full shape. Why should he not resign his commission in Guise's and become permanent Captain of the Edinburgh Town Guard?

He was more than capable of filling the position, knew exactly how he would go about it. He would continue knocking the men into shape, make this part-time militia a force to be reckoned with. He would consult with Professor MacLaurin at Edinburgh University over the parlous state of Edinburgh's city walls and other defences.

Catto had met MacLaurin earlier in December. The good professor feared it would be all too easy for a Jacobite army to breach those defences. Catto agreed with him. Repair and strengthening ought to be undertaken as a matter of urgency. Before a Jacobite army simply scrambled over those crumbling stones and took control of the city. Catto's mouth tightened. Which might – God Almighty – be sooner rather than later.

To be sure, Edinburgh's Lord Provost John Coutts likely wouldn't be happy about any repairs and strengthening of the walls. Duncan Forbes of Culloden suspected Coutts had connived at their decline into their current sorry state, believing the man to be a covert Jacobite, secretly sympathetic to the Stuart Cause. Like Duncan Forbes, Coutts had yet to return to Edinburgh after a prolonged Christmas visit elsewhere.

Once Lord President Forbes came back to Edinburgh, the pretence that Catto too was a covert Jacobite would end. It would have to. The intelligence he had gathered, the dispatch from Glasgow adding to the evidence of a very real threat of armed rebellion, meant action had to be taken. Arthur Menzies of Edmonstone, Cosmo Liddell and the other inept Jacobite plotters Catto had fooled were in for a very rude awakening.

Catto suspected Culloden would strike hard bargains with all of them, discreetly of course. Not only because that was the Lord President's preferred way of going about things but also in the hope of flushing out yet more Stuart sympathisers. The chances were high he would tell them – make that *order* them – to go about their lives as normal. Which meant they would be out and about in the world again. Where they would be baying for Robert Catto's blood.

Hideous unease seized him as he stood there. Arthur Menzies and Cosmo Liddell now knew the secret of who his father was. Loathing the deception, he'd been forced to use it as a way of convincing them he was indeed sympathetic to the Stuart Cause.

Despite the threats Culloden would be holding over their heads, they would still be free to move around, talk to others, drip poison in their ears. Couple Catto's parentage with the inevitable realization he had been working for the Lord President all along and Edinburgh's Jacobites could paint him as not to be trusted by either side. That wouldn't do his chances of advancement much good, either in Guise's or as permanent Captain of the Town Guard.

On top of all this, how could he expect Christian Rankeillor to forgive him for gathering information against her father and their friends? In Meg Wood's brother, he now had confirmation another of those friends should be added to the tally. How could he expect her to allow him to make love to her, far less want to spend the rest of her life with him? He was back in Cloud Cuckoo Land.

'Twas worse even than that. Much, much worse. A few days ago he had seen another of her closest friends onto the boat for Banff. He had persuaded Anna Gordon, against her own better judgement, that she could best help Christian Rankeillor by leaving Edinburgh before Christmas. He knew very well that she too was a committed Jacobite, might well have been involved in the plot to smuggle the Jacobite agent out of the city. But, God forgive him, it had suited him to leave Kirsty Rankeillor isolated.

He had stayed there on The Shore at Leith for a while, watching as the vessel glided out through Leith Roads to the wider Firth of Forth and the open sea beyond. Until Anna Gordon, standing on the deck looking back at him, had grown smaller and smaller and he could no longer see the worried expression on her face. It had come to him then what part the uncaring fates had assigned to him in this developing drama. He was the angel of death and the destroyer of worlds.

He could destroy Christian Rankeillor's world. He was already on the way to doing so. Whichever way you looked at it. If her Jacobite friends found out about her and him, she would be tainted forever in their eyes. His blood ran cold at the thought of what might happen to her if – despite all the odds against it - a rising in favour of the Stuarts met with success.

His dream of yesterday had not stood up to the clear, cruel light of day. All that was left to him was duty. He started walking again. One foot in front of the other.

Emerging a few strides below where St Mary's Wynd became the Pleasance, he called in at the Cowgate Port to exchange a few words with the guards there.

'Anything to report?'

'Been a quiet day so far. That's the way we like it, young Captain Catto, eh?'

He went on through the High School Yards and up to the Rankeillor house. Despite his despair, he remained aware of a flicker of hope. As though he had lost his footing on Salisbury Crags and slid over the edge of the ridge but was up there holding on for dear life, clinging on by his fingertips.

Chapter 17

'Professor,' Robert Catto said. 'Please be seated.'

Patrick did as he was bid. Christian was already sitting down. Robert Catto followed suit, taking the upright chair she had previously set between the two armchairs.

'Firstly,' he said, 'before we come to your own situation, Professor, we need to discuss Miss Rankeillor's position. I trust I have your agreement she should say nothing about any involvement she had with the concealing and spiriting way of the Jacobite agent. Or,' he added, 'that she was the cartographer of the map of Scotland which I found the night you and Balnamoon met the Jacobite agent at Surgeons' Hall.'

He smiled thinly when Patrick could not totally hide a start of dismay. 'She did not tell me she had drawn the map. I worked that out.' He stirred the abruptly very still air of the library with his index finger. 'The map which lists roads, ports and military garrisons among other features. All the information an invading army needs,' he said, his voice very precise. Then hard. 'Maps can be dangerous. Lethal, even.' He let those words lie for a moment.

Steel, thought Christian. In his voice and in his eyes. This was him at his most austere, the Redcoat captain and officer of the law. She remembered thinking that the night they had first met when he had invaded this house with his men. Arrogant. Unbending. Dismissive of her. She had seen a very different side to him since then. Yet he remained an officer of the law and a man determined to do his duty to the absolute utmost. She was unsurprised when it was he who broke the silence he had created.

'I ask you again, Professor. Do I have your agreement your daughter should not implicate herself in any way? *Must* not implicate herself in any way?'

'Do you doubt it, laddie?' There was steel in Patrick's voice too. He had donned his best frockcoat and his full-bottomed wig shortly before Robert Catto had arrived. Christian found it lamentably old-fashioned but she could not deny the abundant grey curls tumbling over his shoulders gave him quite an air. Of authority, certainly. Professorial too, learned and wise.

She had often thought of the long wig and the formal robes he wore at official university and hospital events as his armour. He was going to need those defences now. The man who was about to interrogate him was more than twenty years younger but he too radiated authority. In the current situation, he also had the upper hand.

'I don't doubt it in the slightest, sir. But I fear Miss Rankeillor may have to be persuaded to do as is undoubtedly best for her.'

Patrick looked at his daughter. 'Aye, she can be a wee touch thrawn when the mood takes her.'

'So I have observed, sir.'

Now they were both looking at her, studying her as though she were some kind of a specimen such as might be found over at Surgeons' Hall. *Example of a canker. Example of a diseased foot. Or in her case, example of a disobedient young woman who fails to realize what is in her own best interests.*

This unexpected alliance was not to be borne. She wanted to leap to her feet and pace around the room. The only thing stopping her was the certainty she'd be told in no uncertain terms to sit down again. Probably by both men in concert. Which was an unfortunate word to have jumped into her head.

As she had recently discovered, her father was a member of *The Concert of Gentlemen,* also known as *The Association,* a secret society dedicated to bringing about the restoration of the Stuarts to the throne of Britain. Which fact Robert Catto now knew. Which fact was enough to see her father hanged for treason.

They continued to study her, challenging her not to agree with them. In lieu of moving her restless body, she lifted her arms in a gesture of profound frustration. 'I cannot simply *abandon* you, Father!'

'You would not be abandoning him,' Robert Catto told her. 'You would be helping him. Immeasurably so. It will do the professor's case no good at all if he is seen to have involved his daughter in Jacobite plotting.'

'Exactly,' Patrick Rankeillor said. 'And ye ken fine, Christian, I did not want to involve you. Not at all!'

He shouldn't have said that. It admitted too much – but the words were out now. Robert Catto's expression gave nothing away. Seemingly unaware, her father made a steeple of his fingers and surveyed her over his hands. 'As we have discussed before, Christian, I have never been the kind of father who demands unquestioning obedience. Have I now?'

'No,' she admitted. 'Only when I was wee and it had to do with my safety. Like telling me not to go too close to the fire. Or not to play with my dolls and my other toys at the top of the stairs.'

'This has to do wi' your safety. Therefore I am demanding obedience now,' Patrick said, adding gravely, 'and also begging you tae give it. For your sake and my own. Young Captain Catto is quite right there.' He sent their gaoler a look which might have been approval. He had fallen silent during this interchange between father and daughter, allowing Patrick to speak again.

'Which is very kind of him. Unexpectedly and exceedingly kind.' There was a tremble of emotion in Patrick's voice. 'But also gey risky from his own point of view. I'd say that puts you under a moral obligation to help him as well as me by saying nothing about anything you might have done over the past two weeks.'

The two men remained focussed on her, expectant looks on their faces. Expecting she would agree. Funny, she thought, they are enemies, on opposite sides, yet in this they are united. Because they both wanted to keep her safe, shield her from any approaching danger.

'If you stay out of it, you will be in the best position to keep Betty and everyone else in our rapidly expanded household safe. All of whom, it would seem, stand in need of as much protection as we are able to give them.'

She considered his words, saw how much sense they made.

Lifting her chin, she looked at both men in turn. 'Very well. I agree. I shall say nothing about any involvement on my part.'

'Make us a promise,' Robert Catto urged, leaning forward in the upright chair.

'I promise.' She drew one finger in the shape of a cross over the bodice of her blue gown. 'Cross my heart.' She decided to leave out the next bit. *Cross my heart and hope to die.*

'Give us your word too,' Robert Catto said.

She turned to him. 'I give you my word.'

Both of her interrogators visibly relaxed. Robert Catto sat back in the upright chair, Patrick stretched out his legs to the warmth of the fire. After two days on the road riding back from Glasgow, he was relishing the comforts of home. This home from which he might be wrenched away permanently. Christian swallowed hard, quelling the flash of nausea the thought brought with it.

'What now, young sir?' her father asked.

'We continue as though life is normal until the Lord President returns to Edinburgh. I expect he will want to speak to you.'

'Aye, I expect that too.' Patrick Rankeillor sounded a little weary. 'Aiblins he'll want to do more than that.'

'His decision, Professor. In the meantime, I shall take your written statement.' He glanced at Christian. 'Without Miss Rankeillor being present.'

'As you wish, laddie. How, until you meet with the Lord President, do you propose we continue as though life is normal?'

'By exercising extreme discretion. On everyone's part. Do you have duties you must fulfil at the Royal Infirmary or the College immediately after the New Year?'

'Not in terms of the College. The students do not return until well on in January and my own classes dinna start until February this term. Although it might look odd were I not to call in at the Royal Infirmary over the first few days of the New Year.'

'Then I must advise a diplomatic illness. Perhaps your daughter could write a letter saying you caught a chill on your journey back from Glasgow and feel it would be wiser to keep to your own house for the meantime.'

'Advise?'

'Just so, Professor. I shall of course read this letter and arrange for its delivery. I am now going to ask for your word of honour. Should any possibility arise within the next two or three weeks – or beyond – of conversation with others, that you will discuss only medical matters or exchange social niceties.'

'You will trust me to do so?'

'I believe you to be an honourable man, sir. I also believe you appreciate how important it is we keep the events of the past two weeks as quiet as possible.'

'Aye,' Patrick said, his eyes going from Robert Catto's face to Christian's and back again. 'I do know how important it is. I give you my word of honour. What about the rest of my household?'

'Alice, Geordie and Joshua must remain here – at least for the immediate future – and not be seen by any callers to the shop or the house.'

Patrick inclined his bewigged head. 'Of course. We shall ensure they remain out of sight.'

'Your housekeeper and your maidservants may go to the markets for provisions, if required. As long as they know not to breathe a word about the new members of the household. I shall speak to them on that subject.'

'There is no need for you to speak to them,' Christian said hastily. 'They all seek to protect Alice and Geordie and Joshua.' While she was seeking to protect Alice and Tibby from being the focus of Robert Catto's attention. The two girls shared an unfortunate bond. As a consequence, both were now scared of all men. In Tibby's case, with the exception of Patrick Rankeillor and Jamie Buchan—

Oh God, but maybe we should all have been scared of Jamie. Will it ever not hurt to think of him and what he did? Of how he ended Jeannie Carmichael's life? All for the Cause. All for the sake of the Cause.

'Miss Rankeillor?'

She blinked. 'I beg your pardon, Captain. What were you saying to me?'

'I hadn't said anything yet,' he said, the grey eyes narrowing. 'I will now. If you will kindly pay attention.'

She gave herself a little shake. 'You have my full attention, Mr Catto.'

'Glad to hear it,' he said drily. 'You may go out and about much as you normally would. Avoiding the Royal Infirmary. I daresay you might want to pay a New Year visit to some of your friends. Life going on in its normal way.'

Some of her friends, the two closest of whom were no longer in Edinburgh? Her breath caught in her throat. Was this him giving her a legitimate reason to be out of the house for a few hours – and had there been the briefest of pauses before he had made that suggestion?

'Miss Rankeillor?' he asked again. Then: 'Ow!' Muttering under his breath, he raised one hand to his brow.

'Something pains you?' Patrick asked with quick medical interest.

'Not pain.' Catto shook his head, proving that point. 'Irritation only. I have some stitches here I believe may need to come out.'

Patrick stood up and went to examine Robert Catto's head, his fingertips tracing the line of stitches at his hairline. 'Aye. I think you are right. How did you come by this injury?'

Unseen by her father, who had his back to her, Christian shook her head.

'A stupid accident,' Robert Catto said. 'Caused by carelessness on my part.'

Patrick was still peering at his head. 'Who stitched this up?'

Christian pointed a finger towards her chest. Again Catto took the cue.

'I took myself to the Royal Infirmary. Miss Rankeillor was kind enough to clean the wound and repair the damage.'

Patrick swung round to Christian. She hoped she was making a good job of looking completely innocent. 'You made a grand job o' it, my dear. Very neat. Why do you not take Captain Catto through tae the shop and remove your handiwork?'

'There is no need. I can take the stitches out myself.'

As her father frowned at him, Christian sent him a swift smile. 'I'm afraid you will have to submit, Captain. There are rules in this house which supersede all others. A patient must be attended to. Made more comfortable.'

Now Robert Catto was glowering too, directing his frown at her. 'I am not your patient. And I am perfectly comfortable.'

'Really?' she asked, piqued by his sharp tone. Her emotions were see-sawing wildly this morning. Small wonder. This was the Robert Catto she had first met. Did he not realize she knew the real man now? She could see through his defences, the dismissive demeanour and acid tongue. Her own voice grew sharper.

'Right at this moment I don't think anyone in this room is comfortable. Forbye, 'tis surely more sensible to allow me to take your stitches out here where we have all the necessary equipment to hand.' She waved a hand towards the door into the shop.

'All right,' he said. 'But not in the shop. I do not want to risk being seen to be here in Infirmary Street either.'

'Then go and fetch what you need, Kirsty,' Patrick said, 'and bring it all back here.'

Chapter 18

Will you sit over here at my desk, Captain?' she asked when she came back into the library a few moments later, her hands full. 'Then I may lay these bits and pieces in front of you.'

He sat down, all too aware of how sharply he had just spoken to her. Wondering how he could make amends with her father listening in.

Unlike Patrick Rankeillor's worktable, piled high as that was with all manner of letters, papers and books, her smaller desk was tidy. Catto's eyes moved over the neat inkstand with its supply of freshly cut quills and the row of pigeonholes along the back of the desk. The papers in those were arranged in good order, reminding him of what his grandfather had always called his *bureau*. Another word came back to him. His grandfather had not spoken of pigeonholes but of doocots, the Scots word for a dovecote.

A table easel was pushed back to one side of Christian Rankeillor's desk. It held a folio fashioned out of strong card and tied with short strips of linen tape. Judging by its bulk, it held a number of drawings. Dead centre, in front of the doocots, sat a polished piece of marble he estimated would fit neatly into her palm, rich brown in colour. Like her hair. He thought he might know where it had come from. That brought another family memory rushing back.

Leaning forward, she laid down the paraphernalia she had brought through from the shop: a small kidney-shaped metal bowl; inside it, a pair each of scissors and tweezers; a second bowl filled with clear water; two folded cloths. She had taken the first two stitches out when the bell on the shop door jangled.

'I'll go,' Patrick said, rising from his armchair.

'Professor.' Robert Catto's head snapped up, a rumble of warning in his voice.

'I gave you my word of honour, laddie,' Patrick said. 'And 'twould seem I have a patient waiting. Nor am I going to try to escape.'

'I did not think you were, sir. I am merely reminding you of our agreement.'

'I've no' entered my second childhood quite yet, young man.' Patrick spoke with some asperity. 'I can remember baith what you said tae me and what I said tae you a few moments since. Wi' nae difficulty whatsoever.'

Catto waited until Rankeillor had closed the door. 'Why does he make me feel as though I'm a clumsy schoolboy again?'

'It's a knack,' Kirsty Rankeillor said, her voice cool. 'Every learned professor I know has it. I think they acquire it after years of dealing with unruly students. My father is usually very kind to his but he keeps the withering looks and stern tone of voice in reserve, in case of need.'

'Unlike Professor Monro, who shouts first and asks questions later?'

'When did you meet Professor Monro—' She caught herself on. 'Oh, when you went to ... *investigate* ... the cells at the back of the Royal Infirmary?'

'Yes.' He left it at that, not wanting to revisit what had happened when he had found evidence of John Roy Stuart's stay in those cells. The tumbled bedclothes and pillows had been bad enough. Finding scraps of poetry composed by the man he refused to recognize as his father had been much worse. Some sentimental tosh about 'the bonnie dark-haired lass, her eyes shining with compassion.'

He'd burned them all, dropping them to the floor and grinding them into fragments with the heel of his shoe. Christ, he'd been so bloody angry with Christian Rankeillor that day!

He'd tried telling himself that was because of the danger she had courted by bringing food and medical attention to a known rebel. Always rigorously honest with himself, it hadn't taken him long to admit he was jealous too. He couldn't bear to think about the care she had shown John Roy Stuart – and despised himself for allowing the man to still have the power to wound him.

'I can't imagine you were ever a clumsy schoolboy.'

'Oh, but I was! Gangly and gawky.' He thought back to his conversation with Marjorie Livingstone. 'All arms and legs and always falling over my own feet. Very unsure of myself. Very shy around girls.'

'Well, you have conquered those afflictions very successfully. Dinna laugh,' she said. 'It makes your head move.'

His momentary amusement evaporating, he moved his head even more, turning and looking up at her. 'I'm sorry if I snapped at you earlier.'

'If?' she queried, moving her hands and the implements they held clear of the wound. *'If?'*

'Kirsty. Let me say something. On my way here today I began to wonder whether you would still want to lie with me – how you could still want to. I know I have no right to expect anything from you. If anyone were to find out it might bring even more trouble to your door. From your friends as well as your foes—' He broke off, thinking his words were both ill-judged and woefully inadequate and for once, unable to interpret the expression on her face.

When she made no comment, he stumbled on. 'I shall probably have to do things for which you will find it difficult to forgive me. I shall certainly have to do things I cannot tell you about. Nor can I predict the future. I can make an educated guess as to the course the Lord President may choose to follow after he returns to Edinburgh but I cannot be sure.'

Still she said nothing, only kept looking at him.

'I'd been hoping I might be given permanent command of the Town Guard. Now I can see only too clearly the reasons against that ever happening.'

She spoke at last. 'Reasons? Or just one reason?'

'At least two. Who would be making the decision would also influence the outcome.'

'Yet your loyalties are in no way divided.'

'You know that to be the truth. Others might think I deliberately allowed the Jacobite agent to escape.'

'Or accuse you of having done so.'

'Aye. Depending on where *their* loyalties lie.'

She drew in a breath. 'I could testify as to the truth of the matter. Say what I know. What I have witnessed.'

'No, you couldn't.' His voice was sharp. 'We're going to keep you out of this. Unseen and unheard by anyone who might take an interest in the situation. From whichever side of the divide they might be looking.'

'You really think I could be in danger from my friends as well as my foes?'

'Yes. I really think so.'

'So whatever choices we two may make, we're damned if we do and damned if we don't?'

'That's about the sum of it.' Then, muttering the words as though he were saying them only to himself: 'Keeping you out of this is about all I really can offer you.'

'All you really can offer me?' She repeated the words, her voice rising. *'All you really can offer me?* Have you forgotten the day before yesterday, when you put your heart into my hands? Or what I told you about how I felt while I was waiting for you to return after rescuing Geordie and Joshua from Eastfield? How I was so scared you might not come back at all?' Her voice shook on the words.

'Kirsty—'

'Hold your tongue! I haven't finished yet.' Adjusting her grip on the tweezers, she placed the back of her hand briefly against her mouth before she spoke again. 'I've been having doubts too, Robert. Yesterday I found myself fearing I was betraying so much I hold dear.'

He swallowed hard. 'By lying with me? By not letting your friends know where my loyalties truly lie?'

'Both of those. Until Joshua taught me a lesson.'

'Joshua?' Catto asked, puzzled.

'Och, he didn't know he had! Can we have any idea what it's been like for him having his whole life controlled by someone like Charlotte Liddell?'

'Bloody awful, I should think. Unbearable. Only he's never had any choice other than to bear it.'

'Aye. Yet still he found the courage to help a friend. Dared to run away with him from Eastfield. If he's forced to go back, we know Charlotte will punish him.' She shuddered. 'Maybe even order him to be flogged, as Geordie was. He knows that better than anyone. But still he made the choice to leave Eastfield and bring Geordie with him. He did not allow fear to stop him. Or make him turn back once they were on the road.'

She looked away from him, seeing something that wasn't here. *Somewhere* that wasn't here. 'The thought of the two of them out there in the cold and the dark…' She shivered. 'They must have been so scared.'

'Yes,' Catto agreed as her attention returned to him. 'They must have been terrified. Chilled to the bone. Exhausted too. Beginning to give up hope.'

'Clinging on to it, all the same. For as long as possible. Until you and Mr Livingstone found them. As for you and me, we also agreed there was to be no turning back. Did we not?'

Not trusting his ability to speak, he reached for one of her hands.

'Careful!'

He caught her hand before she could swing it out of his reach. Risking the scissors, he pressed a kiss on the back of it.

'Daftie.'

'Going to keep on scolding me?' he managed.

'That's more than likely. Are we agreed *we're* not going to give up hope? Nor turn back?'

He swallowed hard. 'We're agreed.'

'You said Alice and Geordie and Joshua should stay at Infirmary Street, *at least for the immediate future.* Do you think they might not be safe here?'

'Have you been worrying about that?'

'How can I not? The law classifies all three of our orphans of the storm as *property.*' She pronounced the word with bitter incomprehension. 'Property you have taken away from Cosmo and Charlotte. *Stolen.* In so doing you have broken the law. Which, as the Captain of the Town Guard, you are duty bound to uphold. As is Lord President Forbes. Which I presume is one of the reasons you are not confident about being given permanent command.' She finished in a rush of words. 'Please dinna tell me to let you worry about that!'

'All right,' he said. 'I'll tell you something else instead.'

Chapter 19

'That would be wonderful!' she said a moment later, her eyes shining. He had told her about asking Charles Paterson to draw up the relevant papers and of how Catto would present those to the Lord President.

'It will be wonderful if he agrees to my proposal. In any case, yes, I think we need to move Alice, Geordie and Joshua to another hiding place. Once Geordie is a little recovered but soon enough to give us a week or so's grace before the Lord President comes back to Edinburgh. Some breathing space.'

She frowned. 'You think he might not agree to your proposal?'

'Let's cross that bridge when we come to it. *If* we come to it.'

'Where could they go, though?'

'Archie Liddell's mother's house.'

'In Colinton?'

'So I believe. A few miles west of the city and in a secluded position?'

'Aye. It's a lovely spot. But might this not be dangerous for Mrs Liddell?'

'The lieutenant tells me his cousins act as though his mother doesn't exist. There was no help or even sympathy offered after his father died.'

She nodded. 'I know Archie wrote to Charlotte and Cosmo to inform them of the death of their uncle. I dinna think they ever replied, far less offered their condolences. What lovely people they are. How would we get our charges to Colinton? Without anyone noticing, I mean. At night after the city gates have closed, you having the authority to open them again?'

He shook his head. 'One single horse-drawn cart rolling over the cobbles towards the West Port late at night would draw too much attention. We'll do it during the day, with them in the back of a cart, concealed somehow. Escorted by Archie Liddell dressed as a carter. Now,' he said, with an unexpected rush of hopefulness, 'let us talk about something else.'

'All right. What did you and my father talk about while I was through in the shop?'

'Nothing. We sat in a somewhat uncomfortable silence. I didn't want to start on his statement until you had completed your medical ministrations.'

Unease. That was what he was sensing now. Anxiety about her father. So he would do his best to distract her, if only for a few moments. 'This is torture.'

Her cool and capable hands stilled. 'I'm sorry. I'm being as gentle as I can.'

'You are. The torture is not getting my stitches out. The torture is being so close to you and not being able to kiss or touch you in case one or other of the doors into this room are flung open by either your father or the wee witch.'

'You'll just have to be patient.' His reward was the smile in her voice.

'I can be patient if I know I'll get a reward for my forbearance.'

'Now you've given me an excuse to leave the house?'

'I wasn't confident you would want to use it.'

'Yet still you offered it.'

'Hope,' he said. 'I was *hoping you* would want to.'

'That word again,' she said lightly. 'Have you any thoughts as to where we might go?'

'Only unsuitable ones.'

'You had considered taking me to a house of pleasure?'

Her question brought his head back up again.

'I've h-heard l-lovers can g-go there,' she stuttered.

'Have you indeed?'

She raised her own dark brows. 'I really cannot think why you are giving me such a fearsome look of disapproval, sir.'

'Can't you?' he demanded.

'No. Answer my question, if you please. Were you going to take me to a house of pleasure?'

'The thought crossed my mind and immediately left it. We

cannot run the risk of being seen together. Especially not in compromising surroundings. Do you have any ideas?'

'I might have,' she said, feeling both a nervous fluttering in her chest and the weight of the two heavy keys in the pocket under her skirts. 'Not going to tell you yet, though. You deserve to suffer.'

'I'm suffering now,' he complained. 'With you standing and me sitting I am acutely aware of your breasts. Even though you're in your practical clothes and I can't see them at all. Not even the merest glimpse.'

'Be quiet,' she said. 'You'll make me blush.'

'Oh, is that all it takes? How wonderful. I like to see you blush. Let me think now. I could speak about your breasts at some length. I have only to turn my head to be no more than a kiss away from them. Or to be able to lean said poor wounded head against their soft warmth.'

He felt her excited little breath on his brow. 'Dear girl,' he said. 'Might I be right in thinking those shameless thoughts you haven't yet recounted to me involved either or both of such actions on my part? Which I should be more than happy to carry out.'

She had told him about what she had called her *shameless thoughts* when he had brought Geordie and Joshua back here to Infirmary Street two days before. After Geordie's wounds had been dressed and the rest of the household had gone to bed, she had responded to Catto's request for her to sit on his knee.

Watching her by the light of the fire, he had seen her pick her way around Geordie, lying on his front on a mattress in front of the fire. The boy had been sleeping soundly after consuming the sleeping draught she had helped him drink.

Request? Uncertain of her though he had been on that occasion, it had come out more like a demand. He'd half-expected her to slap his face but she had seemed more than happy to acquiesce. He wouldn't put it as strongly as obey. Not that he would ever want obedience from her. He didn't understand men who demanded that from their wives and lovers. Where was the fun in that?

'You will kindly look straight ahead and continue to keep your poor wounded head still. Dae as you're tellt. Perhaps you might also still your busy tongue. An almost impossible task, I know.'

'There is one way you can get me to shut my mouth. Or at least stop talking.' His voice was a low rumble in his throat, his words warm. 'Are you still blushing?'

'Never you mind.'

'What about my way of getting me to be quiet? Tried and tested on Yule Day. Why don't we try it again now?'

'Because I'm still taking your stitches out.'

'You must be nearly finished.'

'Now I am,' she said a moment later, dropping the tweezers and scissors with a clang into the kidney-shaped bowl. She dabbed a damp cloth against his brow. 'There. That's you done. You may have a very fine scar here but it should fade in time.'

He shrugged. 'No matter.' Like her father, she traced her fingertips over the wound. He had felt little when Patrick Rankeillor had done the same. Her touch was having a very different effect on him.

'Thank you for not telling my father the person who repaired the damage was also the person who inflicted it.'

'I take it you fear he is distressed enough about Balnamoon. You told him about Jeannie Carmichael?'

'Aye. Although not about you and her.'

'May I move my head now?' he asked after an awkward little silence.

'Why do you pretend to obey me when it is you who is in charge? Yes, you may move your head now.'

He looked up at her. 'In some things, I defer to you. Medical matters, of course. Both of body and mind. Apropos of which, how is Geordie today?'

'Desperate to see you. I countermanded that. Don't think he should tackle the stairs again quite yet. Especially not two journeys, down and back up again. Although he looked so unhappy when I said no I almost relented.'

'The wee witch really would have apoplexy if I went upstairs?' He glanced at the paper, quills and inkwell on her desk. 'Would it help if I wrote him a note? Telling him I'm as eager as he is and looking forward to seeing him as soon as he's fit to come downstairs?'

'I think it might help, yes.' She frowned. 'Apart from wanting to see you, he is still rather subdued today. Somewhat withdrawn.'

Determined on smoothing the worried look off her face, he pointed towards the polished stone. 'Do you have this on your desk as a paperweight or to bring good luck?'

'Both,' she said. 'As a practical object and as a talisman.'

'Did it by any chance come from Portsoy, on the Banffshire coast?'

'How did you know that? Oh,' she added, answering her own question, 'You must know Portsoy. Is that where you meant by *at the back of the north wind?*' When she had asked him where he came from, those were the words he had used.

'Maybe.'

Her eyes gleamed with interest. Thank God for curiosity and its power to distract and soothe a troubled mind. He had observed this trait in her before.

'Did my talisman remind you of a day spent there picking up pretty pebbles? Perhaps you and your sister went there once? Or more than once?'

Aside from a terse comment, he had told her very little about his sister, other than mentioning he'd had one. Once upon a time.

'Perhaps we did. Kiss me.' Raising one arm, he slid his hand around her neck, under her gleaming hair. Soft as thistledown, their lips met in a gentle kiss which swiftly grew deeper. He didn't deserve this. He didn't deserve her: but he welcomed her innocent passion with a surge of gratitude. A moment later he heard a much less welcome sound.

'Damn,' he murmured against her mouth. 'Move back.' The door from the shop was being pushed open. By the time her father came through it, Catto and Kirsty Rankeillor were a good yard apart.

'Professor,' Catto said five minutes later, he and Patrick Rankeillor now alone together in the library. 'Perhaps we can start by you telling me what you talked about when you visited Mr Andrew Wood at his workshop in the High Street of Glasgow?'

Chapter 20

Forty minutes later Christian was leading the way through to the back lobby of the house, ready to show Robert Catto out. While he and her father had been closeted alone in the library, she had helped Betty start the preparations for the evening meal, wondering and worrying all the while about what was being said.

Her father looked his usual calm self when the two of them came through to the kitchen, perhaps only a little pale. He even invited his interrogator to stay and eat with them. Despite these very strange circumstances, the laws of hospitality remained sacred.

'I thank you, but no. You have enough hungry mouths around your table as it is, Professor.' Robert Catto's glance swept round the crowded kitchen. Unless they had company, the Rankeillors regularly ate here with the rest of the household.

The housekeeper was standing at the range stirring something. Kirsty Rankeillor was supervising as maidservants Mary and Tibby set plates and cutlery on the table. Alice Smart, sitting on the wooden settle in the comer of the kitchen, was doing her best to render herself invisible. Catto had not missed how she had tried to shrink even farther back when he had entered the kitchen. Joshua too was obviously sensitive to her feelings. He was sitting on the settle but at the other end of it, giving his friend's sister the distance she so clearly craved.

Catto spotted a tray lying on the table, already set with two beakers, two plates and cutlery. 'Is this for Geordie's supper?'

It was Joshua who answered him. 'Aye, sir. I'm taking it up to him. My own too, so as to keep him company.'

'Good man,' Catto said. 'I'm sure he'll be glad of that.' He drew a letter out of his breast pocket. Patrick Rankeillor had waited the few moments it had taken him to write it. 'Take this to him as well, if you please.'

'You *could* stay, you know—' Christian began, suppressing a yelp as Robert Catto grabbed her, slid his arms around her waist and kissed her passionately, hungrily. They had only just reached the back lobby, the bend in the corridor allowing them to be out of sight of anyone in the kitchen. If they were lucky and Betty didn't come after them. Or called out in an exasperated tone of voice for Christian to close the back door and come and sit down at the table so they could all eat.

Throwing caution to the winds, she kissed him back, matching his passion and his hunger. As their mouths came together and their hands roamed over each other's bodies, they stumbled, their feet sliding across the stone floor of the lobby. She drew him back against the door to steady them. The old coats, plaids and cloaks hanging on the back of it came around her shoulders like a cocoon.

'Very resourceful,' he muttered before they renewed their kiss. 'Miss Practical. That's you.' Like her, he was careful to speak in a low voice.

'Stay,' she said, when they regretfully separated, both knowing they could not linger. She took his face between her hands. 'Stay and eat with us.'

'I cannot. Not when all I can think about is making love to you.'

'I think we both have a lot more to think about than that.'

He sighed. 'Aye. We do.' The grey eyes clouded. 'You said you told your father about Jeannie Carmichael. But not about her and me?'

'No. Nor did I tell him about you and … Mr Fox.'

Catto lifted her hands from his face. Lowering them to his chest, he wrapped his long fingers around her own. 'Can you forgive me for what I did with Jeannie Carmichael?'

'It's not my place to forgive you.' Then, after a tiny pause: 'What about your lady friend?'

'Ah.' Ludicrously, he found himself fighting a blush. 'I think you must mean the lady who, as you put it at the time, you saw me embracing with some fervour in the High Street on Daft Friday when you were in a chair being carried up to the ball at the Assembly rooms. There to plot the escape of a known rebel.'

She fixed him with a stern look. 'That accusation does not excuse you.'

'I don't need to be excused. I wasn't spoken for on Daft Friday. I am now. As I told another young lady in the Grassmarket this morning.'

'La, sir, you seem to hold a prodigious attraction for the female sex.'

'I fear 'twas the contents of my purse which attracted the girl in the Grassmarket.'

Christian Rankeillor blinked. 'Does that sort of thing happen in the morning? In broad daylight?'

'It did today. I was a mite surprised myself. I gave her a sixpence.'

'Out of the goodness of your heart? Very generous. Spoken for,' she repeated. 'Is that what we're calling it? Och, dinna smile at me like that!'

'How odd. I could swear you told me you liked it when I smile at you like that. Said it has interesting effects on you. In interesting places.'

'Stop it,' she said. 'Right now. So what about the girl I saw you with on Daft Friday, the one you were indeed embracing with some fervour?'

'Her name is Lizzie Gibson. She was giving me a warning. The embrace was covering up her words.'

'Do I take it she works at the house of pleasure in front of which the two of you were standing? The one which pretends to be a milliner's shop?'

'How does a respectable young lady like you know such a thing?'

'Because I pay attention and I also have two eyes and two ears. I take it you know her through her trade? What was she warning you about?'

He shook his head, kissed her knuckles and dropped her hands. 'You don't need to know, Kirsty. Time I was leaving. Time you were going back through to the kitchen. The wee witch will be flying through on her broomstick to turn me into a frog if we stay here for much longer.'

'Very amusing, Captain. And I like to know everything. Was the warning about Jamie?'

'Aye,' Robert Catto said. He had turned away from her to lift his coat off one of the pegs on the back door.

'What did she say?'

'She warned me not to turn my back on him.'

'As you are currently doing to me. Because you do not wish to speak to me of Jamie.'

Swinging his coat over his shoulders, he shrugged his arms into it and turned back to her. 'Have I not told you enough? Let us leave it there, Kirsty. If you please.'

'All right,' she said, realizing he was once again trying to protect her. 'I thought I recognized her.'

'She knows you.'

'Does she?' Christian asked, surprised.

'I told her about Alice Smart and she asked if anyone was looking after her.

Lizzie was relieved to hear you were. She says you are kind, skilled and do not judge people.'

Now she knew. This was the girl who had called at the shop about a year ago, looking for ointment to clear up a rash on her hand. For some reason she and Christian had struck up an immediate rapport. It had soon become clear how she earned her daily bread and she'd been amazingly frank about it.

Someone who practices my trade has to have smooth, clean hands. My gentlemen friends expect it.

'Who are any of us to judge others? Let he who is without sin cast the first stone. When did Mistress Gibson tell you all this?'

'The day I escorted your friend Anna Gordon down to Leith to embark on the Banff packet.'

When Christian stiffened, he spoke again. 'Lizzie is currently staying with her mother and her son, who live in a tiny fisherman's cottage near The Shore, down at Leith. I have not lain with her since before the Daft Friday ball. Nor have I any plans to do so. Although I am going to visit her to tell her so. I owe her that.' He raised his hands, palms outwards. 'I owe her a lot more, for giving me the warning. Trust me on this, Kirsty.'

'Strangely enough, I do. Which is why I am going to give you these.' Her body relaxing, she slid her hand into the pocket under her skirts, bringing out the two keys.

'The keys to the bagnio,' she said. 'One for the gate to its garden and one for the double doors to the building itself. Can you get copies made and bring these back to me as soon as possible? I dinna think Betty or my father are likely to go looking for them but better safe than sorry.'

'The bagnio?' He frowned. 'It's very close to this house.'

'I know.'

'It's also very close to the Royal Infirmary.'

'I know that too. Although it cannot be overlooked from this house and I shall take the long way round to get there. I think I can also get there without being seen from the hospital.'

He was still looking doubtful. 'Won't it be too cold? All marble floors and tiled walls?' As she had previously told him, although she and her friends had bathed there before heading for the Daft Friday ball, the bath house was rarely used now. The running costs had proved to be too high. He traced the line of her jaw with his fingertips. 'I should always want you to be warm.'

'We can be warm at the bagnio. Although it will involve you in some work beforehand.'

'Gladly. There's coal and kindling over there?'

'Plenty. You have no other objection to the bagnio?' She had worried about that, knowing he must be aware his father had briefly been there before being carried up to the Assembly Rooms in a chair.

'An objection to the chance for us to be alone together? Give me the keys, woman.'

'Are you coming back here tomorrow?' she asked, addressing his bowed head as he slid the keys inside his coat, tucking them into his breast pocket.

'Regretfully not. I have to be on duty at the guard-house all day and into the evening.'

'For Old Year's Night. Hogmanay.'

'I'm told it can be as lively as Daft Friday.'

'It can. Although hopefully you will not have to face down another mob at the guard-house. Tomorrow is also your birthday.'

'Well remembered.' When he had stumbled to the infirmary after Jamie Buchan had hit him over the head, she had clerked him in, asking for a few details about himself.

'I wish we could be together on your birthday. I wish we could see in the New Year together.'

He looked up. 'So do I. On both counts. But I shall definitely call on New Year's Day.'

'When you will stay to eat with us. I doubt if even Betty would refuse you the hospitality of this house on New Year's Day.'

'Well, there's an enticement. A grudging welcome from the wee witch. But it would be too awkward, Kirsty. When can we meet at the bagnio?'

'When I can work out how to get away without my father or Betty working out what I'm doing.' She frowned. 'What if someone else sees us making our way there?'

'We shall plan not to arrive together. You shall take your roundabout route to get there. I shall also make sure I'm not seen on my way there. New Year's Day,' he went on. 'I presume another feast is planned, as on Yule Day? Which means the kitchen is unlikely to be empty at any point.'

'We might be able to snatch a moment or two. We'll have stayed up to bring in the New Year and everyone will be tired after Betty's had us all changing bedclothes and washing clothes tomorrow. Can't go dirty into the New Year.'

'My mother always said that too.' He indicated the small window to the side of the back door. 'If you can be in the kitchen alone, watch for me from here. You can open the door without me having to knock and alert the house to my presence.'

'I can now. Since you fixed the door when it got stuck, it no longer shrieks in protest when anyone opens it.'

'So the gods are with us. I'll aim to be here for 10 of the clock. With a bit of luck we can have some quiet conversation before anyone else knows I'm here.'

'Quiet conversation, is it? That's as good as you being *spoken for.*'

He responded to her impish smile with one of his own, lighting up his handsome face. 'You'll want to wish me Happy Birthday, won't you?'

She reached up, taking his face between her hands. 'You look a lot happier now than you did when you arrived here earlier.'

'Your doing,' he told her. 'All your doing. You've changed me, Kirsty Rankeillor.'

She stretched up and kissed his cheek. 'Maybe I've just helped you find a part of yourself which had got lost.'

He gave her two kisses in return for her own. One on her lips. One into the palm of her hand. She stood with her back to the kitchen door, leaning against the softness of the plaids, coats and cloaks. Soon, she thought. Very, very soon.

Chapter 21

He walked up the High Street with a spring in his step, relishing the feel of the big solid keys against his chest. There was a tune running through his head, one he remembered hearing played on the fiddle, fast, lively and rumbustious. If the name came to him, he would ask the fiddler at what had become a favourite howff here in Edinburgh to play it for him.

'Twas the sort of tune that set your feet tapping and made you want to leap up and grab a girl by the waist and dance her round the room. Not any girl. Not any more. Only one special girl from now on. Pity you couldn't take women into taverns. Not respectable young ladies anyway.

He had danced with Christian Rankeillor at the Daft Friday Ball at the Assembly Rooms, farther up the High Street. That had been a stately measure, stylized and slow, with very little contact between the dancers other than a sedate touch of the hand, the merest meeting of palms and fingertips. He longed to dance with her to a Highland air, a strathspey or a reel.

He knew his outward *persona* could be stern, even dour. He had cultivated that. Armour against the world. Defence against being hurt again as he had been before. Now, here in Edinburgh, despite all the plotting swirling around them both, despite his concern for her, despite how low his mood had been earlier today, he had discovered he was capable of being happier than he had ever imagined he would be again. Nor was he ready to surrender his dream of the future quite yet. Or at all. There had to be a way.

He looked across the High Street at the milliner's shop behind and above where a quite different trade was carried on. Lizzie Gibson wouldn't be back from Leith yet. When she was he would go and see her, thank her again for the warning she'd given him. Would he tell her why he would not be visiting her again? Aye, he would. Would he tell her the name of the girl who had changed him, found the part of himself which had got lost? Probably. Knowing Kirsty Rankeillor was looking after Alice Smart, Lizzie might well have guessed anyway.

Catto drew level with the guard-house, raising a hand in greeting to the man on duty at its door. He walked farther up the High Street, heading for the luckenbooths clustered together in a ramshackle building on Parliament Square in the lea of the soaring High Kirk of St Giles. The compact little wooden shops and booths housed a variety of craftsmen. His first call was to a locksmith.

The man promised the copies of the keys Catto handed him would be ready around noon the following day. He'd asked him to make three copies of each. She could put the originals back in their usual place and keep a pair for herself. Less chance of them being discovered that way. Bidding the locksmith farewell, Catto stood for a moment on the cobblestones of Parliament Square, thinking about those keys.

The keys to her heart. The keys to their mutual pleasure. He did not underestimate her decision to lie with him. It was a huge step for a girl like her to take and an irrevocable one. He did not underestimate the risk she would be running that her father or her housekeeper might somehow find out. Yet she was ready and willing. She must be nervous about the actual act, though. Her first time.

For a moment he stood there, balancing on a knife-edge of tenderness and desire. When she'd told him she wanted to lie with him, he'd told her she had given him a gift. He ought to give her a gift in return. His eyes had been fixed, unseeing, on the row of luckenbooths. Now he focussed in on one of them, where he had previously observed a silversmith practiced his trade.

Charlotte Liddell was as vocal in bed as everywhere else, loudly and coarsely expressing her pleasure, demanding more of what she wanted, batting away any touch which didn't please her. The rougher he was with her, the more she liked it. Which was fine by Arthur Menzies of Edmonstone. He liked it rough too. When the chit was unwilling, so much the better.

Charlotte was only too willing. When she was in the mood. There was no tenderness in her and Edmonstone's relationship. If you could dignify their coupling by calling it that. Nor did they like each other very much. Not at all, really. But he had to keep her and her brother sweet. The Cause needed their money. Or would do, when the time came.

Sitting up, Arthur Menzies swung his legs over the side of the bed. They'd spent the afternoon there and now he was ready to get up, get dressed, go downstairs and meet up with Cosmo to start on the claret and have some masculine company before dinner. Even if Charlotte's brother barely had the brainpower or concentration to discuss anything of importance. Not that Arthur shared much with him anyway. Especially when it came to political matters.

'Stay,' Charlotte commanded, grabbing his bare arm. 'I want you to tell me what the three of you did to the little Smart trollop.'

He half turned to look at her where she lay back against a mountain of fine linen pillows, her fair hair spreading out across them. 'I've told you that already, Charlotte.'

'Tell me again.' A gloating look slid across her face. 'I like to hear how she cried and screamed and begged you all to stop. I like to hear exactly what you did to her.'

'You really are a vicious bitch,' he observed, followed by a yell of pain when she pinched his arm hard before releasing it. Opening her eyes wide, she stretched out, her breasts bouncing in response. 'You enjoyed telling me, Arthur. You know you did. Go on,' she wheedled, 'tell me again.'

'No,' he said, all at once sick of her. She was as stupid as her brother. 'I'm going. I'll see you at dinner.'

Charlotte came up onto her elbow, her hair flowing over her arm. 'When we get them back – the Smart girl and her brother and Joshua – you could do it all again.' Her eyes gleamed. 'Maybe I could watch.'

He stared at her, in distaste and incomprehension. The pleasure with an unwilling and untouched girl was in the spoiling, the forcing, the destruction of innocence. The idea of joining with such soiled goods for a second time was disgusting. Like getting up in the morning and pulling on the crumpled and sweaty shirt you'd dropped on the floor the night before.

Charlotte was still plotting her revenge, asking Edmonstone if he too had been aware of a sexual frisson as they had watched knotted leather lacerating the pale skin of the Smart boy's back. Only she put the question in much coarser terms, laughing wildly without waiting for an answer.

'When we get him back, we'll flog him again,' she said, eyes gleaming and lips parted. 'It'll hurt so much more now the skin is broken.'

Retrieving his nightshirt and banyan from the arm of the chair where he had laid them, Edmonstone turned and spoke. 'His skin will have healed by the time you get him back, Charlotte. *If* you get him back.'

'Don't be ridiculous, Arthur,' she snapped, sitting up and glaring at him. 'Of course we'll get him back. The other two as well. All three of them are ours by right, mine and Cosmo's. Our useless lawyer had better be doing something about that right now!'

Edmonstone pulled his nightshirt over his head. He would change into his evening clothes in the bedchamber he thought of as his own here at Eastfield before he went downstairs. 'It might not be so easy.'

Charlotte launched into a stream of invective, cursing him, Charles Paterson, Robert Catto and *that superior little bitch Kirsty Rankeillor.* 'Who' she demanded, 'does she think she is to look down her nose at me? The daughter of a sawbones? You should have seen how she smirked when she saw my painting of the Prince. Everyone else thought it was beautiful!'

No, Charlotte, everyone else lied. Arthur Menzies had seen the painting too. Charlotte continued to rant. He stepped back to the bed, seizing her flailing arms, trying to calm her down. Bloody hell, she really was hard work. 'You cannot know for certain she has taken them in.'

'Oh, I know all right. She's going to regret it. I can promise her that. I'll see her in the gutter.' The angry movements of her arms had stopped, as her voice had grown softer: laced through with venom.

'What idea has crept into that head of yours, Charlotte? I can see from your face it's not a pleasant one.'

'How do you fancy teaching Kirsty Rankeillor a lesson, Arthur? One she'll never forget. One she'll never recover from. She won't be acting all superior with anyone after that! She really will be in the gutter!' She laughed wildly. 'All three of you together, like you did with the Smart girl.'

A vicious bitch and a stupid one too. You didn't force a woman of your own class. You might want to but you couldn't take the risk. A girl like Kirsty Rankeillor was protected by her position, her father and their many friends. Edmonstone didn't deny he might fancy a taste of the prim and proper surgeon-apothecary's daughter. Whenever he'd encountered her at a social gathering he'd always had the feeling she was looking down her nose at him too.

She'd also witnessed his humiliation at the Assembly Rooms, when Catto had ordered him and Cosmo to be subjected to that kicking in the balls. Revenge would be sweet – but he didn't want to end up in the Tolbooth. Much though he disliked it, there was another consideration too.

'Don't be ridiculous, Charlotte,' he snapped. 'She's one of us. She and her father. Strong in the Cause.'

The expression on Charlotte's face changed. Cunning. That's how she looked now. He felt the stirrings of unease.

'You sure of that, Arthur? That she and her father are strong in the Cause?'

'What do you know?' he demanded, gripping both of her wrists. 'Tell me. Tell me now!'

Her eyes fluttered shut and she shifted on the bed, raising her shoulders and thrusting out her breasts. 'Squeeze as hard as you like, Arthur. You know I like a firm hand.'

He released her wrists and spoke through gritted teeth. 'Tell me what you know!'

'I know she has a fancy for the Town Guard captain. I know he has a fancy for her. I've seen them together. He's not strong in the Cause, is he now?'

Wrong, Charlotte. Wrong, wrong, wrong. Yet in that very

moment, Edmonstone's doubts about Robert Catto coalesced.

Fifteen hundred miles to the south, on a mild winter's afternoon in faraway Italy, a young man leant forward over his writing desk, studying the document lying there. It had been drawn up and signed at the Jacobite court-in-exile here in Rome a few days before Christmas. It was an official declaration from his father James, appointing his elder son Regent of Scotland.

Charles Edward Stuart straightened up. Unable to contain his elation, he punched one hand into the cupped palm of the other. It was happening at last, oh, sweet Jesu, at long, long last. He squeezed his eyes tightly shut, his emotions threatening to overwhelm him. He would be the man who would win back not only Scotland but all his father's kingdoms for the House of Stuart. Prove himself to his father and the whole wide world.

He opened his eyes again, commanding himself to be calm. He was 23 years old. Often he felt as though he'd lived double those years, spent a lifetime waiting for this chance to fulfil his destiny. He'd been born for this. Now his father had passed the standard to him and he would live up to what was expected of him. Meet and embrace his destiny.

In Rome and in Edinburgh, man planned and God laughed.

Chapter 22

Agnes Moncur was on her morning rounds, checking everything and everywhere was clean and tidy and the patients comfortable. It was a routine daily task but today being Hogmanay gave an added impetus to her inspection. Edinburgh Royal Infirmary would sail into the New Year as the well-organized place it was.

She always worked from the top down. The operating theatre was on the uppermost floor, where skylights allowed as much natural illumination as possible. This morning it was empty and quiet. There were no operations planned for today.

On the floor below were two wards, one for male patients, the other for female. The cavernous central stone stairs of the Infirmary with their draughty landings formed the dividing line. Nurses and orderlies on both sides of the stairwell assured her all was well. She had a walk round each ward herself to make sure.

Satisfied, she went on down to the ground floor. The necessary houses at either end of the building were clean and the two kitchens, also at opposite ends of the ground floor, were already busy with preparations for the midday meal for patients and staff. After a check of the pantries, the apothecary's shop, the library and the laboratory, Agnes walked across the main entrance hall and unlocked the solid oak door which gave access to the cells at the back of the building.

There was very little natural light in the corridor here, the only windows small and set high up in each of the cells. A shelf inside the main door held a brass lantern, a box of candles, stone and flint. Lit lantern in hand, Agnes walked along the corridor. She'd cleared away the evidence of Mr Fox's stay in these cells after Daft Friday, annoyed with herself for having done so too late to stop the Town Guard captain from having seen it. It wouldn't hurt to make doubly sure she hadn't left anything behind.

Back in her own room ten minutes later, she sat down at her desk and started on her mail. According to the orderly who had brought her letters this morning, the one on top of the small pile had been delivered directly to the hospital by a caddie. Nothing odd about that. People often used them to send letters and small parcels. She frequently did so herself, suspicious of the Post Office. Everyone knew they intercepted mail to and from suspected Jacobites: of whom she was one. As were the Rankeillors.

She supposed it wasn't odd either that Kirsty had sent a letter rather than walking the short distance to the hospital. If her father had caught a bad chill on the journey home from Glasgow and she was caring for him.

If Patrick Rankeillor really had caught a bad chill.

Sitting there in the quiet of her room, Agnes looked up from the letter. Suspicion. Once it slid into your mind, it didn't easily leave. This letter compounded what she had felt when Kirsty had left the last batch of physic at a time when she knew full well everyone would be busy on the ward round.

The man who delivered the carrots and turnips for the soup which formed a large part of the patients' diet had already discreetly told Agnes what the coffee house keeper at Leith had told him. James Nicholson, a loyal friend to the Cause, had given shelter to John Roy Stuart and Jamie Buchan of Balnamoon on the snowy night when they had escaped from Edinburgh after the Daft Friday ball.

Robert Catto had called past a few days later, after the snow had cleared. He had asked if 'our guests' had got away all right. James Nicholson had denied any knowledge of any guests, telling the Town Guard captain he had no letting rooms. Whereupon Catto had amicably wished a firm 'Godspeed' to any travelers obliged to make their journeys at this time of year. The implication that he had Jacobite sympathies had been clear.

Another friend to the Cause had reported a visit paid by Robert Catto to Charles Paterson a few days before. The lawyer's Jacobite sympathies were well known, especially to those who shared them. Agnes trusted those who had given her these reports but she needed to be sure. People could dissemble, pretend to be what they were not.

She had learnt this lesson the hard way. She'd been twenty years old when her jovial, jesting father and her handsome and gentle new husband – her childhood sweetheart – had marched off in support of James Stuart and the Jacobite Cause.

Both men died at Sheriffmuir, the battle both sides claimed as a victory. Devastated, Agnes and her mother were struck another blow. The tavern the family had run at the harbour in Montrose was seized by a platoon of redcoats, mother and daughter turned out onto the street with barely more than the clothes they stood up in. Too many men who'd long been regulars at the tavern did nothing to help, standing silently watching as the two women were evicted.

Only the kindness of the Coutts family caught them when they fell. Prosperous local merchants, they took the women in, gave them a roof over their heads and food to eat. They were grateful beyond words. Despite that, Agnes' mother was left a broken woman. A pale ghost of her former self, she died less than a year later.

Agnes grieved bitterly for all she had lost but at some point steel slid into her soul. Her devotion to the Cause which had taken her father and husband had grown stronger with each passing year. Now it was unshakeable. Edinburgh Royal Infirmary and the restoration of the House of Stuart were the two central pillars of her life: and she was determined those she had loved so much would not have died in vain.

Which was why she had to be sure about the Rankeillors and Captain Robert Catto. Folding Kirsty Rankeillor's letter, she put it to one side, to be filed when she next stood up. Which would not be until she had written two letters of her own. She would certainly not send them via the Post Office. The hands of those all-important trusted friends would make the deliveries.

Chapter 23

'Good morning. I hope I am your first foot.' It was New Year's Day and Christian had just opened the back door to Robert Catto. He wore his tan leather coat, a well-worn satchel of the same colour and material slung across his chest.

'You are.'

'Then I wish you a very Happy New Year, Kirsty. Even if I do not possess the dark hair which is supposed to bring luck.'

'I like your hair as it is. As you know very well.'

Leaning forward, he kissed her on the cheek. A butterfly touch. His lips bore the cold of the outside world. Yet they were warm too.

'Happy New Year to you too. We shall have to hope it will be a happy one, anyway.'

'It's a new year,' he said gently. 'A fresh start.'

'Aye. Did you have a busy night?'

'Most of the drunks bouncing down the High Street were amiable. At least two told me I was their best friend.'

She laughed. 'Funny how it takes some folk that way. Happy birthday for yesterday. I am sorry I do not have a present for you.'

'I'm hoping to get my present from you very soon,' he said, laughing when she blushed. Sliding his hand into his pocket, he brought out a small irregular shaped parcel wrapped in rough paper. 'Here,' he said, handing it to her. 'A lump of coal. So you will always be warm throughout the year.'

'Is that yon one at the back door?' came Betty's voice.

Robert Catto rolled his eyes. *'Yon one,'* he repeated. 'I do have a name.'

'So does she. And it's not the wee witch.' Christian tugged at the sleeve of his coat. 'Come in out of the cold.'

He kicked his feet against the doorstep to rid his shoes of any clinging dirt or ice and stepped into the back lobby. He was all height and broad shoulders and masculine vitality and he brought the small space to vibrant life.

'Is it unlucky to come in at the back door on New Year's Day?'

'I dinna think so. Since I let the old year out here last night. It's away to wherever the old year goes. I should not have thought you were superstitious. Will you take your coat off and I'll hang it up? What's in the satchel?'

'Clothes for the boys,' he said, lifting the satchel over his head. 'A pair of breeches and a waistcoat apiece, three shirts likewise, stockings and small clothes. Not new but still with a lot of wear in them. Or so Sergeant Livingstone's wife tells me. I asked her to get them for me and she obliged. Very speedily too. I'll have to see about getting a pair of shoes for Geordie.'

'They stripped him bare, didn't they?' She raised the back of her hand to her mouth, knowing she could be feeling only a fraction of Geordie's humiliation at the hands of the Liddells.

Robert Catto pulled her hand down and kissed the back of it. 'He's safe here now. One of the men is a cobbler. I've asked him what measurements to take of Geordie's feet. He thinks he might have a suitable pair of shoes in his workshop. An order that was never collected.'

'Are the guards wondering what's become of Geordie?'

'One or two. Once the Daft Days are over and life gets back to normal more of them will be curious. I've told those who've asked he's had to go home for a while to care for a sick relative. Sergeant Livingstone knows the truth, of course.'

'But you can trust him implicitly.'

'Yes. I can.'

'What about the shoemaker?'

'Fortunately he is a man of few words. With a quite astonishing lack of curiosity.'

She took the leather bag from him and slung it over her own shoulder. 'Feels a bit heavy for a few clothes. Something weighing it down, I think. Another New Year's gift?'

'In a manner of speaking. There are also two sets of keys in there. In an inside pocket at the back of the bag. As for being superstitious, soldiers tend to be.' He turned his mouth down in a gesture of self-mockery. 'Always trying to strike bargains with the Almighty. Or providence. 'Tis also hard to shake some things off, especially those learned in childhood.'

'Things your mother brought you up to believe?'

He slipped his arms out of his coat and let her take it from him to hang it up on the back of the door. 'My mother brought us up to believe in unicorns.'

'She must have been a very wise woman. By us, you mean you and your sister, I take it. What is her name?'

'Charlotte.'

'Like Charlotte Liddell.'

'Nothing at all like Charlotte Liddell.' He shook his head in emphasis. 'Thank God. Besides which, to my mother and me she was always Lottie.'

She wanted to know more. Much, much more. She wanted to know about his life before he had come to Edinburgh. She wanted to know where his sister was now, when he had last seen her or written to her. When Lottie had last written to him. In the guard-house on Daft Friday, he had spoken about his sister selling herself to the highest bidder. *Not that I blame her*.

Considering how cagey he was about his past, she contented herself with an observation. By his lights, he had told her a lot. She hoped they would have the time and the opportunity to get to know much more about each other. She hoped with all her heart the Lord President was going to take his time about returning to Edinburgh from Inverness.

'Charlotte in honour of the—' She stopped short, drawing forth a mocking look.

'Pretender?' he queried. 'Is that the word you were looking for, Miss Rankeillor?'

'No. It is not. But you were not christened Charles or James.'

'I was named for my grandfather. My mother's father.'

Christian wanted to know more about his grandfather too. Her friend Anna Gordon had said there were Cattos around Methlick in Aberdeenshire. Was that where his grandfather's house was? Would she ever find out?

'Did you have the big clean-up yesterday? A redd-up, my mother used to call it.'

It was her turn to roll her eyes. 'What do you think? Betty is never satisfied until the house is cleaned from top and bottom and everything washed. Every*one* too.'

He laughed. 'Except the cat, I take it.'

'Aye. Lucy does her own ablutions.'

'But you did not go to the bagnio to bathe?'

'Not this year.' They exchanged a look full of meaning. And longing.

'When?' he asked.

'Soon,' she said, giving him the words she had said to herself after he had left the day before yesterday. 'Very, very soon.'

Catto unfastened the buckle on the satchel and took out what Christian Rankeillor had surmised to be a lump as solid as the piece of coal he had handed her. He laid it on the kitchen table, a wash-leather pouch bulging with coins. 'Contents fourteen shillings,' he announced. 'To cover expenses incurred in feeding and housing Alice, Geordie and Joshua.'

Patrick Rankeillor gave him one of his withering professorial looks. 'We dinna require any money for that, young man.'

'No,' his daughter echoed. 'We do not.'

'I require to give you this money. Regulations,' Catto added crisply. 'I am obliged to do it. Nor am I spending my own money. I have a fund available to me to pay for such eventualities.'

'That's as maybe,' said Patrick Rankeillor, still visibly bristling. 'Put the money back in your bag, laddie.'

'You cannot be expected to keep people who are in your house because of me and the decisions I made.'

Standing beside her father, Christian folded her arms. Looking from one to the other, both with decidedly fierce expressions on their faces, Catto was momentarily nonplussed. Until his brain cleared. He tapped the purse with his fingertips. 'Look at it this way. This is King George's money.'

When the stern expressions facing him relaxed, if only by the merest smidgeon, he pressed his point. 'Surely the two of you can have no objection to spending King George's money. Quite the reverse, I should have thought.'

A gleam showed in Rankeillor's eyes. 'You're gey persuasive, laddie.' At which point Catto assumed agreement had been given.

'I shall of course require a receipt. I can't go about spending the king's money willy-nilly.' Patting his breast pocket, he looked at Christian, now narrowing her eyes at him. 'I have taken the liberty of preparing one. Perhaps you and I might repair to the library, Miss Rankeillor, so you can count the money and sign the receipt.'

Realization dawned in those narrowed green eyes. His own signaled a silent warning.

Chapter 24

Glad you managed to keep your expression neutral,' he said a moment later as she sat down at her desk in the library. 'You're learning.'

He propped himself against the wall between the side of the desk and the double doors which led out into the front lobby of the house. They had come that way from the kitchen and he had closed the doors behind them.

'Not the lost cause you first thought me in that direction?'

'I never thought you were a lost cause. Although you know what I do think is. And wish you and your father would also recognize as such.' Folding his arms, he went on without breaking stride. 'I'm wondering why the wee witch is allowing us to do this, not having a fit of the vapours because I've closed the doors. Not insisting on one of your maidservants being on sentry duty in the open doorway.'

'Because she knows it's important for Alice and Geordie and Joshua that the doors are kept closed. Also because she is still too occupied fussing over my father. She misses him when's he's away.'

'Are they more to each other than master and servant?'

'No!' She swung round, so she was sitting sideways in her chair, the fingers of one hand curled over the back of it. 'Of course not!'

He shrugged. 'It wouldn't be an unusual arrangement. I imagine it happens in many houses.'

'Not in this one.' Christian shook her head. 'Definitely not. He would not take advantage of her in that way.'

'She might not see it like that.'

'What?'

'Surely you know, Kirsty. Surely you've noticed. She's in love with him.'

'Don't be ridiculous!' She glared at him. 'That is the most stupid thing I've ever heard!'

He studied her for a moment before unfolding his arms and raising his hands, palms outward, in a placatory gesture. 'I'm sorry if I've offended you.'

She was still glaring at him. 'Did you want us to come through here to gossip about my father and Betty? Or do you really require a receipt?'

'No.' He came forward to stand behind her, resting his fingers on her shoulders. 'What I require is this. What I require is you. Turn back round to face your desk.' Pushing her hair to one side, he began to drop soft little kisses on the nape of her neck. She arched her back and let out a low moan of pleasure.

'Count the money,' he commanded, his lips very close to her ear. 'Sign the receipt.'

'How can I when you're distracting me like this? Oh…' she said again. 'I wanted to stay annoyed with you but I find I cannot.'

'So you don't want me to stop kissing the back of your neck?'

'No… I don't want you to stop.'

'Count the money,' he said again. 'Sign the receipt.'

'I'm sure I can trust you. If you say the purse contains fourteen shillings, then it does.'

'Count it all the same. To give us a little longer through here on our own.' His fingers were dancing around the edge of the white kerchief tucked into the neckline of her dress. He pulled the edge of it down, exposing more of her skin to his lips.

'Butterfly kisses,' she said. 'I like those.'

'Good. Meet me at the bagnio. Very soon. Very, very soon. Shall I give you the keys now?'

'Maybe wait till I've finished counting the money.'

'I could slip them into your pocket for you.'

'No, you could not. What if one of them were to come in?' Half-turning again, she looked up at him, a little shocked … but excited too.

'It'll not take more than a moment.' Before she knew it, he had taken the keys out of his satchel and was sliding them through the slit at her skirt's waist, unerringly finding the opening in her pocket.

'You seem to know your way around women's clothes.'

His soft laugh stirred the waves of her hair. 'Want me to take my hand away now?'

'Yes … no…'

He laughed again. 'I won't go any further. Not today. Although I'll leave my hand where it is for the moment. I'm going to do a reconnaissance of the bagnio later. Tell me what I'm going to find.'

'There's a central lobby. Off that there's a pantry and a drying room for towels and sheets. There are two bathing rooms, the little bagnio and the royal bagnio. The little bagnio has two bathtubs, the royal bagnio has three. There are also two robing and disrobing rooms,' she began, hearing how dreamy she sounded. 'They are also bedrooms, with wooden floors and divans, that is to say, beds in the Turkish style.'

'I know what a divan is.'

'I'm sure you do. I daresay you've visited a few bagnios in your time. The kind which are more than simple bath houses.'

'Do you really expect me to respond to that statement? Do the butterfly kisses still feel good? And having my hand where it is?'

'More than good…' she said, rolling her shoulders and revelling in the feel of his fingers through the thin material of her shift and his lips on her skin.

'Just think how much more pleasure we can give each other when we're not stealing snatched moments. Surely it must be time for you to pay that New Year visit to one of your friends?'

'Now that my gaoler has given me his permission to do so?'

'Answer the question. When will you meet me at the bagnio?'

She took a quick little breath. 'How about Thursday of this week?'

'Excellent. In the afternoon?'

'Yes. At three of the clock. I think Anna might invite me to stay on for supper. If so, I expect she'll ask me to stay overnight. So I dinna have to walk home in the dark.'

His hands stilled. 'Oh. A whole night together. I had not expected that. Had not dared to dream it might be possible. Och,

Kirsty…'

He said her name with such longing it made her smile.

'You haven't told your father or the wee witch that Miss Gordon is no longer in Edinburgh?'

'I haven't told them a lot of things,' she said, turning to face him.

'Which makes you feel bad?'

'Not as much as it should. When we meet at the bagnio, will you…' She stopped.

'Will I what?'

'Bring something with you … wear something … so we do not risk…' Her voice trailed off.

'Armour, you mean? Of course I will. Protection,' he said. 'We might also call it that.'

'Anna would need to send me a letter.'

'I'll arrange for that. I'll get a caddie to deliver it. Don't let anyone else read it. I'll write something but I do not think I can pretend to be your maidenly friend.'

'She might not be so maidenly.'

'Really?'

'She has a sweetheart.'

His handsome face was bright with interest. 'And they have—'

'I have no idea what they might have done! Or not done. You really are a gossip, Robert Catto!'

'Just interested in people,' he said loftily. 'Now. Count the money and sign the receipt.'

A few days, then. A few more days till she and Robert Catto would lie together. After which she would no longer be a virgin. Sitting on the edge of her bed, Christian studied herself in the big cheval glass which stood a few feet away from it. She wondered if she would look any different afterwards, if her expressive face would give away how she had spent the night away from Infirmary Street. Most of all she wondered if Betty would be able to tell. Och, but that would be awful!

A week or two ago the housekeeper had challenged Christian on having feelings for Robert Catto.

Feelings that I know can go nowhere.

Those can be the maist dangerous kind o' feelings.

Until she'd made that observation, it had never occurred to Christian that Betty might once have had a sweetheart. Or that maybe she still did. Which was a profoundly uncomfortable thought.

She knew her father and Betty were fond of each other. Nothing more and certainly nothing less. Heart-warming in one way. Yet if Robert Catto was right about Betty being in love with Patrick Rankeillor, heart-breaking in another.

The rigid structure of Edinburgh society would never have allowed a distinguished professor to marry his housekeeper. Which might not have stopped Betty from dreaming about it. Had she perhaps longed to bear him a child, a wee brother or sister for Christian? Continuing to gaze at herself in the cheval glass. she blew out a sigh. Life could be very sad.

For some folk, life could be brutal. Geordie and Joshua, Alice and Tibby. What savage and heartless men had inflicted on those two girls had nothing to do with love. Alice and Tibby would not be able to understand – how could they? – that Christian would willingly give herself to Robert Catto, allow him to make love to her, do her best to make love to him.

It's different when you both want it. That's what Anna Gordon had said – and she would know. Although Christian hadn't satisfied Robert Catto's curiosity, she knew Anna and her sweetheart Alick Forbes had not yet lain together but, as Anna put it, had *taken a few steps along the road.*

In a few more days Christian would travel right to the end of it.

Chapter 25

Christian was halfway down the stairs when she saw Mary walking through from the kitchen, a besom and a dustpan in her hands.

'Good morning, Mary.'

The girl looked up at her young mistress and returned the greeting. Christian walked on down to meet her.

'There's good news today,' she told her. 'Joshua is giving Geordie a hand to get dressed in the clothes Captain Catto brought yesterday. Then he'll help Geordie come down the stairs. I'm going to wait here for them.'

Mary beamed. 'Och, that's grand, Miss Kirsty! I'm right glad Geordie feels well enough!'

'Aye,' Christian agreed, and was interrupted by someone outside the front door tirling the pin. The brass wire to which it was connected jumped and jangled above their heads high up on the wall of the lobby and along its way to the kitchen. Mary propped the broom and the dustpan against the wall of the lobby.

'Dinna you worry, Miss Kirsty. I'll no' open the door very wide. You bide here and make sure Geordie and Joshua stay upstairs.'

Secretly amused by this hitherto unseen confidence, as well as a wee bit nervous as to who might be at the front door, Christian waited. She was relieved when she saw Mary accept a letter from whoever was proffering it. Closing the door, she glanced down at the letter and brought it to Christian.

'For you, miss. I think. It's your name on the front, is it no'?

'It is, Mary. Well done.' She'd been teaching the girls their alphabet, progressing to how to recognize names, their own and the other members of the Rankeillor household. She turned as her father came out of the library and Betty came through from the kitchen.

'A letter. Delivered by…' She swung round again to Mary.

'I dinna ken. A man. Maybe a caddy, I think.'

'Very probably,' Christian said, realizing she was going to have to open the letter and read it out loud with an eager audience watching and listening to her.

My very dear Kirsty,

You'll remember we agreed you would pay me a visit early in the New Year. I hope tomorrow would not be too prodigiously short notice? Will you come in the afternoon before it gets dark and stay over? I'm afraid Meg has had to go back to Glasgow early but hopefully you and I can chatter enough to make up for her absence. I don't think we'll have any problem diverting ourselves! Quite the opposite, I'm sure!

If you can come, no need for a reply.

Your loving friend,

Anna Gordon

She read it out, bemused by the lack of a tremble in her voice. Feeling no blush staining her cheeks. Her hands steady on the sheet of paper. She looked up and found her father frowning at her. For a moment all she could hear was the rushing of blood through her ears. Had he guessed something was amiss? She didn't dare look at Betty.

'I hope Miss Meg hasn't had to go back to Glasgow early because of any family trouble.'

Family trouble. They might all be in danger of experiencing that.

She relaxed when Patrick smiled at her. 'You should go lass, it would be a nice wee outing for you. Especially after all the alarums and excursions over Yuletide. We can manage without you for a night, can't we Betty?'

'Of course we can. You go and enjoy yourself with Miss Anna.' Betty was smiling too.

A young voice called from the upstairs landing. 'Is it all right for us to come downstairs now?'

Everyone looked up. Geordie was standing with his left hand resting on the bannister. His right arm was curled through Joshua's left. Both boys were dressed in the respectable but plain and simple clothes Marjorie Livingstone had got for them. She had included several pairs of woollen stockings in the bundle. Geordie had no shoes yet but his legs and feet should be warm in those until he got a pair.

One boy so dark. One boy so fair. Yet they were brothers under the skin.

'Down you come, lads,' Patrick said. 'Take it slow and steady.'

An hour or so later Christian walked into the kitchen and found it empty apart from Geordie. When she'd been told Robert Catto had now given permission for her, Mary and Tibby to leave the house, Betty had given a great big sniff of disapproval. This morning she'd wasted no time in taking advantage of her regained freedom.

After two festive meals, the larder was sorely in need of replenishing. It was high time too for the girls to learn how to buy the best food at the best prices at Edinburgh's various markets. With the Daft Days over, those were getting back to their normal routine.

Geordie was in the comfortable chair by the kitchen range often occupied by Betty once her day's work was done. Cushions sat on top of a wooden frame which could be stretched out to form a footrest, as it was now, turning the chair into a daybed. He had a blanket over his legs and two plump pillows behind his damaged and tender back. Lucy the little cat lay curled up on his lap.

He was holding *The Adventures of Robinson Crusoe* but it was obvious he wasn't reading it. Gazing over the top of the book, his eyes did not seem to be focussed on anything. She had to say his name twice before he turned his golden head towards her. His hair was cut short but he had a mass of waves.

'Miss Kirsty? Can I do something for you?'

'I thought I might be able to do something for you, Geordie. Where are Joshua and Alice?'

'Out the back chopping sticks for kindling. Joshua said he was going to do it and Alice said she'd better show him how to so he doesna cut his leg off.'

Christian laughed. 'Is that what she actually said?'

'Aye.' A trace of what Robert Catto had called his sparkle returned to Geordie's face.

She drew up a three-legged stool and sat beside him, pointing at the book. 'Are you not enjoying it? We could easily swap it for another one. Whatever some folk might think, you don't go to hell for not finishing a book you don't like.'

'I'm enjoying it fine, miss,' he assured her. His attempt to rouse himself to show some enthusiasm clutched at her heart-strings. 'It's a grand story. I'm just finding it a wee bit hard to…' He broke off, obviously not knowing the right word to use.

'To concentrate?' Christian suggested. 'Give your full attention to it?'

'Aye,' he agreed. 'I'm finding it a wee bit hard to con-cen-trate.' He rolled the syllables around his mouth, as she had learned he always did when introduced to a new word.

'Is that because you can't stop thinking about other things? Bad things?'

He turned his golden head away. 'Aye, miss. I can't stop thinking about what happened at Eastfield.'

She took the book out of his hands. 'I should make you a bookmark.'

'I've got one, miss. The letter the Captain sent me. I put it at the back when I'm reading.' A tinge of pride warmed his voice. 'Nobody's ever sent me a letter afore.'

Keeping his place with her thumb, she flipped back to the end to find the neatly-folded letter and transferred it to where he had read to so far. Robert Catto had addressed it formally, to *Master George Smart.*

'There,' she said, laying the book beside his legs. 'Now you'll know where to start from when you feel like reading it again.' She laid a comforting hand over his hands, which he had lowered to rest on the blanket. 'Would you like to talk about it, Geordie? There's no-one else here, only you and me. Sometimes it helps to tell someone what's bothering you. I promise not to tell anyone else. Unless you want me to.'

He turned his head again to look at her out of his clear young eyes. 'Ah dinna want ye tae tell Alice or Joshua. What was done tae Alice was much worse than what was done tae me. They were horrible tae Joshua too. For a long time. For *years*, Miss Kirsty! He says he canna remember no' being Miss Liddell's *wee pet.*' Geordie said the words with a bitterness which struck Christian to the core. A boy of his age should be too young to know that emotion.

'He tellt me that's what she used to call him. Lots o' bad names too. When she wasn't slapping him or hitting him. Or ordering folk to throw buckets o' cold water over him. With her screaming and shouting that no amount o' water would ever turn him white. That's what happened after I was flogged, Miss.'

Christian drew in a breath. What a truly vile woman Charlotte Liddell was.

'He's worried they're going to find him and take him back. He's real worried about that, Miss Kirsty. That's why I dinna want to burden him, or Alice. I might want ye tae tell the Captain, though. Although I dinna want him tae think badly o' me.'

'Why on earth would he think badly of you, Geordie? You've done no wrong.'

'But I must have done wrong, miss.' Swallowing hard, he drew the back of a shaking hand across his nose. 'Otherwise why would they have done what they did tae me?' The words were tumbling out now. 'Miss Liddell asked her brother if he wanted to whip me. She said she would but she wouldn't be able to hurt me enough! Why did she want to hurt me at all? I've never done them any harm! But they wanted to hurt me! Which makes me think I must be worth nothing!'

'You are worth so much, Geordie!' she assured him, giving his hands a quick squeeze to reinforce her words. 'Loved by Alice. Liked by Joshua, who took such a big risk to get you away from Eastfield. You two are likely going to be friends for life. Captain Catto took a big risk too, going out looking for you, bringing you back here. Because he too thinks very highly of you. Calls you his right-hand man, is that not so? I think very highly of you. So does Mrs Betty. Mary and Tibby too. I'm pretty sure it won't be long till Professor Rankeillor feels the same way. Once he gets to know you and finds out what a fine person you are.'

Geordie wasn't in a fit state to take in what she was telling him. Under her hand, his fingers curled in frustration and bewilderment. 'They took my clothes away, miss. My braw new clothes. I felt really smart in those.'

'Living up to your name, young Master Smart,' she said, and got a ghost of a smile in response.

'They stole them from me.'

'Aye. They did.' She squeezed his hand again. Dare she hope she had heard indignation in those words? That would be a much healthier emotion than him feeling he was worthless.

'They think they're so high and mighty but they're nothing more than common thieves. They stole from Alice, too. You ken what I mean, miss,' he added, looking at her out of those clear blue eyes.

'Aye, Geordie. I ken what you mean.'

'They stole from Joshua too. Stole his *life*. He's a human being like the rest of us.'

'Yes, and another very fine one. Tell me something, Geordie. Do you think Alice and Joshua are worthless?'

'No!' he burst out. This time there was no mistaking the indignation in his voice. 'Of course ah dinna think that! Oh—' He broke off, realization dawning in his eyes. 'You're crafty, Miss Kirsty.'

'You see what I'm driving at? You see the logic?'

'Logic,' he repeated. 'Which would mean the sensible conclusion tae draw in the light o' a' the evidence?'

She grinned. 'You're a grand talker, Geordie. How do you know all the things you do?'

'Because I listen afore I speak, miss. And you're a grand healer. You're right kind, too. Like the Captain. Even though he tries no' tae show it.'

'I've seen it, Geordie. I know he's kind.'

'He likes *you*, Miss Kirsty.'

'I like him.' She gave his hand one last pat and stood up. 'Now, shall I go and make sure Joshua hasn't cut his leg off?'

Chapter 26

'Don't be scared.'

As they stood facing each other in the central lobby of the bagnio, he reached out a hand and drew his fingertips down the side of her face. He had already been there when she had arrived a moment before but they were both still dressed as they had come in from the chill of the January afternoon. It was cold in here too, although very bright.

There were no windows around these internal walls but the lobby was flooded with winter sunshine streaming down from the cupola on top of the building. In a curved niche opposite the double front door sat a life-sized brass statue of an eagle, wings upraised, gleaming in the light striking it from above.

Their cloaks fell from their shoulders, his grey, hers dark blue. Beneath her cloak he could see she wore a fine woollen gown in a rich dark brown. The hem of her skirts brushed the black and white marble tiles of the floor. As she bent forward to set her wicker basket down he saw neat little brown leather shoes with a low curved heel and a tantalizing glimpse of her ankles, clad in white stockings.

He was carrying his leather satchel, slung bandolier-style across the waistcoat he wore below his cloak. That was of fine brown broadcloth, much the same shade as her gown.

'We match today,' he said, his cold fingertips still tracing the line of her jaw.

'So we do.' Her eyes fluttered closed, then opened again as she wrapped her fingers around his wrist, under his ruffled shirt cuffs, stilling and capturing his hand. She wore knitted mittens, fashioned to leave the tops of her fingers free. 'A butterfly touch,' she observed. 'Like those little butterfly kisses the other day.'

'I'm trying not to frighten you away. Startle you so you'll flutter off like a pretty little butterfly. Although it's not too late for you to change your mind, Kirsty.'

'Would that make you angry?'

'No. But I'd be very disappointed. Which is vastly to understate the case.' He tugged her hand away from his wrist, lifted it to his mouth and kissed it.

'I'm not going to change my mind.'

'Glad to hear it.' He looked at her over the back of her hand. 'One thing though Kirsty, before we go any further. I should probably have asked you before. You know you will bleed? Also that it may hurt? Although I hope only very briefly.'

She took a breath. 'I know both those things. There are towels in the linen press through in the bedroom. We can put one under us. For the blood.'

'Miss Practical,' he said, wondering if he could love her any more than he did right now. 'We match in this too, it seems. I've already made up the bed through there, with a towel beneath us.'

'When did you do that?'

'On my first visit here this morning. While it was still pitch black.' He gestured towards the gleaming brass eagle. 'Struck a light and got the fright of my life when that thing loomed up in front of me. Thought the king of the birds was going to pick me up and fly me to his eyrie. What's an eagle doing in a bagnio? I haven't seen that before.'

'He's one of the symbols of the calling.'

'The calling?'

'The College of Surgeons. Possibly connected with surgeons having to be eagle-eyed. What did you do after you recovered from your fright?'

'I set a low fire under the boiler. That amount of water in a cistern takes a long time to heat.' He looked around him. 'Very ingenious system of pipework here. To draw the water in from the well outside and run it through under the floors to heat the different rooms.'

'There speaks the engineer,' she teased.

Or the man who's as scared as you are. Only for a very different reason. That's why I'm babbling about pipework. Very romantic.

'You want us to bathe?' she asked shyly.

'I thought you might like to. Afterwards.'

'Oh,' she said. 'Afterwards.'

His mouth curved. 'That's a rather faint little voice. At the risk of embarrassing you even further, I'd love us to bathe together. The bathtubs look long, wide and deep enough for two. Have I shocked you?' he asked, as her hand flew up to her mouth.

'Y-yes,' she stuttered. 'N-no… Maybe… I dinna really ken if I'm shocked or not.'

'You can mull it over. Water won't be hot enough for quite some time. One more thing. If it hurts too much or if you simply do not like it, tell me and I will stop. At any point.'

Her eyes searched his face. 'You would do that? You *could* do that?'

'If it's for you, I can do anything. Wouldn't much like it but I'll stop if you ask me to.'

She dropped her eyes, obliging him to speak his next words over the top of her head. 'You did this the other night, you know. When I brought Geordie and Joshua back from Musselburgh. Once you and I were alone in the library – apart from Geordie, our sleeping chaperone – you apparently found my neckcloth deeply fascinating, It seems to be exerting the same fascination over you now.'

Flipping one edge of his grey cloak back, he gripped the thick belt of the satchel and swung it round his back. She kept her head down, one mittened hand resting against his black silk neckcloth. Over her hair she wore a white cap with a narrow frill, a fashionable little hat on top of it. He flicked its brim. 'Can we get rid of all this, d'you think?'

'Not yet.' Hampered by her bowed head, her voice came out as not much more than a squeak. 'Not until I say what I have to say.'

'Which is?' he encouraged, stooping and leaning sideways in an attempt to see the expression on her face.

'That I dinna ken how to do any o' this. That I am woefully ignorant.'

'Och, Kirsty…'

His soft laugh brought her head up. 'Dinna make fun of me!'

'I'm not making fun of you. I'm amused, that's all.' His deep voice was as soft as his laugh. 'I rather like what you call your woeful ignorance. I think it's sweet. You dinna need to ken how to do any o' this,' he added, in affectionate mimicry of her accent. 'All you need to do is let me make love to you. *Are* you scared?'

'Maybe a wee bit nervous.'

'I'll be as gentle as I can. Hold you as I would a precious piece of porcelain. As I would those dainty little teacups of yours. The ones you keep in your bedchamber for when your friends visit.'

'Which you know about from the night when you invaded my bedchamber. I like the metaphor, all the same.' Earnest again, she looked up at him. 'I want to make love to you too, Robert. Give you pleasure.'

'You already do. You *will* do. I guarantee it. You know how to kiss, don't you? And caress? Everything else will come naturally.' His voice dropped to a murmur. 'Are those not beautiful words? Kiss,' he repeated. '*Caress*.'

'Yes,' she agreed. 'Those are beautiful words.'

'Wonderful. We're making progress. Let's make some more. Take your hat and cap off. Better still, let me do it.'

After he had freed her hair, they kissed again before he moved both arms to encircle her waist, spreading his fingers under her cloak. Damn her stays – but they would soon be rid of those.

'I'll put more coal on the fire under the boiler soon. Not quite yet. But before we come together.' He clicked his tongue against the roof of his mouth. 'You may have liked my metaphor but that was an unfortunate turn of phrase.'

'Isn't that what we are going to do, come together?'

He laughed. 'That's the ideal, yes—' Then, seeing her puzzled frown: 'You have no idea what I'm talking about, do you?'

'No. So tell me.'

He spared one hand to tap the end of her nose with his finger. 'I'll tell you later. At the appropriate moment.'

'Will there be one of those?'

'I'm hoping for several. I'm glad you don't want to change your mind. I might have become unhinged if you had. Driven mad by unrequited lust.'

'Lust, is it?'

'Nothing wrong with honest-to-goodness lust,' he said, delighted to see his words had made her eyes sparkle. Green as a summer meadow, those eyes. Along with the defiant upward tilt of the chin, one of the first things he had noticed about her. Among other attributes and characteristics. She was such a beguiling mixture, shy one moment and bold the next.

'I'd jalouse you ken a great deal about lust, Captain Catto.'

Triumphant. That was the only word to describe the look on her face now. Idiotically happy, he pretended to glower at her. 'I was going to add, especially when lust goes hand in hand with love. Now, Miss Rankeillor,' he asked, deliberately arch, 'what about those shameless thoughts of yours? As I recall, you were going to share them with me. Anytime you like, madam.'

'Och, Robert…' she said, her whole body softening.

'Och, Kirsty,' he responded, glad he had slid the satchel out of the way. Stays or not, the feel of her body against his was intoxicating. No barrier below her waist other than fine wool, the petticoat and thin shift covering her hips and legs and what lay between. 'Och, Kirsty,' he said again. This time there was no teasing in the words. 'I love it when you melt against me like this… Oh,' he moaned, feeling his body react to hers. 'You're willing, then?'

'Aye. Dinna want to be responsible for you losing your wits.'

'Only for that reason?'

'Stop fishing for compliments.'

'*Kiss*,' he said. '*Caress*. Several of both, if you please.'

They did that, ending with both of them a little breathless, foreheads pressed gently together. 'You'll have to guide me too. I've never lain with a virgin before. Never wanted to. Until now. Let us go through to the bedroom.'

Picking up her basket he led the way out of the lobby and into the bedroom. There were two divans in there, standing on honey-coloured varnished floorboards. The wider one was neatly made up with sheets and a couple of blankets.

'You did this earlier today?'

'Yes. Shall we take our cloaks off and sit down on the edge of the divan?'

Following both suggestions, she untied her cloak, laid it over the foot of the divan and sat down. He set her basket on the floor to the side of the bed. 'What's in here? Apart from your night clothes, I take it.'

'Sustenance,' she said, looking up at him as he swung off his cloak and laid it on top of hers. 'Not wearing your horseman's coat today?'

'I thought my cloak might add an extra layer of warmth later on. Along with yours. Should we need that.'

'I've brought gingerbread and ginger tablet. Couldn't bring anything more substantial. Not when I'm only supposed to be taking a wee New Year's gift to Anna. But I thought you'd appreciate the ginger. What's in your satchel?'

'My banyan. As requested. I brought sustenance too.' Swinging off the satchel, he laid it on top of his cloak and sat down next to her. 'My contribution to the feast is a loaf of bread, butter and some slices of ham. Although I shall indeed look forward to the gingerbread and the ginger tablet. The second time you've brought me some.'

'I remember. When I called at the guard-house trying to work out whose side you were on. When you discovered Geordie had been hiding Alice there.'

After the assault on her, Geordie's sister had been taken, bound and gagged, to a squalid brothel in Edinburgh, told she would work there from then on. When the woman who ran the place succumbed to drink, Alice had found the courage to make her escape and go looking for her brother.

Catto touched Kirsty Rankeillor's cheek. 'Don't dwell on it. She's safe now. They all are.'

'Reading my thoughts again?' she asked ruefully. 'Will your men not think it odd that you have taken food away from the guard-house? Or wonder why you will be absent from there overnight?'

'I do not have to explain myself to my men. Besides which, nobody is keeping much of an eye on the guard-house pantry with Geordie not being there.' He lifted one of her hands. 'Can you bear to take your mittens off? I promise it will be warmer in here very soon. I'll add the coal to the fire as soon as daylight has faded. So no one will notice any smoke coming out of the chimney.'

She nodded her agreement before holding out her hands to him. 'Why don't you take my mittens off?' Growing bolder and more relaxed though she was, there was a tremble in her voice.

'Happy to oblige,' he said, peeling off the little gloves. Tucking one inside the other, he rolled them into a neat bundle and tossed them into her basket. Raising her hands to his lips, he planted a delicate kiss on the inside of each wrist, relishing her visible pleasure at his touch. She was still nervous, he could see that. Maybe even scared, despite having denied it. He had to do something about that. Some inconsequential talk might help release the tension he could sense building up inside her.

'I also brought some wine. There's a bottle of hock and a bottle of claret in the pantry. This morning I found some glasses and rinsed them out and dried them. I even polished them with a cloth I found in one of the drawers.'

'You've thought of everything.' She had a deep voice for a woman but that comment had come out more highly pitched, breathy and nervous.

'I'm not finished yet. I brought some coffee too. Also a packet of tea so you can have your favourite drink tomorrow morning. Or whenever you like.'

'Tomorrow morning,' she repeated. 'By which time everything will have changed. I shall have changed.'

'You'll still be you. What would you say to us loosening up a little more? Doesn't mean we're going to do anything yet. There's no rush. Not till you're ready.'

There was a tiny pause before she spoke, her hands rising to his neckcloth. 'I'd say this.' She slid the smooth strip of fabric from around his neck, rolled it up and sent it to join her mittens in the wicker basket on the floor. She looked very serious. Getting her courage up.

Tentative fingers touched his skin. She followed those fingers with her lips, kissing his bare throat. Once. Twice. He tilted his head back, savouring her touch as she had savoured his. Not that he was going to let her do this for too long. He wanted her first time to be as good as it could possibly be, which meant he was going to have to muster every last ounce of self-control.

'My turn again now.' He tugged the white linen fichu out of the neckline of her bodice, folding it before tossing it down to the bottom of the divan to lie on top of the satchel and their cloaks. 'Ah. This is a much better view.' Bending his head, he began kissing the tops of her breasts.

When he felt her fingers on his black satin hair ribbon, he raised his head again. 'Not yet. Not till I add the coal to the fire. We'll light a few lanterns soon too. Found three this morning. I've got them all ready in the pantry. I think it would be best to leave the sconces unlit.'

An idea leapt into his head. 'Turn around. With your back to me.'

'Why?' she asked, although she was already obeying him.

'So I can do this.' He slid his arms down over her shoulders and her half-exposed breasts, his fingers sliding down under her stays and shift to cup them.

'Oh!' she yelled. 'Your hands are so cold!'

Chapter 27

Behind her, he was shaking with laughter. He was also luxuriating in the feel of her soft breasts, warm under her clothes, her nipples springing into life under his questing fingers.

'W-well,' he spluttered through a heady mixture of mirth and arousal, 'What do you expect? I'm not wearing mittens and it's cold out there.'

'Oaf! Idiot! *Oh…*'

'*Oh?*' he asked, his lips against her ear. His breath was as warm as his hands were cold.

'Oh, nothing! Oh, I want to hit you!'

'Be my guest,' he said, laughter still bubbling through his voice.

'How can I in this position? You have me trapped.'

'Totally against your will, of course. That'll be why you're leaning back against me. That'll be why you're arching your back like a cat stretching in the sun.'

'Oaf,' she muttered again.

'But not a liar. I think my hands are warmer now.'

'This is relevant because?'

'Because I want to do some exploring. Turn round again.'

'You really cannot get out of the habit of issuing orders, can you?'

'It's in your own interests, Kirsty.' Sliding his hands out of her bodice, he smoothed it and the quilted petticoat below it up over her white stockings.

'Pretty. But should you not be wearing sensible woollen stockings on a day as cold as this?'

'I thought you might like these ones.'

'You thought right,' he growled. A bolt of desire shot through him as he imagined her naked apart from her fine white stockings and their pale blue ribbon garters. Lying back on this divan, ready for him to make love to her as he gently nudged her legs apart.

Not quite yet. His cupped hand slid up over her knees. 'Will you let me go farther?'

'I'll let you…' Her voice was slurred. 'Oh yes, I'll let you…'

His long, strong fingers moved up over the smooth skin of her thigh, dancing onto the most intimate part of her body. 'Oh…' she moaned again. '*Och, Robert…*'

He kissed her, long and deep, tasting her lips, tasting her mouth. Encouraging her with a teasing tongue when she responded.

'You,' he said, lifting his lips away from hers, 'who knows so much about the human body, do you know you have a tight little bud right here? Like a rosebud. The source of so much pleasure.'

She gasped when he touched it.

Afterwards he held her close, kissing her brow and murmuring soft little endearments into her hair. 'Good?' he asked when he heard her breathing begin to slow down.

'Good … is vastly to understate the case. I think that must have been one of your appropriate moments…'

'Yes. You just came.'

'Came?' she said dreamily. 'Is that … what it's called? I never knew it would … feel so good…'

'You can feel it again,' he said, holding her more tightly still, caught between laughter and elation at her response. 'As many times as you like.' Smoothing down her skirts with one hand, he rose to his feet and extended the other to her. 'But first come and keep me company while I put more coal on the fire and light the lanterns. Then we'll have a glass of wine.'

She looked up at him as he stood there beside the divan. 'What about you?'

'What about me?'

'Y-your pl-pleasure,' she stuttered.

'Oh, darling girl, I'm having so much pleasure!'

'Really?'

'Really.' His voice softened. 'Kissing you. Touching you. Watching you receive pleasure at my hands. I'll keep. For a while.'

They were in the pantry. Christian was sitting on a tall stool next to a high and narrow side table. Robert Catto was standing in front of it, opening the bottle of hock. She was enjoying seeing him in more casual garb than usual. He had unbuttoned his brown waistcoat and rolled up the sleeves of his white linen shirt, securing them by their cuffs to his elbows. He'd done that before he had added coal to the fire under the boiler, washing his hands, wrists and forearms afterwards.

He had lit two lanterns and placed them on the high table. Catching the fine dusting of coppery hairs on his forearms, their light was needed now. Above their heads, all that could be seen through the cupola on the roof was darkness streaked with grey. The January night was upon them.

He poured the wine, handed her one of the glasses and raised his own. 'Shall we have a toast?'

She threw him a speaking look. 'Could we agree on one?'

'I'm hardly going to ask you to toast the king, Kirsty.' His voice was very dry.

'I have no objection to toasting the king. Quite the reverse.'

He cast a glance around the pantry. 'I see no bowl of water here. No way of passing your glass over one to indicate your toast is to the king over the water. As you would call him.'

She lowered her wine glass.

'I'm sorry,' he said. 'I should not have said that.'

'I should not have said what I did either. But when it comes to politics we are on opposite sides, Robert. Us being here together tonight does not change that.'

Her stomach lurched. Being here with him tonight could be seen as a betrayal of the Cause which had shaped her life. There were those who would think so if they knew.

'Divided loyalties, Kirsty?' he asked gently. Then, when she nodded: 'Can we try not to think like that tonight? Just be here and with each other, forget about politics, kings and princes? Safe in our own world, where no one knows where we are. Even if only for one night. A world where all things are possible.'

She studied him for a moment before lifting her glass again.

'To us,' she said, clinking it against his. 'To a world where all things are possible.'

He echoed the toast, adding: 'And to love. And to Sergeant Livingstone.'

'What does Mr Livingstone have to do with it?' she responded, wrinkling her nose in perplexity.

'He's an observant man. Before we found Geordie and Joshua on the bridge at Musselburgh, we stopped to let the horses drink from a burn. Sat there looking out to sea. The moon was very bright. Shining down on the dark water like a yellow path through the waves.'

'Making you moonstruck again? Enough to tell Mr Livingstone about us?'

'*He* told me. Said he thought I'd met a special someone here in Edinburgh. Asked if my intentions were honourable. He has a young daughter.'

'He asked you that!' Christian took a gulp of wine. 'How did you answer him?'

'I told him I wished to God my intentions *could* be honourable. Asked him how that was possible when you and I are in the situation in which we find ourselves.'

'What did he say?'

'That only one thing really matters. Love.'

She took a moment, considering, then nodded. 'He's right, is he not? Love is the source. The well from where all other good feelings flow.'

Now. He should do it now.

He watched her in the lantern light, thinking how beautiful she looked, thinking how much more there was to her than her lovely face and glorious hair. She was a source, a deep well of goodness. Kind. Brave. Thoughtful. Intelligent. Much too good for the likes of him. Playing with the stem of his glass, his eyes dropped to her empty one. 'More wine?'

Her answer brought his gaze back up to her face. 'Maybe afterwards.' Standing up, she held out her hand. 'Let us go back through to the bedroom.'

'Warmer in here now.'

'Aye,' she agreed. Once again they were sitting side by side on the divan.

'Will you permit me to unpin and unlace you?'

'I will. What do you seek?' For he had turned his head away and was looking around the bedroom. Not an easy task when it was so shadowy, lit only by the lanterns they had brought through with them from the pantry and stood on the floor in here.

'A little dish or some such to put your pins into.'

She slid her hand into the side of her gown, finding the pocket beneath it. 'Here,' she said, handing him a small roll of quilted cloth. 'After I've taken them out I secure them here.' She raised one hand, palm outwards. 'You dinna have to say it. Miss Practical again.'

'I like my Miss Practical. You and I have our differences but we also have a lot in common.' He dropped light kisses on her brow, the tip of her nose and her lips before starting to slide out the pins which fastened her stomacher to her gown. There were only eight of them. It didn't take long.

'Tell me what we have in common.'

'This,' he said, holding up the last pin. 'We both like order and method.'

She glanced down at the little roll of cloth. He stuck the pin into it, completing two neat rows of four. 'So we do. That's how I put them in too.' She lifted her stomacher and shrugged out of her gown. Standing up, she freed its skirts and stepped out of her underskirt. She returned the pins in their quilted roll to her pocket and untied the ribbons holding it around her waist. He took the gown, stomacher, underskirt and embroidered pocket from her and laid them over their cloaks and his satchel at the foot of the bed.

'I'll move all this in a minute. Apart from our cloaks. Shall we take our shoes off?'

'Our stockings too.'

'I shall. But I want you to leave yours on.'

'You like them that much?'

'I like them that much.' His attention returned to her stays. 'I hope,' he said as he began to unlace them, 'that you appreciate the iron self-control I'm exercising here. Have you ever calculated how many yards of lacing and ribbons are wound around the average female?'

'You seem to be enjoying finding out.'

'I am.' Once he had unlaced her, she rolled her shoulders to free the stays. He took them from her, placing them with the rest of the clothing at the foot of the bed.

She looked down at herself, clad only in her stockings and her shift. 'I am undone.' She spoke in mock tragic tones.

'So you are.' His gaze rested on her freed breasts, their curves and rosy nipples visible through the thin linen of her shift. 'Happily, I hope.'

'Very happily.' She reached under his hair, curving her fingers around the nape of his neck. 'Should you not also be undone?' she asked when they pulled apart. 'Your hair, certainly.'

'Untie my ribbon, then.'

She rolled up the strip of black satin and sent it to join the pile of discarded clothing at the foot of the bed. Her hands went towards the waist of his breeches. His own shot out to stop her.

She blushed. 'Oh. Because you might…'

'Aye,' he agreed. So she knew that much. 'Because I might.'

'I don't know what to do now.'

'Permit me to remove what's left of my clothes and your shift. After that you can lie back and look beautiful. That's all you have to do.'

'Am I allowed to touch you now?' she asked a moment later, turning in to him as he lay down beside her.

'Not yet.' His hand slid down her body. 'Some more of this first. Which will also get you ready for me. Now,' he said a moment or two later. 'All right?'

'Very all right…'

'Allow me only to don my protection.'

He entered her as gently as he had promised, stopping when she drew her breath in on a hiss of pain.

'You can still tell me to stop. It's not too late.'

She slid her hands around his shoulders. 'I don't want you to stop!'

He stayed still, murmuring soothing words, stroking her hair back from her forehead.

'Better now?' he asked a moment or two later.

'Much better…'

He began to move again, slowly filling her. She said his name. Once. Twice. Then over and over again. That was when order and method were forgotten, as their legs pushed everything off the foot of the bed.

Chapter 28

The bedroom of the bagnio was warm now, the air within it still. The lantern on the floor beside the divan shone steadily, bathing them in soft light. Relishing the feel of the strong arms encircling her, Christian stretched her body within his warm grasp, pointing her legs and feet as far as they would go before relaxing back again.

He pressed a kiss against her brow. 'All right?'

'More than all right. A lot more.'

He propped himself up on one elbow and looked down at her. His chestnut brown hair slid over her breasts like a length of silk. 'It gave you pleasure? *I gave* you pleasure?'

She turned into him, mumbling her answer against his chest and the fine hairs covering it. 'Couldn't you tell?'

'Aye. I could tell.' He was smiling, she could hear it in his voice. 'Even though you didn't use many words. To be more precise, *because* you didn't use many words.'

Remembering how she had moaned against his mouth, how his lips and his fingers had rendered her incapable of coherent speech, the sounds she had made when they had joined together, she kept her face where it was. He was clearly enjoying himself too much to stop.

'Not many words at all,' he mused. 'Apart from my name. Over and over again.' He paused for a moment. When he spoke again, his voice was husky, no teasing now in his words. 'I loved hearing you say my name over and over again!'

Those words brought her head up. 'Och, Robert…' She took a strand of his hair between her fingers and tugged, bringing his face closer to hers. 'Did I give you pleasure?'

'Couldn't you tell?' he countered.

'I thought I could. But I want to hear you say it.'

'Aye. You gave me pleasure. So much pleasure.'

'Could we maybe do it again? After we bathe?'

A flash of devilment in his grey eyes, he pretended to consider her question. 'Oh, I daresay you could persuade me. Using your womanly wiles. For now, let me go and run our baths. Or should that be *bath*?'

His mouth widened into the broadest of smiles at her answer.

He came back from the little bagnio with a bowl of warm water, a cloth folded into a pad and a fresh towel. Christian came up onto her elbows. 'I can clean myself up.'

'All right,' he said, dipping the cloth into the bowl, squeezing it out and handing it to her. He squatted down beside the bed. He'd shrugged his shoulders into his banyan before he'd left to run their bath. It was a sumptuous garment, with a pattern of red and turquoise dragons rising out of a yellow background. He'd been wearing it over his nightshirt the day she had called at the guard-house.

'I ought to be embarrassed about doing this in front of you,' she said, glancing up from the task in hand.

He cocked his head to one side. 'And you're not? That's good.'

'Maybe it means I really am shameless.'

'You have nothing to be ashamed of. All done?'

When she nodded, he sprang to his feet and took the blood-stained cloth from her, dropping it back into the bowl of water. 'Let us slip the towel out from under you and you can transfer your … eh … posterior, to the clean one. I'll dispose of all this and you can get your wrapper out of your basket. Did you bring slippers too?'

Made of lead, the bagnio's bathtubs were always lined with a white linen sheet. He'd done that and the bath, one of two in the little bagnio, was nearly full. One of their three lanterns lit up the room.

'I have the towels ready.' He indicated them with a wave of his arm. 'Couldn't find the soap.'

'I'll get it. There are a few bars in one of the cupboards in the pantry.'

Back in no more than a moment, she crossed over the black-and-white floor tiles to where he stood beside the bath. She felt as if she were gliding towards him, floating above the floor tiles. She told him so, adding: 'It's as though we're in a different world to the one outside the bagnio. A thousand miles away from it.'

'We are.' Taking her in his arms, he held her close. 'Our own world.'

'The world where all things are possible?'

'That's the one.'

After they had tossed their dressing gowns aside, he took her hand to help her step into the bath. 'As though you're helping me into a coach,' she said. 'Politely. Like a gentleman. Nothing at all like the man who threatened to throw me over his shoulder the night we first met.'

'I'd have done it too.'

'I know you would.'

'No point in making threats if you're not prepared to carry them out. Going to sit down, Miss Rankeillor? And slide forward a bit?'

'Not easy to slide on a linen sheet. The bagnios you've visited before must have had marble baths. I'll have to lift my … eh … posterior. I'd jalouse you normally use a coarser word.'

'Hah!' was the only response she got to that before he stepped into the bath behind her. Bent at the knees, his strong legs fitted in on either side of her body.

'Lean back against me. And give me the soap.' He dipped it in the water, moved it to and fro. 'Lemons,' he observed as it released its scent. 'I love the smell of lemons.'

'They grow outdoors in Italy, I believe.'

'In great abundance.' He drew the soap up from one of her wrists to her shoulder and down onto her breasts, smoothing it over both in turn. Sighing, she relaxed even more against him, with the inevitable result.

'Something else growing here.' He said the words into her hair.

'So there is. Could I turn round so I can see it?'

His hand stilled. 'What?'

'I've seen the male organs of generation before, made drawings of them several times, but I've never seen them on a living body— Oh, what's the matter?' For behind her, he had begun to shake.

'Nothing,' he howled. 'Not a bloody thing!' He got the words out, then dissolved into helpless laughter.

They ate their supper at 8 o'clock, registering the time by the ringing of church bells. They had retrieved the satchel and clothes from the floor at the foot of the divan and put them out of the way. Now they sat cross-legged on the divan, facing each other. He wore his colourful banyan, she her cream-coloured cambric wrapper. He had brought a tray of food through from the pantry and set it between them, going back for the tall wooden stool and placing it beside the bed to hold their glasses of wine.

'Noisy place, Edinburgh,' he observed once the church bells had stopped ringing.

'Are not all cities noisy?'

He smiled at her. 'How many cities do you know?'

'Edinburgh, Glasgow and Aberdeen. I have been furth of Edinburgh, you know.' A sheepish look followed her momentary indignation. 'I suppose that's not a very long list.'

'Would you like to visit other cities? London or Paris or Berlin or Dresden or Rome?'

'I should love to visit all those cities. Do you know each one?'

He nodded as he set out their supper. 'I've lived in Paris and I've spent time in the others. I'd love to take you to Rome. You would find much to sketch and paint there among the antiquities.'

He handed her a plate with a thick slice of ham, two slices of bread, a few curls of butter and a small knife to spread it with. 'While I should enjoy sitting there watching you. You would have to wear a straw hat with a nice wide brim. The sun is very strong in Italy. We wouldn't want your pale Scottish skin to get burnt.'

He served himself and raised his plate. 'Eat,' he urged, when she made no move to do so.

'You'd love to take me to Rome,' she repeated. 'Pray tell, Captain, how would we manage that?'

'We're in our own world tonight,' he reminded her. 'One where all things are possible.'

'Our own world may only last for this one night. We cannot know if we will ever be able to be together like this again.'

She looked so sad, sounded so wistful. He wanted to lift the sorrow from her, assure her they would have many more nights together, promise her the Earth – and knew he could not. *Promises made and not kept are worse than promises not made at all.*

So he could not give her the present he had brought for her. Could he?

'Hope,' he said, his voice not quite steady. 'We have to hold onto hope. Now let us eat.'

He came back into the bedroom after clearing away their supper things and drew in a sharp breath. In the warm lantern light, she looked like a painting. One which moved, as she raised both arms, lifted her mass of dark hair and flipped it over her shoulders to tumble down her back. In response to the movement, her wrapper fell open at the front. Catto's eyes flickered downwards. Spotting him in the open doorway, she tugged the two sides closed and crossed her hands over her breasts.

He walked over to the divan and sat down on the edge of it. 'Too late for that. I've already seen them. And very lovely they are too. Will you let me look again? I like to look. Just like you do.'

She allowed her arms to fall to her sides. Leaning forward, he moved the fronts of her wrapper apart, adjusting the soft fabric so one breast was half exposed, the other fully bare.

'Artistically draped. Like a beauty in an Italian painting. If I could draw as well as you can, I would draw you as you look now.'

'So you would have something to remember me by?'

He raised his eyes from her breasts to her face.

'We must part, Robert. Sooner or later. You know that as well as I do.' A tear slid down one smooth cheek. He reached out to blot it with his thumb – and made his decision.

Springing to his feet, he walked across to where his clothes were laid over the back of a chair. He knew she was watching him, knew she was wondering what he was doing. Digging into his waistcoat pocket, he brought out a small paper packet, came back and handed it to her. 'A gift. From me to you. With all my love.'

He was holding his breath as he watched her open it and place its contents in the palm of her hand. A brooch. Two hearts entwined, surmounted by a crown. Small and dainty and beautifully wrought in silver.

She looked up at him. 'You do realize what a luckenbooth brooch signifies?'

'That's why I bought it,' he said, sitting back down on the edge of the bed, his voice carefully light. 'Had to endure insult to do so.'

'Which unfortunate person incurred your wrath?'

'The silversmith who sold it to me.'

'What did the poor man say?'

'He winked in a damned impertinent manner and said he hoped the lassie was bonnie.'

'Did you glower at him?'

'I do not want to talk about the silversmith. I want to know if you will accept the brooch. As a token of a promise made from me to you and you to me.'

'A promise that can only be made – and kept – in our own world, the one where all things are possible?'

'Yes.'

'You are most certainly moonstruck.'

'Undoubtedly. Will you be moonstruck with me?'

She raised her free hand, trailed her fingertips down the side of his face. 'Even though our moon may be buffeted by storm and wind, tossed about like a ship on a stormy sea, at times obscured and hidden from view?'

'Aye,' he said, his voice husky. 'All of that.' He took her hand and kissed it.

The pause before she spoke again could only have lasted seconds. To him it seemed much longer.

'On that basis, I'll accept the luckenbooth. I should really give you a silver coin in exchange but I did not bring my purse out with me. So the pin of the brooch does not pierce our friendship,' she added, responding to a puzzled look.

'What is between us is vastly more than friendship. I thought you might wear the luckenbooth in some concealed place. Kept secure in the little roll you keep for your pins, perhaps. Tucked inside your pocket.'

She curled her fingers, wrapping the little brooch in her hand. 'Thank you,' she said, and found herself incapable of saying anything else. He had one final question for her.

'Tell me something, Kirsty. Maybe this is no more than a forlorn hope…'

'Go on,' she said when he hesitated.

The words were rattled out, as though his courage might fail him if he didn't say them quickly enough. 'If it were possible for us to wed, would you want to?'

'Of course I would, Robert. Och, of course I would!'

Leaning forward, he drew her into his arms. They held each other for a long, long time.

Chapter 29

'I do not like leaving you alone here.'

'I'll be fine.' It was the following morning and they were standing together in the central lobby of the bagnio, his hands on her waist, her hands flat against his chest. They were both dressed but only he was wearing his cloak. There was a dim light coming into the lobby from the lantern in the bedroom, enough for them to see each other.

'You have to go first, while it is still dark. We cannot risk leaving together. Especially not once it's broad daylight. I cannot leave before then. 'Twould look very strange if I arrived home before 10 of the clock.'

He sighed into her hair. 'I know all that. I still don't like it. Lock the door behind me. The minute I leave.'

'Of course.'

'I don't like the gate to the bagnio garden not being locked either.'

'Who would open it? I'll be fine,' she said again.

'What will you do till it's the right time for you to leave?'

Her voice was warm. 'Maybe I'll sit on the edge of the divan and think about everything we did here yesterday evening and last night.'

'Oh,' he murmured, his voice as warm and intimate as hers. 'Don't forget what we did first thing this morning. I liked how you woke me up.'

She dropped her eyes. 'I lay there for ages wondering if I should.'

'Didn't want me to think you were too bold?'

'Yes,' she said, looking up again. 'Was I – too bold, I mean?'

'You were a delight. You *are* a delight. Shall I tell you

something? I was awake from the first touch. Thought I'd pretend to still be asleep for a little while longer, lie there and enjoy the moment.'

She hit him. Not very hard. Making him laugh.

'You can wake me up by that method anytime you like, Miss Rankeillor. I also liked how you finally told me what your shameless thoughts were.'

'I liked how you acted them out. I can still feel … certain sensations … in certain places.'

'I hope you are not sore. In certain places.'

'Not sore. I have what you might call an … *awareness*.'

'Then I shall spend my day thinking about your body remembering mine.'

She kissed him for that. 'Although I don't believe a word of it. You'll spend the day doing your duty. You always do. Go,' she urged. Before dawn breaks.'

'One question before I leave. When can we do this again?'

A few hours later, halfway through a chilly but sunny morning, Arthur Menzies obeyed a discreet request from one of the footmen at Eastfield to go to the kitchen door. A man stood a yard or two away from it beside a horse and well-laden cart. In one hand he held the animal's bridle, in the other a letter.

'Mr Jamieson?' he queried, using an alias Arthur Menzies often went by when he was on business for The Association.

Edmonstone nodded towards the letter. 'That for me?'

'Aye. I'm instructed to wait till you read it. In case you want to send a reply.'

Arthur Menzies unfolded the letter and quickly scanned it. The story it told was couched in careful language but he understood what was being said. It confirmed his own thoughts, those same suspicions which been growing inside his own head. He looked up.

'You had this from the lady's own hand?'

'Via another trusted hand. I am to take any reply directly to her.' He lifted his chin, indicating the contents of his cart. 'Later on today, when I deliver these carrots and neeps.'

'Then give her this message. *I shall do what I can as soon I can.'*

Watching as the man climbed up onto the cart and gave his horse the command to walk on, Arthur Menzies crushed the letter into his fist. He would throw it on the fire as soon as he went back into the house.

As soon as I can. He needed to make some preparations first, work out how best to get at the truth, establish once and for all which side Robert Catto was on. He'd have to get the arrogant bastard alone, none of the ruffians of the Town Guard standing by ready to do his bidding. The agony of the kicking doled out to him and Cosmo at the Assembly Rooms had passed. The humiliation rankled still. It always would.

Turning the tables on Robert Catto might be a tall order. The man was so sure of himself. Nor did Edmonstone have any doubt the man could handle himself in a fight. Yet surely there had to be some way of putting him at a disadvantage. He must have a weak spot, an Achilles heel.

Charlotte's voice rang around his head, ranting about Robert Catto, ranting about Kirsty Rankeillor, about having seen the two of them together. About how she was sure they had a fancy for each other. Now there was a thought. Maybe the surgeon-apothecary's daughter was Catto's weak spot. If he could get her on her own, she could be his route to finding out the truth about Catto.

A surge of pure malice coursed through Arthur Menzies. He would do what he had to do for the sake of the Cause. If there were some sport to be found in it, so much the better.

Rage against his confinement here at Eastfield though he might, it could be dangerous for him to head for Edinburgh now. Even if he found himself some shabby clothes and avoided the drawing rooms and supper parties of the well-off, his was a well-kent face in the oyster cellars and taverns in the less salubrious parts of the town. He might easily be spotted and his presence reported.

Catto had made it clear he expected him to stay at Eastfield until he told him otherwise. That rankled too. Who did the bastard think he was to command a messenger for The Association? Whoever the hell his father might be.

As soon as I can. Edmonstone frowned, thinking it through. He could not risk leaving Eastfield yet awhile but he could dispatch a messenger of his own, have him scout out the lie of the land, gather what information he could. The brute of an overseer would do his bidding for a few coins.

After an evening which seemed to go on forever, on the alert for any awkward questions even though none had come, Christian was sitting up in bed holding the quilted roll in which she kept her pins. The wee silver luckenbooth was there now too, wrapped in a handkerchief to keep it from being scratched by the pins. It was of exquisite workmanship. Robert Catto had chosen well.

He was also off his head, of course. Clearly, so was she.

Lucy the cat was padding up the bed towards her. With her free hand, Christian tickled the little creature's furry head before putting the luckenbooth away and slipping the quilted roll under her pillow.

She thought about what he had said today about wanting to draw her 'as you look now.' Her hair loose about her shoulders, her breasts half bared. Swinging her legs over the side of the high bed, she stood up and walked across to the desk in the window embrasure where she kept a set of drawing materials. Taking them over to her dressing table, she slid the free-standing oval mirror which stood on it towards herself.

She sat for a moment, listening until she was as sure as she could be that everyone else in the house was fast asleep. Shrugging out of her wrapper, she loosened the neck of her nightgown, pulling it down over her shoulders and breasts, adjusting it as he had done.

Artistically draped. Like a beauty in an Italian painting.

Once she had a self-portrait in front of her she returned to her artist's desk and slid the drawing into a sheaf of other sketches. They included the one she'd made of him when he had fallen asleep in front of the library fire here at Infirmary Street. She took it out and studied it for a moment.

He had looked very peaceful that evening, relaxed and loose-limbed in the firelight, his sarcastic mouth stilled. She had offered to make him a copy of the drawing. She would make him a copy of the one she had just drawn too, a belated birthday present.

A thought flew into her head. How she would love to make a drawing of him entirely naked. Without an artistically draped fall of cloth. She laughed, clapping one hand over her mouth to muffle the sound. Would he let her? She could always tell him what was sauce for the gander should also be sauce for the goose.

She had looked her fill today. Clearly amused, he had lain back and let her do it.

'You seem to be enjoying looking at the male organs of generation on a living body. There are less formal words for them, you know.'

'I do know. And I am. Enjoying looking. Very much. I dinna like this, though.'

She reached her hand out to the trace the scar on his thigh.

'How did you come by it?'

'A musket ball fired by some misbegotten French bastard.'

'At Dettingen? I wondered if you had fought there. How long did it take you to recover from the wound?'

'Let us not talk of tiresome things.'

'I'll just keep looking, then.'

'Good. I am finding it rather … stimulating.'

She giggled. 'So I see— Oh, what are you doing?'

For, so quickly she had no time to react, he had turned over and whirled her over too, pinning her beneath him.

'Enough looking,' he murmured.

Going back to bed, she blew out her candle, licked her fingers and pinched the wick to make sure it was out. She slid down the bed, pulled the covers up and turned onto her side. Purring gently, Lucy settled herself into the small of her back. Lulled by the rhythm, Christian gave herself over to more memories of the night before.

She slid one hand under the pillow, resting it on the quilted roll which now held the luckenbooth brooch.

Hope. She would hold on to hope for as long as it lasted. As she would stay for as long as she could in their own world, the one where all things were possible.

Chapter 30

The letter was couched in the politest of terms. Lord Provost Coutts requested that Captain Robert Catto kindly call on him at 11 o'clock this morning. He would be in his banking house in the Parliament Close, off the High Street. Above the flourish of his signature, he assured Catto that he remained his most humble and obedient servant.

Catto snorted as he laid the letter on his desk at the guard-house. It was the other way round. As the Captain of the Town Guard, he was Coutts' servant. In theory. In reality he answered to Lord President Forbes. They were well into January now but that gentleman was still at his estate near Inverness: and Coutts *was* the Lord Provost.

There was no request here. This was a summons. Catto knew, because he had made it his business to know, that the Provost had come back to Edinburgh the previous afternoon. He and his wife had been on a visit to relatives out in the country, extended because the heavy snow on and around Daft Friday had rendered many country roads impassable.

Catto had learned from Duncan Forbes that Coutts had a reputation as a convivial man, a lover of good food and good company, all washed down with copious amounts of claret, port and brandy. Unable to return to Edinburgh in time for the Infirmary's Daft Friday ball, the banker had extended his stay away from the capital even further, enjoying those pleasures to the full.

Duncan Forbes suspected Lord Provost Coutts of having Jacobite sympathies. What Catto suspected was that Coutts had found a letter waiting for him from Charlotte Liddell. That would be what this summons was about. Going on the basis of the letter the vicious little bitch had sent to Charles Paterson, he had no doubt she would be accusing him of harbouring fugitives from the law.

Harbouring was the word she had used in her letter to Paterson, alleging that in so doing Catto had broken the law and was therefore not a fit and proper person to captain the Town Guard of Edinburgh. That he had broken the law was undeniable: and Kirsty Rankeillor was right. He had compounded the offence by bringing Joshua back to Infirmary Street with him. He'd have to think on his feet to get out of this one.

The Provost's banking house and his home on the floor above were only minutes away from the guard-house. Catto walked the few yards up the High Street and turned left into the Parliament Close. Hemmed in by the dingy building housing the luckenbooths, the narrow passageway ran back from the High Street under the lee of the High Kirk of St Giles. This morning its soaring tower and crown spire looked like a painting, a cloudless blue sky the backdrop to the grey stonework of the cathedral. It was a bright, crisp, sunny day.

As Catto plunged down the steep steps of the close, he left the fine day behind him. The tenement land on his right in which Coutts lived and carried on his business was one of the loftiest in Edinburgh. Fifteen storeys high. The banking house was at the foot of the close, where one side of the building faced onto the Cowgate, the other onto the close. Its top floors might reach up to the sky but its feet were planted in dirt and glaur. A metaphor for Edinburgh. For life itself, in these dangerous times.

As he neared the bottom of the steps, he stumbled. Steadying himself by slapping his palm on the wall of the building, he turned to see what had tripped him up. Three of the steps were crumbling away at their edges. A reminder from the gods he had to tread carefully here? Then again, he had to tread carefully everywhere in Edinburgh.

Heads down, two clerks were working in the room into which Catto walked from the close. He'd tried the big solid door and found it unlocked. One head came up, its owner rising to his feet and coming forward.

'Can I help you, sir? Captain?' he offered as Catto flipped one corner of his grey military cloak over his shoulder, exposing his dark red Town Guard uniform.

'I believe Mr Coutts is expecting me.'

'I am indeed,' came a voice from behind the clerk. 'Come away in, man.' He ushered Catto into a room beyond the clerks' room, invited him to remove his cloak, asked him to sit down and offered him coffee.

'Or perhaps you'd prefer a glass of claret? Although it's a wee touch early for wine.' There was a smile on his face and the twang of the North East in his voice. Thanks again to the Lord President, Catto knew Coutts originally came from Montrose, on Scotland's east coast.

'Coffee, sir, if you please.'

The Provost went to his handsome fireplace, lifted a tall silver coffee pot from a matching stand on its blue and white Dutch tiles and brought it back to his desk. Two porcelain cups already sat there. 'Coffee's not long made. I suspected you would be a punctual kind of chiel.'

The Lord Provost of Edinburgh was serving him coffee. Giving him a cordial welcome. Not what he had expected.

'Indeed, sir,' he said, taking his cup with a murmur of thanks. 'Punctuality tends to go hand-in-hand with my profession as a soldier.'

'As an engineer in Guise's, I believe.' Coutts flicked up the skirts of his elegant dark green frockcoat and sat down in a substantial carved wooden chair which looked not unlike a throne. The king in his counting-house. He wore a fair wig which brushed his shoulders. The room was all gleaming wooden furniture and richly-coloured rugs and upholstery.'

'You'll be anxious to get back to your regiment sooner rather than later, I'm thinking.'

Catto took a sip of coffee, delaying his answer. *Tread carefully.* As at Charles Paterson's house, the coffee was rich, strong and aromatic. He looked across the desk at Coutts. 'In some ways, yes. In other ways no. I like to be where I can be useful.'

To the Cause. Were they the words he was hoping Coutts might be tagging on to what he had said? He himself might be fearing – especially when it came to Arthur Menzies of Edmonstone – that the pretence must surely be wearing thin by now. This cordial welcome would seem to indicate otherwise as far as the Provost was concerned.

'No wife or sweetheart waiting for you on the continent?'

Catto shook his head. 'Sadly no, sir.' Which wasn't sad at all. His sweetheart was here in Edinburgh. *Sweetheart.* It was a word he often used to address girls. Now it had taken on a much deeper meaning.

It was almost three weeks since they had lain together. He knew – because she had told him – that she wanted to lie with him again. *So much, Robert. So very much.* She was scared they might be found out, worried the excuse of staying overnight with Anna Gordon again was too risky. They were back to snatched kisses and hasty caresses. It wasn't enough. It absolutely bloody wasn't enough.

Coutts laid his coffee cup down and picked up the letter lying open at his elbow. 'I have a letter here from Miss Charlotte Liddell. In which she alleges you are harbouring two fugitives, viz two perpetual servants from Eastfield. Is she right?'

So much for the cordial welcome. Catto judged the man to be about the same age as Patrick Rankeillor, in his mid-forties. He had the face of someone who laughed a lot and the nose of a man who liked his claret, port and brandy but there was shrewdness too in those intelligent eyes.

'I'm harbouring no one, sir.' Which was true. Strictly speaking.

'Come, come young Captain Catto. I believe you may be giving shelter to one of the servants Miss Charlotte mentions. A boy called George Smart? She thinks you may have employed him at the guard-house.'

'We did have a cook boy called George. But he ran away over Yuletide.'

First lie. He would have to keep track of them so he didn't contradict himself.

'Miss Charlotte also mentions an African boy.'

'Ah,' Catto said, slapping his knee and thinking fast. 'That would explain the report I got from Leith three days since.'

'A report?'

'That two boys had been seen at The Shore and one was black. I'm told that's not so unusual in itself, Leith being a busy port, with ships coming and going from many different countries. Including some carrying cargoes in which you have an interest, sir.'

'You're well informed, young sir.'

'As Captain of the Town Guard it is my duty to be.'

'Indeed. So I'm sure you can tell me about a rumour I've heard since I came back to town about a disturbance at Surgeons' Hall before Christmas and also at the house of my friend Professor Patrick Rankeillor in Infirmary Street.'

'A disturbance to those who seek to cause a much greater one,' Catto said. 'From my perspective, a planned raid in pursuit of a Jacobite plotter.'

'Indeed? Do you have a name for this plotter?'

'Only a *nom-de-guerre,* sir.' This lie didn't even feel like one. 'Mr Fox.'

'Did you and your pack of Town Guard hounds catch Mr Fox?'

'Regrettably no. He managed to make his escape.'

'Most regrettable indeed. Were you acting on information received when you led the raid?'

'I was informed Professor Rankeillor is well known to have Jacobite sympathies.'

'This information coming from our esteemed Lord President, I fancy. I take it he authorized the raid?'

'As you say, sir. You yourself being out of town.'

Coutts made an indecipherable noise deep in his throat and changed tack.

'You think the danger is real and not exaggerated?'

Reaching the top of the stone steps, Catto came out onto the High Street, glad to be back out of the shadows into the sunshine of the day. His conversation with Coutts had been a tortuous conversation, full of implications, allusions and unanswered questions. On both sides. Coutts had been sounding him out. That much was obvious.

God, he was sick of all this, longed for the pretence to be over. Which it would be as soon as he had his meeting with the Lord President. Not long to go now before he could show his true colours. Pity that him stepping out of the shadows would come with all those people baying for his blood. Pity those people might well now include Provost Coutts. Which would make the chances of him being given permanent command of the Town Guard even less likely.

Oh dear God, did he really want the pretence to be over? He thought of what Kirsty Rankeillor had said, about the two of them being damned if they did and damned if they didn't.

A dismal thought but one he could not dwell on now. He had another urgent task. For the sake of Geordie's wounded back and Alice Smart's fragile peace of mind, he'd delayed the transfer from Infirmary Street to Colinton for as long as he'd dared. For their own safety, he had to move all three orphans of the storm as soon as could be arranged.

Chapter 31

Two days later, the farewells were being said in the kitchen at Infirmary Street, safely away from the front of the house. Christian hugged Joshua.

'Miss Kirsty!' he protested, although he bore the embrace manfully.

'I'd like to hug you too, Geordie,' she said, turning to the other boy, 'but for the sake of your back I think I'd better not. I'll do this instead.'

Before he too could protest, she planted a quick kiss on his smooth young cheek. She stepped back, touched when she saw the look on his face. Embarrassed but pleased.

'I'm going to miss you two.'

'Likewise, Miss Kirsty,' Geordie said, giving her a glimpse of his old smile. He wasn't quite back to his old self but he was getting there, a wee bit more with each passing day. As his next comment proved. 'Hopefully it's no' for too long, though. What's those German words the Captain taught us - *auf wiedersehen?*'

She nodded. 'Until we meet again.'

He and Joshua were heading off to Colinton as soon as the brewer's dray in which they were travelling pulled up outside the house. Mary and Tibby were in the front lobby, keeping watch through the long narrow windows which flanked the front door. Nervous, but relishing the importance of their task.

Here in the kitchen, Alice Smart was holding two pillows for Geordie to put behind his back as he and Joshua sat in a carefully arranged gap between big wooden beer barrels. Covered with a piece of sailcloth tightly anchored at the edges of the dray, it made an effective tent. Donald John Livingstone had organized that.

Archie Liddell, dressed in working men's clothes, was the driver who would take the concealed human cargo out to his mother's house at Colinton, a few miles west of Edinburgh. With a bit of luck, it would look like he was delivering ale to some of the taverns along the way. Fortunately, the weather had turned much milder, so the going should be smooth under the wheels of the dray.

Betty was standing by the kitchen table, her fingers curled around the handle of the basket of provisions she had packed for the boys' journey. There were two larger baskets of food waiting in the lobby to be loaded onto the dray, giving Archie's mother a head start on feeding her soon to be expanded household. Robert Catto had paid for those and also given Archie a purse of money to cover any additional household expenses.

This basket was for the journey only. Patrick was peering down into it, examining its contents. 'Sure you've given them enough?' he teased, replacing the red and white cloth covering the food. 'They're no' going very far.'

'They're boys,' Betty said darkly. 'Boys have hollow legs.'

Patrick laughed and laid a light hand in turn on each lad's shoulders. He was interrupted in wishing them a good journey by Mary, breathless with excitement, running through from the front lobby with the news their transport had arrived.

'I'll take the pillows, Alice,' Joshua said, lifting them out of the girl's arms. 'We'll see you soon,' he added gently. The plan was for Alice to follow on to the West Port and then to Colinton a little later in the day. Betty would go with her and Tibby as though they were all on a visit out to the country. Who would notice one of the maids was a different girl to the two normally seen with the housekeeper?

'I can carry the basket,' Geordie said, only to be met by a chorus of objections.

'Not yet, lad,' Patrick said.

'No, indeed,' Christian said. 'Joshua, can you manage the basket too? I'll carry it as far as the front door. Then it's as quickly and as quietly as you can down the front steps. Mr Archie will help you in and make sure you're covered up again and hopefully no one will notice anything.'

Ready to go, Joshua took one last look around the kitchen and the people in it. 'Thank you,' he said. 'Thank you, everyone. For everything.' The expression on his face was warmest when he looked at Mary.

Mary blushed.

Christian was working with Mary to prepare the midday meal. 'Only three of us. The house is gey quiet with them all away, eh?'

'That it is, Miss Kirsty. I'm no' looking forward to being alone in me and Tibby's room tonight.'

'Do you want to sleep in my room? We could bring the hurly bed through.'

'Och no, I couldna sleep in your room, Miss!'

'Of course you could.'

Mary bit her lip. 'Would it really be all right? I sometimes get a wee bit nervous at night. When it's so dark. So does Tibby. I have tae pretend I'm no' scared so she willna get too scared.'

'Of course it's all right.' Christian stepped aside, allowing Mary to set three places at the kitchen table.

'You like Joshua, I think.'

Mary snorted. 'He's spent too long in a big hoose. He's all airs and graces.'

Behind the girl's back, Christian smiled.

Chapter 32

The Lord President was listening intently. Sitting on the other side of a handsome desk at his comfortable lodgings in Musselburgh, Catto was telling him what had happened during the raid on Surgeons' Hall and the Rankeillor house. Now he had moved on to an account of Daft Friday. Both events seemed now to have happened a long time ago. The Lord President had at last returned to Edinburgh. Catto had received a message from him this morning, requesting his urgent attendance. So much for having some breathing space.

He offered a sympathetic comment when he heard how Catto had faced down a hostile mob outside the guard-house. He shook his bewigged head when he heard how this distraction had helped the prisoners in his custody there make their escape.

Duncan Forbes habitually wore an old-fashioned full bottomed wig, its flaps of grey curls resting on his shoulders. As a boy, observing the long face framed by the long wig, Catto had always thought the esteemed Lord President looked not unlike a friendly and well-disposed horse. Although he could be ruthless too. A lesson Catto had learned through bitter experience.

The older man tapped the green leather cylinder lying between them on the desk. 'You found this when you mounted the raid on Surgeons' Hall, Bob?'

'Indeed, sir. In this map case presumably designed to keep it in perfect condition so it could be taken to an engraver to make as many copies as required. Will you look at it now?'

Another nod of the head had him sliding the map out of its case. He pushed it along his host's desk so he could unroll and spread it out. Unlike Patrick Rankeillor's work-table, this desk was tidy. Aside from the map and its case, the only thing on it was an impressive highly-polished wooden inkstand. As the Lord President pushed it out of the way, the faceted glass and silver lids of its equally impressive inkwells sparkled in the low January sun streaming in through the window behind the desk. A temporary rainbow.

Catto glanced round the room. Following his gaze, his host gestured towards the tall pewter candlesticks on the mantelpiece. 'Aye. Fetch those, lad.'

Weighing down the corners of the parchment with the candlesticks, Catto went round the desk to stand beside his host. Plagued by gout, unable to stand for long without pain, Culloden sat leaning over the table peering down at the map. Catto pointed out various features: Scotland's main cities, towns, ports and roads, all neatly named and laid out.

He indicated the legend written over the German Ocean. It was a list of military garrisons in Scotland, with a note of how many soldiers occupied each. All were woefully under strength. Britain's monarchy, politicians and army commanders had long since ceased to believe the exiled King James and his elder son Charles posed any real danger to the House of Hanover and the Protestant Succession.

He commented on that, eliciting a heartfelt sigh from Duncan Forbes. 'Aye. This map and the intelligence you have gathered gives the lie to such a dangerously relaxed view of the situation. To cap it all, the rumour you spoke of when you dined with me on your first evening back in Scotland in November is no longer a rumour.'

Catto's head snapped up. 'There's evidence the French are assembling a war fleet at Dunkirk?'

'I understand ships have begun to gather at their naval base at Brest. From there it's an easy sail along the Channel. I also understand the Young Pretender has left Rome. Although he and whoever is with him are doing their best to throw us off the scent, he is even now secretly making his way across Europe.'

'Dear God,' Catto breathed. 'So now we know for sure the threat is real. It's actually happening.'

For a moment, as the two men looked at each other, there was complete silence in the room. Even the sounds from the outside world, the hum of a conversation being held out into the street, a woman laughing, a dog barking, seemed to fade into the distance.

Culloden laid a hand on Catto's arm. 'We'll not allow fear to swamp us, Bob. Nor panic either. We'll stay calm and deal with what we have to deal with.'

Catto took a deep breath. 'Assuredly, sir. Is there intelligence as to how they aim to proceed from Dunkirk?'

'Nothing firm but there are two possibilities. As you previously suggested, what they are planning may be more in the nature of a *coup d'état* than an invasion. Enough French troops on those ships to sail quietly up the Thames under cover of darkness and seize control of London before its citizens have woken up the next morning.'

Catto nodded. 'Relying on the London Jacobites and others around the country – in Scotland, the English North Country, Oxford and Wales, among other places – to rise in response. The other possibility?'

'A landing in Essex and a march towards London, with a battle for control of the city shortly before they reach it. In either case, with their hope – perhaps their already elaborated plan – being for Jacobites in those other places and more to rise and seize control of their own areas. The rumour is that the Marshall de Saxe will lead the French troops who will set the match to the fuse. He is a formidable commander.'

'So I have heard, sir. Even his enemies speak highly of him.' He grimaced. 'In a manner of speaking. He strikes fear into many breasts, of friend and foe alike. If the French fleet is getting ready, it looks like whichever plan of attack they propose is scheduled to happen sooner rather than later. Though the weather cannot be relied upon at this time of year.'

'Which we shall have to hope might work in our favour.'

'Indeed. Although an imminent attack would also seem to be indicated by the presence of John Roy Stuart in Scotland,' Catto said in the driest of tones, as always disliking the sound of his own voice saying that name.

The Lord President looked up at him. 'You have my sympathy, Bob. It must have been a shock coming face-to-face with your father like that.'

'I do not think of him as such, sir. But yes, it was something of a shock. Did you know he was in Scotland?' He hoped he was keeping any note of accusation out of his voice. Even if honesty compelled him to admit Duncan Forbes had warned him John Roy Stuart might fetch up here. He had wanted Catto for this mission precisely because of his connections, those passionately unwanted links to the Jacobite Cause.

Culloden held up his hands in a gesture of denial. 'No. Although it does not surprise me that he is here. He has the ear of the Old Pretender and is, I believe, even closer to the Young Gentleman.'

'Yes,' Catto said, fancying he could taste bitterness on his tongue.

'What did you get out of Patrick Rankeillor?'

'An agreement of what I stated to be my idea of their plans.'

'Which you arrived at how, exactly?'

Because Kirsty Rankeillor's so expressive face told me I had it right. Doing his utmost to keep her out of this, he wasn't going to tell the Lord President that.

'There are only so many possibilities, sir. It also seems to me the French will be willing to help but only in a limited way. They are much more invested in the fighting currently raging in Flanders and elsewhere.'

'Indeed.' Culloden tapped one finger against his lips. 'After I got your letter and verbal message, I sent a dispatch by a Royal Navy vessel from Inverness to London, advising them to be on the alert. The information you have gathered also allowed me to reinforce the message that we need to be on our guard here in Scotland. I have people looking out for John Roy in the north.'

'Have there been any sightings or reports of him?'

'Nothing more than the odd rumour and a few scoundrels trying to claim a reward for some scrap of useless and possibly made-up piece of information. I lingered there for as long as I did in the hope of hearing some reliable intelligence of his whereabouts. But he's a wily one. As I know I do not need to tell you."

'I regret very much I let him slip through my fingers here in Edinburgh, sir. I trust you know how very much I regret it!'

'Aye, Bob, I do.' Culloden laid his hand briefly on Catto's arm. 'Be assured of that. I ken fine you would have held on to him if you could. In one way that makes me gey sad. My own Jock and I have had our quarrels but he is a great joy to me. I to him in return, I believe.' The long face lit up. 'Sometimes he even tells me so.'

A loving, if sometimes strict, father figure to his extended family, Duncan Forbes himself was a widower, devoted to his only child.

'There's no need for you to feel any sorrow on my account, sir.'

'No need, Bob?' Culloden's eyes searched his young visitor's face.

'None whatsoever,' Catto said firmly. 'You think the French will not move without the presence of Charles Stuart?'

'They need that legitimacy. To show they are not a foreign power invading another sovereign nation but allies helping restore the rightful king of that nation. As they see it.' Culloden gave another of his wintry smiles. 'I suspect James has already supplied his elder son with letters patent, making Charles his regent.'

'Aye. That would seem to be logical. France's foreign policy has long favoured the ousting of a Protestant king from the British throne in favour of a Catholic Stuart. It is also in France's interest to weaken the British army in Europe by forcing the transfer of troops from the continent to deal with rebellion at home.'

'Which is why we must do our damnedest to prevent such a rebellion from coming to pass.'

'Amen to that, sir,' came the sombre response.

The older man bent his head again to the map. 'A fine piece of work. Who was the cartographer, Rankeillor's daughter?'

Catto groaned inwardly. He could hardly deny such a direct question, especially when Kirsty Rankeillor had told him the Lord President knew she was a talented artist, had seen other maps she had drawn. 'Yes. Miss Rankeillor drew it.'

'The young lady admitted as much?'

'Aye. She did.' *Rankeillor's daughter. Miss Rankeillor. The young lady.* Now Kirsty. The girl who had melted his frozen heart. The girl he sought to protect with every bone in his body and every drop of his blood. Fear seized him, clutching at his heart with the sinister fingers of a skeleton in a macabre print of death and its horrors.

Oh Kirsty, how I wish you had not involved yourself in any of this folly. And, oh dear God, it's really happening. What I did not believe would ever come to pass. What I did not want to believe would ever come to pass. Armed and bloody rebellion sweeping towards Scotland.

'Is she an active participant in the plot, d'ye think? She and Patrick have aye been close.'

'I do not believe so. Her father has sought to shield her from any plotting. If you will look more closely, I think you will agree the information on garrisons was added by a different hand. I suspect that of James Buchan of Balnamoon, the professor's erstwhile apprentice.'

Hunching his shoulders, Culloden leant further forward, and winced. He muttered a curse. 'Appreciate your young joints while you have them, Bob. I see what you mean about the different hand. Now, help me over to the fireside and we'll continue our conversation over a glass of claret. If you will fetch the decanter and the glasses from the sideboard after you have seen me into my armchair.'

'Allow me first to put the map away, sir.' Bloody hell, he had just lied to the Lord President. Previously he had thought that would be like lying to God. Yet he had done so without a blush or a stuttered word. Then again, he had already lied by omission. He had made no mention of Kirsty Rankeillor having been in the supper room at the Assembly Rooms or at the guard-house when Jamie Buchan and John Roy Stuart had escaped.

She had been at the heart of the plot. Firstly to discreetly transport Mr Fox up to the Assembly Rooms, there to meet Cosmo Liddell, whose wealth might potentially help fund an armed rebellion of the Scottish Jacobites. Secondly, to smuggle the man out of Edinburgh and down to Leith to take ship for the Highlands. Catto's mouth tightened. Where even now he would likely be exercising his silver tongue to persuade fools and dreamers to risk life, limb and family for the sake of the sodding House of Stuart.

So be it. He had kept her out of it. He hoped. He allowed the Lord President to take his arm as they moved to the fireside. It was only the middle of the afternoon, a bit early to be starting on the claret, especially with a long evening stretching out before them. As he had expected, Culloden had insisted he stay overnight.

He felt a twinge of unease, hoping everything had gone as planned in the transfer of Geordie, Alice and Joshua to Colinton. Archie Liddell's mother would have a full house tonight. Whereas it would only be the two Rankeillors and one of the little maidservants at Infirmary Street.

He wished he could take his leave of the Lord President now. He'd come out to Musselburgh on Tam, one of the horses for hire from the stables at *The White Horse*, leaving the garron at a nearby change house to be fed, watered and given a stall for the night. If only he could collect the beast before today was very much older. He could ride the few miles back to Edinburgh, throw Tam's reins to Donald Livingstone's son Michael, scramble over a few walls and knock on the back door at Infirmary Street. Stay there for a while. Reassure her.

How the Devil he was going to do that he did not know. Not now he knew there really was a rebellion in the offing. Like pent-up marsh gas, the genie was about to shoot up out of the bottle, cackling madly as it cast its foul stink over everything, turning blue skies grey, staining green grass red with blood.

He did not doubt they could fight it off. He could not allow himself to think otherwise. Oh God, but neither did he believe there could be a peaceful coup d'état and a bloodless transition back to a Stuart monarchy. The very idea was ludicrous. As he had told Kirsty Rankeillor, those who hold the reins of power do not easily surrender them. Couple that with the passion and the desperation of their Jacobite opponents and who knew what the damage to the civilian population might be? Or who might get caught in the crossfire?

Even if he could head back to Edinburgh now – which he could not – there were other compelling reasons why he had to stay here. Despite the profoundly unsettling news he'd just heard, another crucial subject had yet to be raised. Not tomorrow but this evening. Before much more claret had been drunk.

The house was very quiet. Her father was through in the library, looking over his lecture notes for the next term. Quashing any unspoken fears he might not be in the position to deliver those lectures, Christian was sitting now at the kitchen table with Mary, helping her form her letters, hoping the distraction would stop them both from worrying. She'd brought the wee lantern through from the lobby to give them as much light as possible on the sheets of paper.

'Very good, Mary,' she said, as the girl finished copying her own name below where Christian had written it out. 'Tibby's name next?'

Mary nodded. 'Aye. She'll be jealous when she comes hame and finds oot I've had another lesson— Oh! What was that?'

Christian had heard it too, a noise coming from the direction of the lobby at the back door. 'I'll go and see.'

Mary was already on her feet, lifting the wee lantern as she spoke. 'I'll come wi' ye, Miss Kirsty.'

The relief when they found Lucy the cat sitting on the floor of the back lobby looking up at them was palpable. 'Oh,' Christian said, 'those big eyes are too innocent! She must have been up to something.'

Mary looked around. 'Here it is. Yon wee brass bowl that sits on the windowsill. She's knocked it onto the floor, I'm thinking.' Bending over, she picked the bowl up and turned it in her hand. 'It's no' bashed.'

'Och well then, no harm done.' Stooping, Christian picked up the cat. 'On you go, Mary.' Pausing for a moment, she stood looking through the window to the shadows and darkness beyond.

She couldn't quite suppress a shiver, then chided herself. What was she so scared of? Apart from the obvious, she thought wryly. But did she really fear Charlotte Liddell would burst into the house and start shrieking about her *property*? The horrible Charlotte was so high and mighty – not to mention so stupid – she wouldn't even know where to find the back door of a house.

Outside, one shadow seemed to detach itself from the others, moving stealthily away from the building towards the outhouses.

Chapter 33

The Lord President sighed as he took the glass of wine he had asked Catto to pour out for each of them. 'I'm gey sorry to hear Patrick Rankeillor is actively involved. I'd hoped he might have had more sense.' He waved his free hand towards the chair on the other side of the fireplace. 'Sit yourself down, Bob.'

Catto put his own wineglass on the little table at his right hand. Maybe he could delay raising it to his lips for a while, resist the encouragement he knew he was going to get to drink up. Or maybe not. Like Provost Coutts, Duncan Forbes liked his claret, port and brandy. He also liked his guests to match him, glass-for-glass. The chances of Catto not waking up tomorrow morning with a thumping headache and a dry mouth were slim.

'When it comes to men with a cause, I'm afraid sense flies out of the window, sir.'

Duncan Forbes shot him a sharp glance from under his heavy brows. 'Never had a cause of your own, lad?'

Only my own survival and advancement. Until now.

Leaving the Lord President's question unanswered, he posed one in return. 'How do you propose to proceed as regards Professor Rankeillor, sir? I've told him I expect you will want to see him. Although me being seen to escort him here might not be wise.'

'You think he is being watched by his own side?'

Catto shrugged. 'Everyone is watching everyone else. But if he does not resume his duties at the Royal Infirmary and the College soon, suspicion is swiftly going to fester and grow.'

'Aye,' Culloden said, a look of grim amusement crossing his face. 'So now may be the time to give the watchers something to watch. Fire a warning shot across several bows. Let them know we know they're planning something. While not giving them the solace of learning about the French warships assembling at Brest. Do you have more names for me, Bob?'

'Six, sir. I think two of them may not surprise you. I believe another one of the six is very much a minor player.'

Torn between sending a silent apology to Kirsty Rankeillor's friend Meg Wood and fury at the potentially lethal folly of her brother and the other Jacobite plotters, he gave the Lord President the names. He started with Andrew Wood of Glasgow and the two men spotted entering his workshop at what sounded like a secret meeting also attended by Patrick Rankeillor. He went on through Agnes Moncur, Charles Paterson and Murdo Robertson.

He told the older man how he had acquired the information about Andrew Wood but did not mention Murdo Robertson's failed attempt to dispatch him. Lying by omission again. Although he really did not believe the young medical student posed any threat to him. Or ever had.

'Agnes Moncur,' Culloden repeated. 'There's a tragic story. Lost her husband and her father at Sheriffmuir. Never got over it. Although she's made something of her life all the same.'

'That's nigh on thirty years ago,' Catto said, surprised. 'She could not have been long married.'

'She wasn't. That was the tragedy of it. John Coutts and his family helped her and her mother, I believe.'

'I spoke with him two days since.'

'Did you indeed?' Culloden asked with sharp interest. 'How did that come about?'

'He asked me to call on him. He'd had a letter of complaint about me. Sent by Miss Charlotte Liddell.'

'An unpleasant young woman. What is the nature of her complaint against you?'

'I'm afraid she's much more than unpleasant, sir. As is her brother Cosmo and his friends Arthur Menzies of Edmonstone and Hector Grant of Soutra. You asked me to tread a fine line, to treat the Liddells and their friends with kid gloves. As a direct result of their actions, I have not done so. As a direct result of my actions, Miss Liddell is accusing me of not being a fit and proper person to captain the Town Guard.'

'Go on,' Culloden urged.

Catto told him what Cosmo, Edmonstone and Grant had done to Alice Smart and what Charlotte Liddell had ordered done to Geordie and Joshua. He told him how he had gone looking for the boys, found them no distance away from where they sat here now in Musselburgh. He told him about the confessions he'd made Cosmo Liddell and Arthur Menzies sign. Finally, he told Culloden about the documents he'd had Charles Paterson draw up.

He turned his head, indicating the satchel he'd propped against the big desk. 'I've brought the relevant paperwork with me, sir. I'll fetch it now.'

'Hold your horses, Bob. What transpired when Coutts questioned you about this?'

'I told him both boys had run away. Said nothing about knowing Alice Smart.'

'None of which is true?'

'No. I lied to him.'

'Do you think he knew that?'

'I think he might have done.'

'But did not press the point?'

'No. We had a somewhat strange conversation. I felt as though I were in the labyrinth of which you spoke back in November, a place of smoke and mirrors. Where much was left unsaid, with many pauses and unfinished sentences. Although all conducted with great courtesy, especially on his part. Which did not seem to fit in with him having receiving the letter of complaint about me from Miss Liddell.'

'It may mean he does believe you to be a covert Jacobite and does not seek to get in your way. May also be aware of who your father is and supposes you to share the same sympathies.'

'The former, yes. The latter maybe,' Catto said reluctantly. 'I suppose Mr Menzies of Edmonstone might also have written to Mr Coutts. Since he now knows the nature of my relationship to John Roy Stuart.'

As he forced himself to say that name again, the usual litany ran through his head. *Not my father. Never my father.* The day could not come soon enough when he no longer had to give the man so much as a passing thought.

'Coutts did not show you the letter from Miss Liddell?' Then, when Catto shook his head: 'If Cosmo Liddell and Arthur Menzies now know about your parentage, might they not have told her and she included this information in her letter to Coutts?'

'I do not think so.' Catto thought back to his conversation with Edmonstone on the night of the Daft Friday ball. 'Edmonstone does not trust or value her at all. Is rather contemptuous of her, in fact. Although I would not be surprised to learn they are lovers.'

A cynical look passed over Culloden features. 'Trusting or valuing someone is not necessarily a prerequisite for an *affaire de coeur*. Many are most definitely not of the heart.' He changed tack. 'The three young people you have … *rescued*. Where are they now?'

'In as safe a place as I could find. I would not put it past Miss Liddell to send some of her people after them if she could find out where they are.'

'I shall not tell her,' came the dry response.

'Of course not, sir.' Yet he knew he was reluctant to share this information, even with the Lord President. 'They are at the home of Mrs Liddell in Colinton. Archie Liddell's mother. A quite different branch of the Liddell family.'

'I know them well. Must have been quite a task for Jenny Liddell to look after this young lad who'd been flogged.'

Once again Catto spoke with reluctance. 'When I found the boys at the bridge here in Musselburgh I took them first to Infirmary Street. Where Miss Rankeillor cared for Geordie. She has considerable medical skills, as I think you may know.'

'Where was the young lass at this point?'

'Also at Infirmary Street. Where I had arranged for her to be taken some time previously.'

Culloden eased himself back into his chair, rested his hands on its wooden arms and looked at Catto. 'This is quite a tangle, Bob. I take it you first came to know Miss Rankeillor when you raided her home in Infirmary Street. I would not have thought that an auspicious beginning or a sound basis for a … *friendship* … between the two of you.'

'No,' Catto said after a brief pause. 'But Miss Rankeillor

happened to be at the guard-house when I discovered young Geordie had been hiding his sister there. She offered to take the girl under her wing. I could hardly have kept a young girl at the guard-house once I knew she was there.'

'Miss Rankeillor *happened* to be at the guard-house?'

Fuck, this *was* like lying to God. Catto's wits seemed to have deserted him. Why had he not rehearsed this part of the story? All he could think of was falling back on an abridged version of the truth.

'She was doing some investigating of her own. Trying to establish whether I was friend or foe.'

'Although you do not believe she was involved in the plot.'

Damn, damn, damn.

'She was concerned for her father. After the raid on her house, she was well aware something was afoot. They are very close. As you yourself have just told me.'

'Aye. So I did. She's a bonnie lass, don't you think, Bob?'

'She looks well enough,' Catto managed. Bugger, he was losing his grip on this conversation.

'Talented too. With a lively mind. The sort of girl for whom a man might well develop a tendresse.'

Much more than a tendresse... Much, much more. He was struggling to force himself to deny his feelings and hers, struggling to come up with some sort of a convincing response, when Culloden spoke again.

'Why did you lie to Provost Coutts?'

And why are you lying to me? Or trying not to tell me the whole truth? Were those questions also wordlessly being put to him?

'Because I thought it might be useful for you to have something with which to strike bargains with Cosmo Liddell and Arthur Menzies. I had them write and sign confessions about their violation of Alice Smart. They enjoyed reliving it,' he added, his voice very dry, 'but they would not want wider society to know what they did to an innocent young girl.'

Culloden tapped his fingers against his lips. 'So their confessions allow us to stop dead any plotting or funding on Cosmo's part of this most foolish venture. Also ensuring his silence about your own connections.'

'I also thought these confessions could be used to persuade Cosmo and his sister to sign the relevant documents.'

'The relevant documents?'

'The ones which I have brought with me. All properly legal, drawn up by Mr Charles Paterson, with the assistance of Archie Liddell. Manumission for Joshua, so he may live his life as a free man. Freedom from perpetual servitude for Geordie and Alice Smart so they too may live freely.'

Culloden held up an admonishing hand. 'A commendable aim on your part. But you're getting ahead of yourself here. Cosmo and Miss Charlotte have to be handled carefully.'

'Even when it comes to treason?' Catto replied, trying – and failing – to keep his voice from rising in disbelief.

'Even then. There are those amongst us whom we cannot afford to antagonize. Aye, and I see very plainly you dinna like that answer, Bob.'

'Surely to God they must suffer some sanction?' he demanded, in a tone of voice he knew very well he should not be using to the Lord President of the Court of Session of Scotland.

'Oh,' Duncan Forbes said, his own voice as smooth as silk. 'I'll make damn sure they do. But there's that balance to be struck, that fine line to be trod. There are powerful factions in Scotland – and they are not only the aristocracy and the gentry. The people who create wealth also wield considerable influence.'

Catto kept silent, apprehensive as to where this conversation was going next.

'Commerce,' his host went on. 'Trade. Coal. The mine owners across the Lowlands, down in Ayrshire and up in Fife form a powerful group. Have a good conceit of themselves too. Like the ironmasters. All of these might well see the freeing of one slave and two perpetual servants as setting a dangerous precedent.'

One slave and two perpetual servants. Joshua, Geordie and Alice were so much more than that.

'You are saying they might take enough umbrage to throw their weight against the political status quo in favour of a dangerous alternative?' He had to struggle to keep the scepticism out of his voice.

'I'm saying it cannot be ruled out. Politics is volatile. As are people.'

'Sir, they cannot be sent back to Eastfield. After what they have all suffered at the hands of Cosmo and Charlotte Liddell and their friends, it would be inhuman!'

Horrified by the very prospect, he looked at the Lord President. There was compassion in his craggy face but other emotions too. Conviction. Determination. Ruthlessness.

Catto listened to Culloden's next words in growing disbelief and dismay.

Chapter 34

'That was lucky,' she began, 'I'd only just come through from the shop to start heating up the broth for midday. Wouldn't have heard you knocking otherwise.' She swung the back door more widely open. 'Och, what's wrong?'

He knew he must look pale and tired. Bone weary. He didn't immediately reply, only threw his arms about her and held her tight. Until he let her go, kicking the door shut with his foot. 'Sorry, I've let the cold in. Come through to the kitchen and I'll tell you. If there's nobody else there?'

'Nobody. Mary's upstairs finishing off the sweeping and dusting, my father's busy in the library and Betty and Tibby aren't due back from Colinton until later on this afternoon. Can I get you something?'

'Some physic to take away my headache would be good,' he said as he followed her through.

When they reached the kitchen he told her what the Lord President had told him. Her eyes widened with every word.

'It's all about striking a bargain, then?' she asked a few moments later. 'However grubby the bargain might be? With Geordie, Joshua and Alice merely bargaining counters. Like pieces on a chessboard.' She shivered. 'Powerless pawns.'

'That's about the sum of it,' Catto said, his mouth set in a grim line. 'The Lord President says he cannot afford to antagonize the coal owners and the ironmasters. Says he needs their support. To secure which, Alice, Geordie and Joshua may have to go back to Eastfield.' His voice dripped with sarcasm. '*Sacrificed to the common good* is how he put it.'

'You told him what was done to them? To all three of them?'

'I told him. He said he was sorry for it. He also said they may bide where they are for the moment.'

He swore comprehensively. *'For the moment?'* he repeated. 'That will only make it worse for them.'

Pulling one of the kitchen chairs out from the table, she dropped into it. 'I've been thinking that too. To have tasted freedom and kindness, only to be wrenched away from it again. Back to brutal treatment and never a kind word. For the rest of their lives if Charlotte and Cosmo and the bloody law has its way.'

She looked up at him, her face anguished. 'It's too cruel. We cannot allow it to happen.'

Anger had propelled Catto from Musselburgh to Edinburgh this morning, urging Tam forward at a brisk canter. He'd wanted to gallop, go hell-for-leather. There had been too many other horses and carts on the road to allow greater speed, frustration fuelling his anger to an even higher pitch.

Here, sitting with her in this kitchen, he felt his anger fade. It was replaced by a feeling of resolve.

'No,' he agreed. 'We cannot.'

'But how are we to stop it?'

'I don't know yet. But I'll think of something.' He pulled a chair out for himself, sat down sideways on it, beside her, and took her hands in his. 'Kirsty, I'm afraid I have some more bad news. The Lord President has commanded me away from Edinburgh.'

She gave a little gasp. In the grip of his, her fingers also reacted to his words. 'Are you coming back?'

He lifted their joined hands, spared one thumb to steady her trembling bottom lip. 'Wild horses wouldn't stop me,' he said gently. 'He is sending me on a journey, that's all. As his envoy. I sail from Leith on tomorrow afternoon's tide and I'll be back within two weeks. He has promised me he will take no decision about Geordie, Alice and Joshua until after I come back.'

'Two weeks,' she repeated. 'So you are going to London.'

He squeezed her hands. 'You did not hear that from me.'

Nor would she hear why Culloden was sending him to London. He couldn't tell her without swearing his bloody head off even more than he already had.

'Tell me,' she said. 'Tell me what I must do while you are away.'

'Do as we agreed and go about your life as you normally would. If you need help with anything, send your housekeeper to *The White Horse.* Or go yourself if you can do so with as few people as possible seeing you.'

She nodded. 'Not at midday or in the evening where there will be lots of people there.'

'Exactly. Sergeant and Mrs Livingstone will be your friends and allies. Archie Liddell will let you know how all is going at Colinton. Probably by letter rather than by calling past.'

'Anything else I can do?'

'I don't think so.' He lifted one of her hands to his lips and kissed her knuckles. 'Given that I don't think there's any point in asking you not to worry.'

'No, there's absolutely no point in you asking me that. But I think there is one more thing I can do.'

'Which is?'

'I can spend tonight with you at the bagnio.'

The eyes which could look as hard as gunmetal softened to grey silk.

Maurice de Saxe surveyed the scene before him with a jaundiced eye. He was beginning to tire of the endless dunes. Here in the port of Dunkirk, they stretched for miles to either side. The sand got everywhere, blowing whichever way the wind took it. The scattered and scrubby clumps of tall grasses waving in the breeze did not hold it fast.

Close in to the dunes, warships of the French navy bobbed at anchor. Others had calmer berths in the basin a few minutes' walk behind him, linked to the sea by a short canal.

This war fleet was awaiting his order to set sail for England. He in his turn was waiting for the command to do so. This was not his plan and his heart wasn't in it. He was a soldier, not some grubby assassin, approaching his prey silently in the dead of night. They were to take the English by surprise, sail over from Dunkirk to Essex, then march on London. All to restore the

Stuart family to the throne.

The young prince was here, waiting to lead the attack. Which was a joke in and of itself. He was a personable young man. After two or three conversations with him, De Saxe had reached the conclusion that he was also passionate, rash and impulsive. He was going to be a hindrance rather than a help on this campaign.

Maurice de Saxe was a battle-hardened veteran. His experience had seen him elevated to the highest military rank: a Marshall of France. When it came to war, he knew what he was about and he knew it shouldn't be this. What was needed right now in the ongoing European power struggle was a march into Flanders to fight the Dutch and the Hanoverians, a bold and decisive move to take the ongoing war to the enemy.

A gust of wind blew along the dunes, whipping the sand up into whirling circles. De Saxe rubbed the grains from his face with an irritated oath. The weather wasn't right for this endeavour either. Nothing was.

Arthur Menzies was struggling to hold on to his temper. Damn the man for his insolence, his leering eyes and the smirk twisting his mouth. This was Charlotte's fault. Allowing the brute to make free of her body had given him too great a sense of his own importance.

He might be overseer of the mine but Edmonstone saw little difference between him and the men, women and children struggling to survive under his brutal rule. They were the lowest of the low, which made him nothing more than a rooster crowing on a dung heap. But he had information Edmonstone needed.

They were in the stables at Eastfield, where he had been waiting for him for what felt like hours. Now the brute was spinning out the story of what he'd seen in Edinburgh the night before and earlier on today. He was embellishing the information with the story of a cat's gleaming eyes, staring at him through a window.

'What else did you see?' Edmonstone snapped. 'Who else was in the house?'

'A man and two lassies. One the mistress, one the maid.'

'No one else?'

'Och, I saw one other person. Someone who came tae the hoose while I was watching it this morning.'

'Who?'

'He didna introduce himself tae me.' The man laughed at his own joke. 'Didna see me either. Good job I'd tucked masel into an oothoose. It was bloody freezing there last night,' he complained. 'I'm thinking I deserve a bittie mair money for that. And,' he wheedled, 'for telling ye whit ye'd like tae ken aboot this other person I saw.'

Exasperated but not seeing he had any choice, Edmonstone took his purse from his pocket and handed over another half crown. 'Well?' he demanded.

'He was a tall chiel. Another shilling?'

'Telling me he was tall isn't worth what I've already given you. There are plenty of tall men in Edinburgh.'

'Plenty of tall men in Edinburgh,' the overseer repeated, as though he was weighing the words and pondering the truth of them. 'Aye. Mebbe so. But they dinna all hae a lassie open a door tae them and fling herself at them. He's getting his leg over there, I'm thinking.' He licked his lips. 'The wee hoor looked like a right tasty handful. I'd like fine tae back her up against a wall.'

Edmonstone stayed in the stables after the man had left, his anger mounting. How the hell had he ended up having to pay for every tiny piece of information he had squeezed out of the bloody bastard? How the hell had he allowed Robert Catto to confine him here at Eastfield? Had he colluded in having the wool pulled over his eyes? Had he been such a fool?

He was a messenger for The Association. It was a hugely important role: and he was an important man. It was time for him to take action.

Chapter 35

'How is your headache?'

'What headache?' Taking the big key out of her hands, he closed and locked the bagnio doors behind her, slid his arms around her waist, spun her round and kissed her. 'You had no problem getting away?'

'I did not even have to produce another letter from Anna. I told my father she had invited me to visit and spend the night again and asked him to tell Betty once she gets back from Colinton.'

'He did not think it odd you had not mentioned the invitation before?'

'He was deep in his papers,' she said, sliding her own arms up and around his neck. 'I could have been telling him the house was on fire and he would barely have paid attention. Fortunately I also told Mary I would be away tonight.'

She gestured towards the brass statue of the eagle in the rounded alcove in the back wall of the entrance lobby. 'As long as the king of the birds doesn't fly off and tell any tales, I think we should be safe.'

'What about the wee witch? Will she suspect anything when you go home tomorrow morning with a twinkle in your eye and a spring in your step?'

'La, Captain, you're gey sure of yourself.' As she swayed in his arms, mockery softened into concern. 'Also very light-hearted compared to how you were a mere few hours ago. Even though our troubles have not gone away.'

'You're here,' he said simply. 'We're here together. In our own world. Our troubles can wait till tomorrow. Kiss me again, beautiful girl.'

'A glass of wine and a bite to eat?' he asked an hour or so later.

'I'm not sure I have the energy to do more than just lie here,' she said, suffused with the lassitude which had followed the passion and release of their lovemaking. She was pleasantly warm too. He had arrived at the bagnio before her, giving him time to set a fire under the boiler which heated the water for the bath tubs and ran through the pipes under the rooms.

'Och,' she protested as he slid his encircling arms away from her body, 'don't go…'

'I'll be back in a moment,' he promised, stooping to kiss her bare shoulder.

He returned with a meal very like the one they'd eaten here before and the high stool from the bagnio's pantry on which he placed a bottle of wine and two glasses. The wine had been here since their previous tryst, unopened. She had been intoxication enough.

They sat as they had before, cross-legged on the divan facing each other. Night had fallen but the two lanterns he'd previously brought through from the pantry bathed them in more than enough soft light.

'Thank you,' she said as he poured the claret and served them both.

'What for?'

She smiled. 'One or two things. Right at this moment, for waiting on me. Feeding me.'

'Had an incentive.' He raised his russet eyebrows at her. 'Making sure you recover lost energy. Although I did not see any sign of it failing you.' He glanced at her wicker basket, stood against the wall of the room. 'Were you able to bring something to eat?' He laughed. 'If there's anything left in the cupboards at Infirmary Street after the supplies the wee witch insisted Geordie and Joshua took with them to Colinton.'

'Only some tablet.'

'From the looks of it, there's more than tablet in your basket.'

'You're quite right. I brought my sketch pad with me. In the hope you will be my subject. For a study of the male nude.'

He was biting into a thick slice of bread topped with a similarly thick slice of ham. Her answer made him splutter.

She spoke in an idiotically sweet voice. 'Should I come round behind you and slap your back, sir?'

He raised his hand to his mouth, swallowed, reached for his glass and took a generous swig of wine. 'Thank you for your concern, madam, but there's no need. I'm quite recovered.'

'I'm glad to hear it. I'm rather enjoying the view from here.'

'I could swear you said something about the male nude. But maybe it's me in my banyan you want to sketch.'

Her eyes ranged over him, admiring the garment and its red and turquoise dragons. 'Gorgeous though your banyan is, what lies beneath it and is not quite covered by it is rather impressive too.'

'So impressive you want to sketch it in all its glory? Oops.' For its glory was growing as they spoke.

'Yes,' she said, dropping and lifting her eyes. 'Do you have any objection to me sketching it – and you, of course?'

'Might I not be artistically draped in said banyan?'

'I'd rather have you completely nude.'

'Before or after we make love again?'

'I think you know the answer to that, sir.'

It was late, nearly midnight. Agnes Moncur had taken a tray of food and a jug of claret to the cells at the back of the Royal Infirmary. Arthur Menzies received it somewhat gracelessly. He seemed belatedly to realize this and set out to charm her. Or tried to.

She didn't like this young man very much. Not at all really. She had to tolerate him turning up at the hospital late in the evening and asking her to take him in for a night or two. She had already thought of a quiet corner where he might bivouac without anyone else knowing he was there. He was an important link in the chain which bound all those who were strong in the Cause. He also had an idea how to establish once and for all whose side Robert Catto was on.

Agnes didn't like his idea very much either: but they needed to know. Even although she was wrestling with her conscience about giving him the piece of information which would enable him to carry out his plan.

Thanks to those trusted friends who could move about Edinburgh without anyone noticing them, she was pretty sure she knew where Kirsty Rankeillor was spending tonight: and where she might be found tomorrow morning.

Chapter 36

She had stayed too long at the bagnio after Robert Catto had left. Sitting there looking at the sketch she had made of him, remembering how he had played the fool as she was doing it. While she jokingly told him off.

'You don't want me to look happy? Because I am, you know.'

'You can look happy. I'd rather you didn't cross your eyes at me, though.'

She had asked him to lie on his side facing her, propped up with one arm thrown over the pillows, the chestnut brown silk of his hair tumbling over one shoulder. She was sitting beside the bed on the high stool, knees drawn up to serve as a platform for her sketch book.

'Maybe I'll cross my legs rather than my eyes. Preserve my modesty.'

She made a rude noise. 'Don't you dare. Hold that pose, if you please.'

'For how long?'

'Until I'm finished.'

'If I'm naked, shouldn't you be naked too?'

'I'm not wearing much,' she said, concentrating on her drawing. 'Only my wrapper.'

'Pull the fronts back a bit. Fair's fair, Miss Rankeillor.'

He was such a complex man. The formidable Captain of the Town Guard had been comfortably naked in front of her, laughing and relaxed despite their looming separation. Two weeks seemed like an eternity: and she would not think of the much longer – or even permanent – separation which might be heading towards them. Rushing in like a stormy sea.

She pushed those crashing waves back by revelling in the

memory of their lovemaking. Still feeling the sensations, of how he had used his hands and his mouth to give her pleasure. Startling her by where those hands and that mouth had chosen to go. Hearing herself moan in pleasure, her body melting under his touch. Remembering how she had shyly begun to offer him her caresses in return.

Somewhere outside, a clock struck the quarter hour. Fifteen minutes to twelve. Although she really wasn't sure her father had been listening to her when she had taken her leave of him yesterday, she had told Mary to expect her home before midday and to let Betty know that too. Swinging her cloak over her shoulders, she tucked her sketchbook into her basket and left the bagnio, closing and locking the double doors and the wrought-iron gate behind her.

She decided not to take the long way home. Instead, she set off through the narrow close which led to the courtyard of the hospital. At this hour everyone would still be busy on the ward round. She was halfway through when she felt a prickle at the back of her neck. For a moment she froze to the spot, before whirling round to look back along the narrow passageway. Nothing and nobody.

The ward round was over. It had finished a little early this morning. Agnes Moncur had seen Professor Monro to the front doors of the hospital before returning to her own room. Sitting down at her desk, she lifted her head to gaze out of the window at the rooftops and spires of Edinburgh. Her dilemma of last night had been very real but this morning she had made up her mind.

Edinburgh Royal Infirmary and the Cause, those were the two guiding lights of her life. Attachments to other people, like Professor Rankeillor and his daughter, could not be allowed to stand in the way of her loyalty to the House of Stuart.

There was a knock at her door. She called out the instruction to come in and saw one of the hospital's porters standing there. She beckoned him into the room. The information he gave her had her standing up and snapping into action.

Silently telling herself to stay calm, Christian reached the courtyard and made her way round the edge of it. The open space bounded on three sides by the Infirmary, with its two projecting wings, was deserted. The grand entrance doors were open, as they usually were during the day, come rain, snow or shine. She became aware that she was walking too fast, her shoes beating out a rapid tattoo on the paving stones beneath her feet. Someone standing inside the hospital's cavernous entrance hall might hear her and look out.

Despite her urge to put the courtyard and the hospital behind her as quickly as possible, she slowed down. With the pang she knew she would always feel when she thought of Jamie Buchan, she remembered the advice he had given her when she had been taking food and medical aid to Mr Fox while that gentleman had been hidden in the cells at the back of the Infirmary.

Look confident. Look as though you have every right to be there. If anyone does challenge you, be ready with a good reason for why you are there.

She could manage the first bit. Maybe. It might help if she switched the focus of her thoughts. Like an arrow flying towards its target, they went to Robert Catto. Right now he would still be riding down to Leith. Soon he would be striding up the gangway of the ship bound for London. She imagined the Lord President was sending him there with an important dispatch, one requiring a special envoy to give its delivery due weight.

Wondering what could be so important, she felt a rush of excitement and stopped dead for the second time. Oh dear God, it couldn't be. Could it? Maybe the dispatch Robert Catto was delivering to London was news the rising was about to start. In Scotland rather than London?

Behind her, she heard someone call her name. Agnes Moncur. Christian put a smile on her face and turned around. Pity she didn't have that good reason for why she was here.

Catto dismounted at the change house in Leith and tossed the reins to the stable boy he recognized from the last time he'd been here.

'You'll ride him back up to *The White Horse?*' The two inns, like many others, had a reciprocal agreement.

'As soon as I've fed and watered him, sir. Then I can walk back down here while it's still daylight.'

Catto nodded, dug into his pocket, pushed open the strings of his purse and brought out a silver coin. 'For your trouble.'

The lad grinned and sketched him a cheerful salute. Watching as he led Tam back to the stables, listening to the clip-clop of the hooves on the cobblestones, Catto felt an odd chill run through him. A shiver of fear. With Kirsty Rankeillor at its centre. A feeling she was in danger.

He stood for a moment, applying his rational brain to this almost overwhelming sensation. She *was* in danger, although not any more today than she had been yesterday. He was loath to leave her here in Edinburgh but she had people she could go to for help if she needed it. Added to which, it wasn't his place to question the Lord President's decision to send him on this mission. His place and his duty was to carry it out.

He still had to force himself to walk onto the quay at The Shore and find the London-bound packet.

'Kirsty,' Agnes said. 'Not coming in to see us?'

'I'm afraid not.' Panic put more words into her mouth. 'I've been taking some physic to a patient who's not well enough to come and see us at the shop.'

Agnes threw a glance over her shoulder. The narrow close only really led to the bagnio. If you were going to any of the houses some distance beyond it, you would take a different route. Turning, she looked back at Christian. 'Might I have a word with you?'

'Betty will be expecting me for our midday meal.'

'She can surely wait a few moments.'

Christian refreshed her false smile. Her face was beginning to hurt from the strain of it. 'Of course. How can I help you, Agnes?'

The other woman look tired. Maybe something else was bothering her.

Or maybe I'm clutching at straws. Because I am beginning to feel scared.

'Not here. It's too public.'

'Your room, then.'

Agnes gave her no reply. By the time Christian realized they were bypassing her room and heading for the cells in the back corridor, the lady governess had already unlocked the big oak door separating those from the rest of the hospital and ushered her in. Christian whirled round when she heard the sound of the key turning for a second time. Locking them both in. She had walked into a trap.

'Third cell on the right, Kirsty.'

'Agnes, what's going on?'

'I think you know, Kirsty. Third cell on the right,' she said again. 'On you go.'

Where Mr Fox had stayed. Where Robert Catto had been waiting for her when she had tried and failed to post a warning letter to her father while he had been through in Glasgow before Christmas. Someone else was waiting for her there today.

Arthur Menzies of Edmonstone.

Chapter 37

'Duncan,' Patrick Rankeillor said, rising from his chair as his unexpected guest came into the library, leaning heavily on the arm of his devoted manservant Fergus Chisholm. Betty was following on behind. 'I take it you're not here to consult me about your health.' He frowned as he watched the Lord President's tortuous progress across the room. 'Forbye I'm thinking you could be doing with some medical advice. Take my arm, man.'

'Not here about my health, Patrick, no. Hoping it'll look like that if anyone's taking an interest in thee or me.'

'Less claret and brandy,' Patrick said as he and Fergus Chisholm saw Culloden into one of the armchairs in front of the fire. 'More plain food. Less rich food. Ca' canny on the cheese. You should try it.'

'What sort of a life would I have if there was no enjoyment in it?' Duncan Forbes asked as soon as he got his breath back.

'A longer one.'

Culloden cast him a steely look but waited until they had jointly dismissed Betty and Fergus Chisholm to the kitchen. He did not speak again until the door had closed behind them.

'There are other ways of shortening one's life. More dangerous ones, forbye.' He lifted his bony hands in a gesture of exasperation, the shirt ruffles at his wrist dancing in response to the movement. 'What the Devil were you thinking of, Patrick?'

'Ye ken my views, Duncan. You always have. We've aye been able tae agree tae disagree.'

'When it was all in the abstract. Now it's real.'

'Is it?'

Duncan Forbes shook his bewigged head. 'Too late for pretence, Patrick. I've read your written statement. I ken what was going on here over Yuletide.'

Arthur Menzies pushed her down onto the wooden board which served as the base for a bed. There was no mattress to soften it as she had done for Mr Fox. Her hip and her back made painful contact with the bunk and the stone wall behind it.

'Now,' he said harshly. 'Tell us everything you know.'

'Everything I know about what?' Her heart was pounding. The look on his face was venomous.

'Don't play the innocent with me, you smart-mouthed little trollop.'

Agnes Moncur frowned. Christian saw her reaction, knew Edmonstone hadn't. His attention was totally fixed on her.

'You know exactly what I mean. Tell us everything you know about Robert Catto. Right now.'

'I d-don't know anything. How w-would I know?' If she'd heard the stutter in her voice, he had too. Blind instinct warned her she mustn't show him how scared she was. Somehow she had to talk her way out of this. Beg Agnes to help her.

Arthur Menzies leaned closer, blocking her view of the other woman. 'You would know,' he said, 'because you've been opening your legs for him. Isn't that where you were last night? Where you've come from this morning?' He flicked a glance over his shoulder. 'So she says.'

Christian's heart sank. Agnes had led her here, into this trap. She could not hope for her help.

Catto sat on the edge of the narrow bunk he would occupy for the next few days, listening to the sounds of a ship about to cast off and leave port. Swift, purposeful footsteps. Shouted commands. Snatches of laughter. Grunts of effort. Strings of curses.

He was a good sailor, had always enjoyed the experience of being at sea. It was a welcome pause in his life as a soldier. Time away from bone-wearying treks through hostile territory and long stretches of mind-numbing boredom punctuated by bloody and brutal outbursts of violence.

A chance to reflect. A chance to think about nothing at all. Clear his head of all the detritus life put into it. He had relished some storms in his time, awed by the power of nature. Put the petty but destructive squabbles of mankind into perspective.

Right now he was fighting an impulse to grab his portmanteau, get off this boat and head back up out of Leith. He wanted to be with her, wanted to stay in Edinburgh, wanted to protect her. He wanted not to have been sent on this sodding mission, carrying three fucking stupid dispatches.

Two were letters. One was to the Marquis of Tweeddale, Secretary of State for Scotland. The second was to the Duke of Argyle, chief of Clan Campbell and another of Scotland's most powerful men. The third missive was an address to King George, assuring him Scotland was loyal to the House of Hanover and well-affected towards him and his family. Catto made a rude noise.

He'd succeeded in not doing so when Culloden had read the loyal address out to him but he knew his face had shown his feelings. The wording of the document disgusted him, too much for him to be able to dissemble. Absurdly deferential and self-abasing, praising George to high heaven, promising undying loyalty. A man of the calibre of Duncan Forbes should not have to humble himself like this. Nor humble Scotland either.

'Aye,' Culloden had said. 'I ken fine it's obsequious in the extreme but it's a damn fine example of arse-licking. They expect it, these folk, and it helps protect us. If we can assure those buggers in London the Jacobites are nothing but a small faction of madmen and adventurers, it will help disarm and reduce any retaliation there might be. Keep Scotland safe. Help you too, Bob.'

Retaliation. The word made his blood run cold. Scotland had been a thorn in the side of England for centuries. An invasion and attempted overthrow of King George by a Popish Pretender backed up by French soldiers and a ragtag army of deluded homegrown Jacobites would give those buggers in London the excuse to come down hard on Scotland.

'How will it help me?'

'I doubt you'll get as far as the king but Tweeddale and Argyle will receive you and pass on the loyal address. As my messenger, they'll know you have my complete trust and confidence. Which will stand you in good stead when it comes to your own loyalty, Bob. Should any rumours start circulating to the contrary.'

Catto bowed his head, cradling it between his hands, fixing his gaze on the gently creaking wooden boards on the floor of his cabin. That sodding unwanted inheritance again. Would he never be rid of it?

'Open your eyes, you little slut. And tell us what you know.'

'There's no call for that kind of language,' Agnes said sharply. 'Let me talk to her.' Shoving Edmonstone out of the way, she sat down beside Christian. 'Kirsty,' she said. 'We need to know where his loyalties lie. Think of the Cause, lass!'

'Leave her with me for a while, Mrs Moncur. I'll soon get some answers out of her.'

The way he was looking at her made Christian's skin crawl. Thoughts were chasing themselves around her head. She wondered how far he would be prepared to go to get those answers out of her. She wondered if not answering their questions was as good as an admission of guilt, an acknowledgement that Robert Catto was no Jacobite. There was a plea swirling around her head too.

Help me, Robert. Please help me.

He could not hear her. She knew he could not hear her.

Chapter 38

Kirsty,' Agnes pleaded. 'Tell us what you know. For the Cause, Kirsty. For the sake of the Cause.'

'Leave her with me,' Edmonstone said again. 'I'll soon get the truth out of her.'

'Agnes,' Christian said, grabbing the other woman's hands. 'Don't leave me alone with him. Please, Agnes. Do you know what he and his friends did to an innocent young girl?'

'Shut your bloody mouth!' Arthur Menzies said, starting towards her with his hand upraised.

'No!' Agnes Moncur shouted, springing to her feet. 'You'll not hit her!'

'Then what?' he demanded, his face set in a sneer. 'We just let her go home? We've gone too far for that.'

'Stand by, fore and aft! Single up!' The commands were bellowed out. Catto heard the scrape of wood as the ship's gangway was pulled back on board. The ship was tethered to the quay by heavy ropes at bow and stern. That would be one at either end being untied from their heavy iron mooring rings on the quay by the port workers onshore. Mere moments remained until the vessel glided away from The Shore.

His feeling of foreboding had not faded. She was in danger. At this very moment. He was sure of it. As he was sure she needed him. At this very moment.

Duty. He always did his duty. As she had observed, duty was all he had ever had to hold on to, the one constant in an unpredictable life.

If he didn't stay onboard on this ship he would be failing in his duty for the first time in his military career. He might be cashiered, dishonourably discharged from the army. Worse even than that, he would have betrayed the Lord President's trust in him.

'Let go fore and aft!' The command to cast off the remaining two ropes.

Grabbing his portmanteau, he ran up and onto the deck. The gap between the ship and the quay was already beginning to widen. Amidst shouts of protest and disbelief, he threw his bag ashore and pulled himself up onto the handrail. Grasping a taut rope to steady himself, gripping the hilt of his sword with his other hand, he balanced there for a few seconds. Let go of the rope and jumped.

Agnes Moncur looked stricken. Yet she had made the threat. If Christian didn't tell them everything she knew about Robert Catto, she would tell Patrick Rankeillor his daughter had spent the night with him at the bagnio. Christian looked at her in disbelief. As a child, she had looked up to the lady governess. As a young woman, she had come to see Agnes as a friend.

'How do you know where I might have spent last night?' she asked, hating how her voice had come out as a cracked whisper.

'I know.'

'You cannot prove it,' Christian managed.

'I dinna need to prove it, Kirsty. I only need to tell the Professor. That will be enough. Think how disappointed he will be in you.'

'Enough!' Arthur Menzies said savagely. 'This is getting us nowhere. We'll leave her to stew for a while. Then she'll be more amenable. Give me five minutes with her beforehand.'

Agnes stood up and turned to face him. The expression on her face was unreadable.

'The Cause, Mrs Moncur. First, last and always.'

'You do not need to tell me what is owed to the Cause.'

'So give me five minutes with her now. I won't hit her.'

'Do you give me your word?'

'I give you my word.'

'Very well. I shall wait for you at the end of the corridor.'

He didn't hit her. He grabbed her by the hair with one hand and clamped the other over her mouth. He spat vile words into her face. He told her in obscene and gloating detail what he would do to her if she didn't give him the answers he wanted.

'I don't care for other men's leavings but you need taking down a peg or two. You always have done. I'll have the additional pleasure of telling Charlotte all about it afterwards. Every last little detail. Won't be long before everyone in Edinburgh will know. You'll be ruined.'

'They'll hang you!' she hissed back though his imprisoning fingers.

'Not if I've gone to France or Italy. High time I claimed my place beside the Prince. You'll still be ruined. A slut and a harlot. Soiled and sullied. There's no coming back from that. Think Catto will still want you after I've had you?'

Keeping his grip on her hair, he pulled her in close, back against his body. 'Feel that, you little slut? That's what you'll be getting.' Lust thickened his voice. 'Maybe I'll make you choke on it.'

Every sense heightened, Christian heard Agnes call from along the corridor.

'Mr Menzies?'

His mouth was very close to her ear. Too close. 'Don't rely on her to save you. I'll find a way to come back here without her. Here's a taste of what I have in store for you.'

Sliding his free hand down the front of her bodice, he grabbed one of her breasts and twisted it hard.

Catto landed awkwardly, twisting his ankle as his foot struck the stone of the jetty. He let out a yell of pain, took a moment, and righted himself. At punishing speed he headed over the cobblestones towards the change house. Sod it. Now he had a fucking limp. Tam and the stable lad were gone but he hired another beast and hurriedly promised to swap the horses over if he caught up with them on the way to Edinburgh.

Agnes Moncur sat at her desk wondering where they went from here. Arthur Menzies was right about one thing. They couldn't just let Kirsty go home. He had escalated the situation too far for that.

'Mrs Moncur?' Murdo Robertson put his head round the door. He always knocked. Had he done so and she hadn't heard him, lost in her troubled thoughts?

'Mrs Moncur?' he said again.

Chapter 39

Christian sank down onto the bunk and put her head in her hands. She was shaking, as much with anger as with fear.

How dare he?

How dare he make those vile threats, call me those disgusting names?

How dare he touch my breast? Hurt me so much?

She didn't know how long she sat there. Maybe till it occurred to her that he could dare to do whatever he liked to her. Somehow she had to get out of here.

She stood up and went out into the corridor. Neither he nor Agnes had thought to lock or even close the cell door. She didn't have high hopes they would have been so remiss about the main door and she was right. Thick and solid, it was designed to keep people in. Even if she'd had something with which to try to prise it open, there was no hope of doing so.

For a moment as she stood there she swayed, the hopelessness of her situation hitting home and turning her legs to jelly. She could not hope Agnes would save her. Arthur Menzies was cunning enough – and, oh dear God, angry enough – to find a way to come back here alone. He would not need so long to do what he had threatened to do to her.

Despair threatened to overwhelm her, had her sliding down the wall and crouching there like a cornered animal. She squeezed her eyes tightly shut, wished as hard as she could for Robert Catto to come bursting through the door, knew that was impossible. The ship he would have boarded at Leith this morning would not yet be so far away but he was as unreachable as though he were on the other side of the world.

Her eyes shot open and her skin tingled. Someone else was

here in this shadowy corridor with her. She could feel it. The only light was coming from what was cast by the high window in the third cell on the right. It formed a bright column, dust motes swirling round it. Almost as though someone was standing there.

From out of nowhere, a feeling of calm wrapped itself around her. As though the unseen person had spoken, she heard words in her head.

Don't despair. Think of something. Do something.

Her thoughts flew to Mr Fox. He'd had a pistol to defend himself when he had been hiding in here. Such a weapon wasn't available to her.

Another one might be. The sweeping brush. The big sturdy one he had used as a crutch when he had hobbled his way to the necessary house at the end of the corridor.

He had knocked once and was about to knock for the second time when the back door was flung open. The housekeeper stood there, her face lined with worry. Grabbing him by the sleeve of his coat, she pulled him into the lobby.

'Is your mistress here?' he asked, breathless with pain and exertion. His sprained ankle was taking no prisoners. The wee witch yanking him into the house hadn't helped.

'No. D'ye ken where she is?' She gestured to the young girl who stood behind her. 'She tellt Mary she would be back by twelve. It's past two o' the clock now and she still isna hame. I'm that worried aboot her! Ah was about tae send Mary tae call on Miss Gordon.'

'I'll go and look for her,' Catto said. 'Does the Professor know she hasn't come home yet?'

The wee woman shook her head. 'I dinna want tae worry him unless I have tae. Forbye which, he's been closeted wi' the Lord President for a lang while noo. Asked me no tae disturb them after I had fed them baith.'

'The Lord President's here?' All he bloody needed. Although he couldn't think about that now.

'Aye. Come through tae the kitchen wi' me and I'll gie you something tae eat too.'

'I don't have time.' He had already spared a few precious

moments to brief Sergeant Livingstone and enlist his aid.

'Ye've time tae drink a cup o' milk. I'll bring it tae ye. Forbye ye dinna want tae come through tae the kitchen and sit doon for a wee minutie.'

Leaning back against the deep windowsill, he took the weight off his injured foot. 'Better not,' he said, giving her a swift smile. 'I might not be able to stand up again.'

'I'll fetch the milk,' the maid said, and sped off. The housekeeper looked Catto up and down, taking in his posture and the raised foot. 'Whit have ye done tae yersel noo?'

'Don't ask.'

The girl was back in no time, handing him the cup of milk. He thanked her, downed it in one gulp and wiped his mouth with the back of his hand. 'Right,' he said. 'I'm off. Should the opportunity arise, please don't say anything to the Lord President about having seen me.'

'I'll think aboot it,' the housekeeper said. 'How will ye ken where tae start? Looking for her, I mean.'

'I have an inkling as to where she might be.'

The wee wifie's eyes searched his face. Did she have an inkling too, a suspicion that Christian Rankeillor had not spent last night with her friend?

She nodded. 'Go and look. And bring her hame!'

She was ready. She had tried holding the sweeping brush in different ways, by its shaft and by its end. She had worked out how it would find its balance in her hands. Both hands. Now she was standing here by the big door, listening for it being unlocked. She would let him step into the corridor and then she would crack him over the head with the brush end. She'd be sure to hit him hard, enough to make him stumble and fall. After which she would step over him and make her escape.

When she heard the sound of the key in the lock she was ready for it. The door was pushed open. Whoever was about to come in was a man. She could tell by the heavier sound of the footsteps. She waited, holding her breath. Then she brought her makeshift weapon down on his head.

His reaction was lightning swift. Grabbing the shaft of the

brush, he deflected the blow from his head to his shoulder. Yelling in pain, he spun round and saw her. 'Bloody hell, Kirsty,' he howled, 'I'm already walking wounded!'

She let go of the brush. It fell with a crash onto the stone floor. 'Robert? Och, Robert! You're here!'

He caught the door so it didn't slam, came in and put his back to the wall of the corridor. 'Got to sit down,' he muttered, and slid to the floor.

Chapter 40

'No,' he said again, as they sat side-by-side on the floor of the corridor. 'First I take you home. Then I come back here. After I've rested my foot for a moment.'

'But Robert,' she said, turning towards him and laying one hand on his chest, 'he's vicious. Who knows what he might do? He's got nothing to lose now.'

'Exactly,' he said grimly. 'So I'll make sure he knows that. I have reinforcements coming. Sergeant Livingstone is in charge of those.'

'How will they know where to come? How did you know where to come? Where did you get the key? Why are you not on your way to London?'

'The answers to those questions can wait. Did he hurt you?'

She took her hand from his chest and turned her head away, not wanting to tell him, not wanting to see the look on his face when she did. For she knew she had to.

He raised his right hand, winced, but continued the movement, bringing her head back round so they were looking at each other. 'Whatever he did, Kirsty,' he said gently, 'the shame is his. Not yours.'

His face darkened as she told him what Arthur Menzies had threatened to do to her. 'Calling me vile names all the while. I cannot bring myself to repeat the words he used. The worst names a man can call a woman.'

'I called you one of those names once.' His voice was soft with regret.

'You did not grab me by my hair, tug so hard I thought he might pull it out. You did not squeeze my breast so hard it still aches.'

'I'll kiss your hair better,' he said. 'Take his touch away.' He planted a series of soft kisses on her hair and her brow. 'Would it help if I did it for your breast too?'

'Yes,' she whispered. 'It would help.'

'Then, with your permission...' Wincing again as the movement jarred his injured shoulder, he slid one hand down her bodice and let it lie there. He laid his free hand over hers where it rested in her lap.

'Healing hands,' she said a few moments later.

The long fingers resting so gently on the curve of her breast twitched. 'Your hands, yes. Wrong word for mine.'

'I don't think so.'

He kissed her brow again, then put a finger to his lips and turned his head towards the big door. Someone was putting a key into the lock.

They scrambled to their feet, each helping the other up. Catto drew his sword from its leather scabbard and shoved her behind him. 'Keep well back, Kirsty.'

Arthur Menzies pushed the door open to find Catto's sword levelled at his chest.

'Well, well, well. That answers the question this little strumpet wouldn't.' He glanced towards Christian, who was standing in the open doorway of the third cell down. 'Your slut is loyal, if nothing else. Can't imagine she's much good between the sheets. Too prim and proper.'

'You'll never know. As you will say nothing more about her. As you will come with me. Now.'

'Oh, I don't think so. We'll finish this here. Once and for all.'

Muttering a curse, Catto took a step back, stumbled on his twisted ankle. Although he swiftly righted himself, the mishap gave Edmonstone enough time to draw his own sword.

'Don't be a bloody fool!'

'It's you who's the fool!' Edmonstone lunged forward, his blade heading for the side of Robert Catto's neck. Standing his ground, he parried the attack, hitting the other sword up and away from his body. Arthur Menzies stepped back, drew his sword in an arc through the air, brought it round and attacked again. This time he aimed for Robert Catto's arm. Again, he blocked Edmonstone's sword, forcing his own close to its hilt and pushing it away, grunting with exertion. Beads of sweat broke out on his forehead.

Edmonstone danced back and for a moment the two men stood and took each other's measure. A year ago Christian and Anna Gordon had attended a demonstration put on by one of the fencing masters here in Edinburgh. He had described it as the noble art of swordsmanship. She had silently begged to differ on the nobility of what they had seen. She had to admit there was a certain grace to it. Obviously rehearsed, the movements of the two fencers had been as much a dance as a fight.

She saw the same showiness in how Arthur Menzies moved but there was no grace to this contest: and there was too much at stake. As the two men renewed their grips on their swords, she saw and heard Robert Catto's sharp intake of breath. Curling his fingers around the hilt must have sent a jolt of pain up to his injured shoulder, the wound she had inflicted on him.

The two swords met and clashed again. Once. Twice. Three times. They were of the same type, slender but deadly lengths of flashing steel. She watched in an agony of fear. Robert Catto had experience of battle. She doubted Arthur Menzies did. Robert Catto was physically stronger too, but he was hampered by his injured ankle and shoulder. He was beginning to drag his foot. She knew Edmonstone had spotted that too, was trying to force him back, make him put weight on it.

She gasped as he stumbled again. Arthur Menzies lunged forward and hit his sword up. Robert Catto kept hold of it but his chest and the rest of his body was now exposed to the other blade. The look of triumph on his adversary's face made Christian's blood run cold.

Something happened then. Afterwards she could never describe exactly what. It was as though some unseen person had stuck their foot out and tripped Arthur Menzies up, making him stumble too. He lurched towards the wall of the corridor and struck his head against it. The impact made him drop his sword. It fell with a clang onto the stone floor. Robert Catto stepped forward and put his uninjured foot on it.

She stood there watching the two of them and did not know

what she wished for. Other than Robert Catto's safety and her own. His face wore the mask it had when she had first met him. Harsh. Unforgiving. The avenging angel. Was she going to see him kill?

He glanced back along the corridor at her and his face changed.

'Bugger it,' he said. Transferring his own sword to his left hand, he limped forward to stand in front of Arthur Menzies where he stood propped awkwardly against the wall, drew his right hand back and punched him hard in the jaw. Edmonstone lost his footing and fell backwards onto the floor. There was a crack as his head hit the stone floor and his eyes fluttered closed.

Shoulders heaving, Robert Catto looked at her again. 'All over,' he said between deep, shuddering breaths. 'Sergeant Livingstone and Archie Liddell will be here any moment now. They can pick up this debris.' He gave the body on the floor a contemptuous kick before lifting his head and tilting it to one side. 'I think I can hear them now.'

The big door was pushed open. Sergeant Livingstone and Archie stepped into the corridor, two more guards at their back. She blinked when she saw Murdo Robertson was there too.

'Looks like you have the situation under control, young Captain Catto.'

'Aye.' Robert Catto rubbed one hand over his face, wiping off glistening sweat. 'Apart from being about to fall over.'

Livingstone and Archie Liddell came forward and put themselves on either side of him.

'Lean on us, Mr Catto,' Archie said. He looked at Christian. 'Where?' he asked.

'In here,' she said, standing back to allow the sergeant and him to help Robert Catto in and lower him down onto the edge of the bunk. Sergeant Livingstone went back out into the corridor. She heard the rumble of his voice as he spoke to the two guards.

'Are you all right, Kirsty?' Archie Liddell asked.

'I am now. Och, Archie! I am so glad to see you!'

Chapter 41

They were sitting next to each other on the wooden bunk. Murdo Robertson had supplied the two guards with a stretcher. They had rolled Arthur Menzies roughly onto it and taken him away. After a brief conference with Catto, Sergeant Livingstone and Archie Liddell had followed on.

'You have ordered them to take him to the Tolbooth?'

'Aye. A more secure prison than Eastfield House.' His mouth tightened. 'A damn sight more.'

Murdo Robertson came back in with a set of wooden crutches from the hospital's stores. 'For you, sir,' he said, handing them to Catto. 'For whenever you choose to leave.'

'Miss Kirsty,' he went on, turning to her. 'I have a request for you from Mrs Moncur. She asks if she might come and speak to you, express her regret for what has happened here today.'

Catto could have answered for her, in no uncertain terms. He'd already had words with Agnes Moncur, short but to the point. Christian Rankeillor beat him to it. 'Not yet, Mr Robertson. Not yet. But I thank you for what you have done for me today.'

After he had mumbled a response to her thanks, Robertson took himself off, leaving them alone in the corridor. She took Catto's hand in her own.

'Ow,' he said, although he was smiling at her.

Raising his hand to her lips, she kissed each bruised knuckle in turn, her lips exquisitely gentle. 'Is this your third wound of the day?'

'I suppose it is.'

'How did you hurt your ankle?'

'Jumping off a boat in Leith.'

'Oh,' she said. 'You couldn't just have walked down the

gangway?'

'They had already raised it and cast off.'

'Oh,' she said again. 'Wish I could have seen you leap from ship to shore. Must have been quite a sight.'

'I think I caused a bit of a stir.'

'Why did you jump off the boat?'

'Had a feeling you were in trouble. Could almost hear you calling my name.'

'A feeling,' she repeated. She raised her hand to stroke a strand of his hair back from his damp brow. 'Are you fey?'

'Why would you think that?'

'Because you seem to have had another feeling today. Somehow knowing I was here.'

'I did try your house and the bagnio first. After not finding you in either place, the Infirmary was the next logical port of call.'

'Mmm,' she said. 'How did Mr Livingstone and Archie know to come here?'

'After I checked the bagnio I had the good fortune to run into another of the guards. I asked him to take a message to the guard-house. I had asked Livingstone to go there to await my further orders. Archie Liddell was already on duty.'

'None of this explains your initial feeling that I was in trouble.'

'Doesn't it?'

She threw him a long-suffering look. 'You're doing that prodigiously irritating thing again. Answering one question with another.'

'Am I?'

'Stop it,' she said. 'How did you know to come specifically to this corridor? How did you get the key?'

'Because when I got to the hospital, I went to Agnes Moncur's room. Murdo Robertson was there. The two of them had obviously been arguing and he told me what had been going on. He also told me he didn't know where Edmonstone was and was worried about what he might do.'

When she shivered, he slid his arm around her shoulders, winced, swore, but kept it there. 'In Murdo Robertson's words, I think we should choose to leave here very soon.'

'Tell me something before we do. Did you have any of these

feelings of yours while you were fighting Arthur Menzies?'

'As though an invisible person had tripped him up? No,' he said innocently. 'Nothing like that.'

'You,' she said, 'are the most infuriating man I've ever met. Although I'm very glad you acted on your feelings.'

'So am I. Let's see if I can stand up without falling down again the moment I get to my feet.'

'Foot,' she said. 'You'll be using the crutches. I fear you're going to be in trouble with the Lord President.'

'Almost certainly. He's at your house, in conversation with your father. Shall we go there now so I can discover if I'm going to be drummed out of the army?'

'Getting our story straight on the way?' she asked, stooping to pick up her basket from where it sat next to the wall of the cell.

'Let us at agree on a shortened version of the truth. Leaving out last night's visit to the bagnio. Whether we're going to get away with that is another matter entirely.'

Holding the door open for him, she turned and spoke back down the now empty corridor. 'Thank you,' she said softly. 'Thank you.'

Chapter 42

Catto walked the short distance from the infirmary with the help of the crutches, cursing under his breath as he tried to work out how to use them while not letting his sword get in the way. With every step the pressure of bearing his weight on his arms was exacerbating the pain in his shoulder.

At the same time, he was acutely aware of her growing distress. She was bearing up bravely, chivvying him along, but he suspected it could only be a matter of time before she succumbed to the shock of what she had been through.

When they reached the house, he struggled up the steps and she ran up them to tirl the pin, turning back round to look at him, her hands on her hips. 'Does the swearing help? Maybe I should try it.'

He was saved from having to reply by the housekeeper opening the door, her face lighting up when she saw Christian Rankeillor. The two women embraced.

'I'm fine, Betty,' she said in response to the anxious questions which followed. 'I really am fine. No harm done.'

'Into the house,' Catto said wearily, wondering how many times he had uttered that command. He was like a sodding parrot.

'I'll tell you all about it later, Betty.'

'No you bloody won't,' he muttered, although he wasn't sure either of them had heard him.

Patrick Rankeillor was already on his feet as they came into the library, a look of growing astonishment on his face.

'Christian?'

'She needs to sit down,' Catto said.

'It's you who needs to sit down,' she responded, pointing to the armchair her father must just have vacated. 'Over there.

Opposite the Lord President. Good afternoon, sir.'

'Good afternoon, lass.' His shrewd gaze swept over her and Catto. 'You two would appear to have been in the wars. Care to explain yourself, Bob? Tell me why you're not now on your way to London?'

He'd been anticipating anger. He certainly deserved it. Yet Culloden did not look or sound angry. His eyes fell to Catto's foot and ankle, both now badly swollen.

'He must elevate his foot, Patrick.'

'Aye,' her father said. His back was to the Lord President but Catto saw him roll his eyes. Culloden fancied himself as an amateur doctor, which must be irritating if you were a real one. Rankeillor was already lifting a footstool. Swinging round, he carried it back to the armchair.

'Sit down,' Christian Rankeillor said.

'You sit down,' he retorted. 'I can sit in one of the upright chairs.'

'Sit down,' she said again. 'Unless you want me to push you into the damn chair!' Her voice quavered on the words. Catto did not miss the look Rankeillor and the Lord President exchanged. He didn't have to be fey to understand what inference they had drawn from the way he and Christian Rankeillor had just spoken to each other.

Every part of his body aching, he gave in. Trying to ease the crutches out from under his arms as he sat down, he fell back and cried out in pain.

'That wasn't your foot,' Patrick Rankeillor observed.

'It's nothing.'

'It's not nothing,' she said. 'He's hurt his shoulder too.'

'Your foot and your shoulder. How did you sustain these injuries?'

'The former from jumping off a ship in Leith. The latter because your daughter tried to crack me over the head with a sweeping brush, Professor. I diverted her aim to my shoulder.'

Rankeillor blinked, looked at her and then back at Catto. 'Had you given her a lot of provocation?'

'On other occasions, yes. On this one, no. Someone else did. She was expecting him, not me. He should be in the Tolbooth by now. Escorted there by Sergeant Livingstone, Lieutenant Liddell and two other members of the Town Guard.'

Opposite him in the other green and gold armchair, the Lord President leant forward, his face bright with interest. Burning desire to hear what had happened seemed to have temporarily soothed his painful joints.

'There seems to be quite a story to tell here, Bob.'

'I'll tell it as soon as Miss Rankeillor sits down.'

Patrick Rankeillor swung out one of the upright chairs from his work table, took his daughter's hand and led her to it. He moved across to the small table and tray where the brandy decanter sat, poured two glasses and gave one to her and one to Catto.

'I'll have another, Patrick,' the Lord President said.

Rankeillor rolled his eyes again. Catto took a sip of brandy.

'I was on the ship at Leith when I had the overpowering feeling Miss Rankeillor was in danger and needed my help.'

Culloden made an indeterminate noise at the back of his throat but waved Catto on.

'I found her at the Royal Infirmary, locked in the cells at the back of the building.'

'How did you gain entry to those?' Patrick Rankeillor asked.

'When I got to the hospital, Murdo Robertson gave me the key. He told me Miss Rankeillor had been tricked into going to the back corridor. By Mrs Agnes Moncur.'

Registering Rankeillor's shocked dismay, he went on. 'Miss Rankeillor found Arthur Menzies of Edmonstone waiting for her there. He proceeded to question her on what she knew about me. He did so very harshly.'

When she stirred in her seat it occurred to Catto she might not want the details of how Edmonstone had ill-used her spelled out in front of her father, nor the Lord President either.

'Kirsty?' her father said, taking her hand again.

'It's all right, Father,' she replied. 'He did not strike me. Nor do me any real damage.'

Hoping that was true, Catto told the rest of the story.

Culloden listened and asked a few questions, seeking to fill in any gaps in the tale. 'Where are the dispatches I entrusted to you?'

'In my portmanteau. Which is under lock and key and currently being guarded by Mrs Livingstone at *The White Horse.*'

'Then I can rest easy. She is an estimable woman. I have a story for you too, Bob. You'll have heard tell of the Protestant Wind?'

Catto nodded. 'Twas the name given to the stormy weather which had foiled more than one attempt by the Catholic countries of Europe to defeat the Protestant ones, from the Spanish Armada onwards. 'It blew up again?'

'Aye,' Culloden said. 'There was a storm. Two, in fact. In the English Channel. As I've been telling my old friend Patrick here, one squadron of French ships fell foul of the first one. The second tempest scattered the ships waiting at Dunkirk. Some vessels broke up and sank. Others are battered beyond repair. There will be no French invasion of England this year. Hopefully not any other year either.'

He shook his head. 'The mails can be unreliable. Especially in winter. So I heard one day of the assembling of the French invasion fleet and the next of its destruction. My dispatches are therefore not now so urgent. Although I would still like you to deliver them. In person. On your way back to rejoin your regiment in Europe.'

Silence descended on the room. Until the Lord President spoke again.

'You must return to Europe, Bob. If we didn't know before, we now ken fine you and Miss Kirsty have developed an attachment to each other. I cannot blame you, lad.' He glanced at Christian Rankeillor. 'Nor her either. But to marry her, the daughter of a committed Jacobite family, would spell ruin for your military career.'

Watching her as she raised her glass to her lips with a hand that trembled, something inside Catto snapped. He was so tired of it all. Of having to pretend to be something he wasn't. Of having to hide his feelings for her. Well, that cat was out of the bag now.

'I have a question for Professor Rankeillor.' He saw her startled look but kept right on going.

'Your daughter and I love each other, sir. Do I have your

permission to ask for her hand in marriage?'

'When did you ask *me*?' she demanded, lowering the brandy glass and sitting up straighter.

'You don't remember?'

'As I recall, 'twas not a formal proposal of marriage! Merely a question of my possible willingness to marry you. At some point.'

He wanted to fire out several rude words but thought better of it. 'I'll go down on bended knee right now if you like. Might need your father's help to stand up again.'

'Kirsty,' Patrick Rankeillor said. 'You are both young. You have known each other for such a short time. You have met at a time of heightened emotion for both of you. How can you know what you feel for each other now is going to last? Tell me though, is there a reason why you might have to marry Captain Catto?'

Catto caught Rankeillor's meaning as soon as she did. She coloured up but answered calmly. 'No, Father. There is no reason why I might have to marry the Captain. Other than wanting to.'

Patrick turned to Catto. 'How would you propose to support my daughter?'

'I hope I might be given permanent command of the Town Guard.'

Duncan Forbes shook his head. 'Provost Coutts will block that. As soon as he finds out where your loyalties really do lie. Besides which, I do not believe it is your destiny to be the captain of a local militia. Much more lies ahead of you. There is another consideration. After the failure of the French invasion attempt, the focus of the war on the continent will now shift to the Austrian Netherlands. It is your duty to go back to Guise's.'

'I think you might have something to say on the matter too, Patrick,' Culloden said, turning his attention to his host. 'I fear those friends of yours with the much to be regretted loyalties would not take kindly to your daughter marrying a man who has done sterling work in counteracting the Jacobite threat.'

'Are those people to decide my future?' she burst out.

He wanted to go to her then, pick her up and carry her out of this house, run away with her. They did not need her father's permission to marry. All they needed was two witnesses and a minister or a lawyer. He could find other work. Any kind of work. They could live in a cottage somewhere. He would labour in the fields if he had to—

Patrick Rankeillor was looking at his daughter. Duncan Forbes was looking at Catto. 'I'm sorry, lad, I truly am. But think of what Miss Rankeillor's life might be like, if she were to be shunned by her former friends. Think of that!'

Culloden drank some brandy.

'I will strike a bargain with you, Bob. If you agree to go back to Europe, I shall countersign the documents relating to the three young people currently staying with Jenny Liddell at Colinton. As long as it's done quietly, they may have their freedom. We'll draw a veil over how they got away from Eastfield.'

'And if I resign my commission and refuse to go back to Europe?'

'Then I shall not sign the documents and the law will take its course.'

Chapter 43

The voices around her seemed to be coming from a long way off. There was something wrong with her vision too. Objects in the room were losing their position and shape, bobbing about as though they were floating in water. The faces of the three men seemed alternately to move closer to her and then recede.

'You're too good a man for the army to lose, Bob.' Framed by the curly grey wig, the expression on the Lord President's face as he turned to Christian was compassionate but determined. 'You must let him go, lass. For his sake and your own.'

'Not now, Duncan!'

'Miss Rankeillor needs to rest.'

'Aye.' That was her father's voice again, followed by a blur of movement as he lifted the brandy glass out of her hand. 'Kirsty, I'm going to take you through to Betty. She'll make you an infusion of camomile. After you've drunk it, she'll go upstairs with you and you can lie down for a while with a hot stone pig at your feet. I'll ask her to stay with you. Come on now, lass. Up you get.'

She rose to her feet, aware of Robert Catto trying to do the same.

'Stay where you are, laddie,' her father said. 'Rest that ankle and it'll mend itself all the sooner. When I come back I'll take a look at your shoulder.'

Frustrated by his inability to rise to his feet, Catto fell back into the armchair. Lifting his head again, he addressed the Lord President as soon as the doors into the lobby had closed behind father and daughter. 'Sir,' he said urgently. 'Surely the law would not return the three young people to Eastfield when my investigations have proved Cosmo Liddell is actively conspiring to commit treason?'

'From what you have told me, there is no similar evidence against Miss Charlotte Liddell. Am I right?'

'Yes,' Catto said, brushing that aside, 'but back in '15, estates of those who had been on the Jacobite side fell to the crown, did they not? Punishments extended to the families, not only to the individuals concerned.'

'Aye. That's true. But Cosmo Liddell is not the owner of the Eastfield Estate. His brother is. He lives in London and is known to be well-affected to the House of Hanover and the Protestant Succession.'

'He knows the right people, you mean,' Catto said bitterly. 'As he knows the coal owners and the ironmasters here in Scotland. The creators of wealth who must be assured their position is secure. Whose loyalty is only to themselves.'

'It's how the world works, Bob,' Culloden said. 'I'm sorry for all of this. I'm sorry for you and Miss Rankeillor. But there is a greater good to be considered here. The safety and prosperity of Scotland. The prevention of armed rebellion, bloodshed and division which might endure for years to come.'

When Catto offered no response, Culloden spoke again. 'Clearly you care deeply about these three young people who are currently under Jenny Liddell's roof out at Colinton. So take the bargain I have offered you.'

'It seems I have no choice.' Catto put his head to the back of the armchair and closed his eyes. He opened them again at the Lord President's next, softly-spoken words, giving his own words back to him.

'An overpowering feeling that Miss Rankeillor was in danger and needed my help. Your grandfather was fey too. It tends to run in families.'

She was confused when she woke up. The light coming into her room was the same as when Betty had seen her into her bed. Had she only slept for a few moments?

Betty herself was crouched down at the fireplace. She threw a glance over her shoulder. 'You've been stirring for a wee while now. Stay in bed and I'll bring you a cup o' tea.'

Christian sat up. 'Didn't you just make me one?'

'That was yesterday,' Betty said, coming over with one of the dainty little cups. 'You've slept the clock round and more. You must have needed it. No bad dreams? You looked peaceful enough.'

'No dreams I can remember. Did you stay with me all night?'

'Maist o' it. Mary and Tibby sat wi' you for a wee while this morning. Drink your tea. Your faither wants tae ken if you'll bide in your bed or get up and come downstairs.'

'I'll come downstairs.' Christian took a sip of tea. 'What about Captain Catto?'

'The Lord President took him off wi' him yesterday afternoon. Sent Mr Chisholm out to bespeak two chairs. The redcoat wasna best pleased aboot that. Even though he could barely walk. Stubborn chiel.' She hesitated. 'There's a letter for you. Came a bittie earlier.' Sliding her hand into the pocket on the front of her apron, she brought it out. 'I'll let ye read it and come back and help ye get dressed.'

Christian took the letter, recognizing the handwriting. She unfolded the paper and read.

At The White Horse. Shall come and see you
as soon as this bloody ankle allows. My
compliance in staying where I am has been
assured by two gentlemen of your acquaintance
colluding in taking the crutches away from me.

'All right, lass?' the housekeeper asked when she came back ten minutes later.

Christian looked into Betty's concerned face and wondered if she was ever going to be all right again. She knew Robert Catto would be coming to see her to say goodbye. The Lord President had left them no other choice.

Chapter 44

At *The White Horse*, Marjorie Livingstone was setting a tray of food on the table in the private parlour at the back of the inn where Catto was sitting. Her husband followed her in, carrying a jug of ale and two small pewter tankards.

Marjorie straightened up and raised a hand, dissuading Catto from trying to rise in response to her entering the room.

'No need, Captain. I understand you're still struggling a wee bit.' Her eyes dropped to his feet, visible under the small dining table. 'Forbye your ankle hardly looks swollen at all this morning.'

'It's a lot better,' he told her. 'I had a walk around the room earlier on. Leaning on your husband's strong arm.'

'If you're not sick of the sight of me,' Donald Livingstone said. 'I thought you might like some company with your meridian, young Captain Catto.'

Catto looked up at him. 'I'd appreciate that very much, Sergeant. Sit yourself down. As long as you won't be run ragged serving your customers without his help, Mrs Livingstone.'

'Dinna you worry aboot that, Captain. The lassie's a hard worker and our Michael is going to give us a hand too. He's just back from delivering your letter. We'll move all this out of the way,' she said, lifting an inkstand and some sheets of paper from the table onto a sideboard.

The other piece of furniture in the parlour was a daybed. Catto had slept there last night, cocooned in sheets, blankets and pillows. Marjorie had gently helped him take off his sword belt and sword without jolting his injured shoulder. Then, making him feel like a child again, the Livingstones had more or less tucked him in.

'I should give Michael something.'

'Well,' Marjorie said easily, 'I'll no' say he wouldna welcome a few pennies but you dinna need to. He was glad tae run an errand for you. Eat up, now.'

Catto and Livingstone ate and talked. They spoke briefly of what had happened the day before. They discussed the new arrangements which would have to be put in place up at the guard house after Catto left Edinburgh. The Lord President had accepted his suggestion that Sergeants Livingstone and Crichton and Archie Liddell should act up until a new captain of the Town Guard could be appointed.

Duncan Forbes had also spent last night here, in his case helped up the stairs to one of the bedchambers by Fergus Chisholm. Catto presumed Marjorie Livingstone had found a quiet corner for the manservant somewhere close by.

He and the Lord President had spoken yesterday evening and again this morning, discussing everything which needed to be discussed. He had pleaded his injury as a reason not to drink too much. He hadn't drunk very much at all, in fact. For once, neither had Duncan Forbes.

He had assured Catto that those who had been involved in the Jacobite plot would be dealt with discreetly. Although it would be a long time till Arthur Menzies of Edmonstone came out of the Tolbooth. Culloden would summon Cosmo and Charlotte Liddell to come and see him, lay down the law. The freeing of the three young people would be presented to them as a *fait accompli.*

Other known Jacobites, including those Catto had uncovered, would be spoken to, and warned, told they were being watched. None were going to end their days on a scaffold. 'Not this year, anyway,' Culloden had said with bitter humour. Catto had no doubt he would be striking his hard bargains with all of them, ensuring their silence.

'Can I hire Tam for tomorrow, Sergeant? I want to ride out to Colinton.'

'You think you'll be recovered enough?'

'I'll have to be. There are some documents I need to take there.' The Lord President had signed those this morning. 'Nor do I want to leave without saying farewell to Geordie.'

'Or Tam,' Livingstone offered.

Catto returned the sergeant's smile. 'Aye. Tam too.'

'Geordie will miss you.'

'I'll miss him.' Then, awkwardly: 'There are other people I shall miss too. I've made some good friends here in Edinburgh.'

Livingstone inclined his head in acknowledgement. 'The feeling is entirely mutual, young Captain Catto. Which sentiment I'm sure holds true for Lieutenant Liddell, Sergeant Crichton and the rest of us. Let us hope our paths may cross again sometime.'

'I would wish so too, Sergeant. Although I fear that can only be a forlorn hope.'

'Who knows what the future holds? Let us wait and see. Not give up hope.' Livingstone fixed him with his steady blue gaze. 'There's always hope.'

When they had paused on their way to Eastfield, looking out over the moonlit sea, Livingstone had offered an opinion. *True love never dies.* He did not say those words again now. Nor had Christian Rankeillor's name been mentioned. Catto could feel the sympathy all the same.

'Can you read it, lads?'

Both boys looked up from the documents lying on the table in front of them. 'I can read some o' the words, Captain,' Geordie said, 'but I'm no' just sure I understand what they mean when they're all put together.'

Joshua nodded his head. 'Aye. The same goes for me, sir.'

'That's not surprising. Lawyers write in their own particular way. I sometimes think they do it so the rest of us won't understand what they mean. Gobbledygook, that's what it's called. There's another good word for you, Geordie.'

He gestured towards the documents. 'What it says is that the Liddells and Eastfield Colliery and Estate no longer have any claim over you or Alice, Geordie. Joshua, you are now a free man. You can go wherever you want to, be whoever you want to be.'

'Free?' Joshua asked. 'They canna take us back?'

'No. They'd be breaking the law if they did.'

'And I'm no' breaking the law as well?' Geordie asked. 'What with having run away frae them twice?' He looked at Joshua. 'Wi' my friend's help.'

'You're free, Geordie. And perfectly lawful.'

Both boys looked at him, quick tears springing to their eyes and a string of emotions racing across their faces. Until they jumped up out of their chairs. Wiping their tears away, they danced each other around the room, whooping and yelling with delight.

Chapter 45

The bell on the shop door jumped and jangled as Robert Catto pushed it open. Behind the counter serving a customer, Christian Rankeillor looked up.

'Captain Catto. I shall be with you as soon as I have finished serving this lady.'

'Of course.' He walked over to stand in front of one of the windows, gazing out at Infirmary Street. He was wearing his grey military cloak today, sweeping down from his shoulders. Once the transaction was completed, he held the door open for the woman before walking back to stand in front of the counter.

'I have come to take my leave of you. I thought it was safe enough to come to the front of the house today. I suppose I should also take my leave of your father.'

'He's visiting a patient. I'm not sure when he'll be back. How is your ankle?'

'Much better. As is my shoulder. Your father gave me some salve to apply. Please pass on my thanks. I don't think I was very gracious at the time. Should you be back working in the shop?'

'I'm fine. Apart from being driven mad by being fussed over and tiptoed around. I needed the distraction.'

'You got my second note?'

'Yes. Mr and Mrs Livingstone's son Michael delivered it. How are they all out at Colinton? Is Geordie upset about you going away?' She caught herself on. 'That was a stupid question, was it not?'

'He and I went out into the garden and had a private talk. Man to man. I told him I was relying on him to be strong and keep everyone else strong. I think that helped. I hope it did. Oh, and I taught him a new word. Gobbledygook.'

'Oh,' she said. 'The legal documents? What did they say when you explained what they meant?'

After he had described the scene, she raised one hand to her face to blot the single tear rolling down her cheek. 'That's something we've achieved.'

'Aye,' he agreed, and had to cough to clear his throat. 'As to how they are otherwise, Mrs Liddell tells me Geordie's back is healing well. He seems already to be seeing himself as the man of the house. Though I think Joshua might give him a run for his money there. They are both making themselves useful. All of which amuses Archie Liddell, who confessed he has often worried about his mother being lonely now he longer lives with her. Alice is quiet, as ever, but Archie's mother is kind. The Lord President is going to make her an allowance. Modest, but enough to cover the costs of feeding the new members of the household. Until it can be decided where their future might lie.'

'We shall help them too. In whatever way we can.'

'I know you will.'

'Did Geordie wish you *auf wiedersehen?*'

'Yes.' Then, urgently: 'Come out to the physic garden with me, Kirsty. Please.'

Betty studied her for a moment before she spoke. Catto had already gone through to the back lobby, was waiting for Christian there. 'All right, I'll mind the shop. Dinna ging intae the summer hoose. And put your cloak on. It's a cold morning.'

'Nothing's going to happen, Betty. We won't be out there for long.'

Besides which, what you fear most has already happened. And I think you know that.

'The Lord President is ruthless, is he not?' she said, seeing her breath turn white in the cold air. Saw his do the same when he replied.

'He's that all right.' They were walking away from the back door, past the outhouses, heading for the physic garden beyond.

'Cruel might be another word.'

'He does what he thinks is best for Scotland. Always.

Whatever the cost.'

'A cost you and I must bear. For the sake of the orphans of the storm.'

'He knew neither of us would be able to stand against that.'

As they walked along one of the gravel paths leading to the summer house in the centre of the physic garden, she stopped, pushed back the front of her blue cloak and slid her hand into the pocket under her skirts.

'I should give the luckenbooth back to you.' She took in a quick little breath. 'I wish I had given you a silver coin in exchange for it!'

He turned towards her and took her by the wrist, bringing her hand out of her pocket. 'Keep it, Kirsty. Please keep it. Perhaps you might tuck it away in a drawer. Bring it out now and again and give it a polish. Think of me. Think of us.'

'I do not need a piece of silver to make me think of you. Nor can there be any us. Not any more.' She looked up at him. 'We were most definitely moonstruck. Were we not?'

'Give me your other hand,' he said, already reaching for it. 'Cup them both. Like so.'

'You did this before. When you came back from Eastfield and we agreed we would try to weather the storm together. When you put your heart into my hands. For safe-keeping.'

'Yes,' he said. 'I did. It's still there. It always will be.'

'But the storm has swept us away too.' Her voice was laden with sorrow. 'Shipwrecked and scattered our fleet. And we cannot see the moon.'

'We can look up at the sky and know it's there. Your hands are cold. Let us keep walking. 'Tis too cold to stand still.'

'When does your ship sail?'

'Tomorrow. I am bid to sup with the Lord President tonight. I have only to gather together my belongings and head down to Musselburgh this afternoon. He is going to see me off from Leith.'

'To make sure you've really gone this time?'

They had reached the little pagoda which was the summer house. A wooden bench stood against one side of it, still white with frost which had not yet thawed. Despite what he'd said about it being too cold to stand still, he did exactly that, folding his arms under the grey cloak, pushing out its sides. His eyes ranged over the summer house.

'Do you often sit in here?'

'In the summer, yes.'

'Reading? Or drawing?'

'Both. With a book or a sketchpad open on my lap.'

'You draw the garden, the flowers and the herbs?'

'Often. When I'm inside the summer house I usually draw from memory.'

He looked at her. 'Will you draw me again – from memory?'

'I don't know. I never gave you copies of the drawings I did make of you. Or the one I did of myself. Artistically draped,' she added softly.

'Pity.' He gave her the saddest of smiles. 'I should like to have had that one.' Sliding one hand under his cloak and into the breast pocket of his frockcoat, he brought out a small packet. 'Sunflower seeds.'

'I remember.' One of the symbols of the Stuarts and the Jacobite Cause, they had been a message, a query as to where his sympathies lay. 'You never had the opportunity to plant them.'

'Maybe you would plant them for me.' He held the packet out to her.

Her eyes went from it to his face. 'In remembrance of you?'

'In remembrance of me,' he agreed. 'Is it too much to ask?'

'Yes,' she said. 'And no.' She took the packet from him and slipped it into her pocket.

'Do you wish we had never met?'

She turned her head away, but not before he had seen she was biting her lip. Of course she must wish she had never met him. He had brought her nothing but heartache.

She turned back to him. The expression on the lovely face which showed too much of what she was thinking made his heart skip a beat.

'I could never wish that, Robert. There's a part of me still thinks there could be a way for us to find. Still thinks we could somehow run away with each other.'

'We are both too sensible for that. For a moment, I had the

same mad notion. Thought I could resign my commission, find other work, any kind of work. But I would not take you away from everything you know to lead a poverty-stricken existence somewhere else. Soldiering is the only trade I know. Nor would I subject you to the life my mother led, moving around Europe, never having somewhere she could call home, somewhere she could settle down and be happy. And a better future for Alice, Geordie and Joshua depends on us parting.'

'Yes,' she said. 'That must be our consolation.'

'I have another. You are safe. Your father and your friends are safe. There will be no rebellion and no bloodshed in Scotland.'

When she said nothing in response, he spoke again. 'You cannot find it in your heart to be glad about that?'

'Glad that years of dreaming and hoping have come to nothing? Whole lifetimes of dreaming and hoping? No, I cannot find it in my heart to be glad about that!'

'Och, Kirsty!' he exclaimed. 'Still? After all the risks you, your father and your friends took? I feared so much for you. So much! Can you not at least be glad your world will stay safe, be the same as it always has been?'

Her eyes flashed. 'How can you say that? My world will never be the same again!'

'Oh, come here!'

She was in his arms, her own wrapped about his neck as he bent his head to kiss her. The kiss was passionate, seeking, hungry. It seemed to last forever. Until they broke apart and stood gazing at each other.

'I must go, Kirsty. I have to go.'

'Yes,' she agreed. Neither of them moved.

'When I go,' he said, 'I won't turn and look back. But if I do,' he added illogically, 'I don't want to see you. It's too cold for you to stay out here for much longer. So I want you to go back into the house, where it's warm. Is that understood?'

'Issuing orders until the end,' she said sadly.

'I want you to be warm. That's all. I should always want you to be warm.'

He didn't look back. She watched as he walked through the physic garden. The last she saw of him was a flash of his grey cloak as he walked past the outhouses and went round the side of the house. When she could no longer hear his retreating footsteps she sank down onto the bench.

Betty found her there. Wearing her own cloak, the housekeeper was carrying one of the old plaids from the back of the kitchen door.

'I know it's cold but I want to sit here for a bit longer,' Christian said, looking up at her.

Betty did not scold her for sitting on the frosty bench. Instead, she unfolded the plaid she was carrying and swirled it around Christian's shoulders.

'I'll sit wi' you. We'll just sit here quietly together. For a wee minute. Then we'll ging back intae the hoose.'

'He's gone, Betty. He's gone.'

'Aye, lass.' Betty tucked the plaid around her and said nothing more.

Christian slid one hand into her pocket and wrapped her fingers around the packet of sunflower seeds and the quilted roll which held the luckenbooth brooch. Two hearts entwined, surmounted by a crown. Small and dainty and beautifully wrought in silver.

Chapter 46

The Following Year: Summer 1745 at Rothiemay House, Banffshire, Scotland.

The sun was warm on their deft hands. Above their heads, their faces protected by wide-brimmed straw hats, plump white clouds drifted across a blue sky. Over at the wall which marked the boundary of the formal policies of Rothiemay House, bees buzzed in and out of the long narrow flowerbed running along its base. Tall yellow sunflowers stood like gently-bobbing sentries against the old grey stone.

The two young women sat on wooden stools in front of their easels. They were painting the ancient stone circle which sat in the field next door to the big house.

'Do you think the rumours can possibly be true? Of the Prince having landed in the west?'

'I don't know. To come without French help would be a terrible risk.'

Like her friend, she spoke in a low voice. Even though the only possible listeners were the old stones. Until they heard the murmur of voices. Male voices, growing louder as their owners drew nearer.

'Kirsty,' Anna Gordon said. 'Look up!'

Two men were walking across the grass towards them. Her eyes went to the one in the red uniform. His hair was neatly tied back but she could see the gleam of chestnut.

She wondered if she was dreaming. Maybe she had thought so often of him she had somehow conjured him up. As if by magic. Maybe if she blinked, he would vanish, go back to those long lonely nights when she had ached so much to see him again, to hear his voice, to feel the touch of his hand.

The man now standing right in front of her looked real, taking a step to one side so he could see her around the easel.

'Kirsty,' said the other man. 'Anna. May I introduce…'

'Oh,' he said. 'I am already acquainted with these ladies. We met in Edinburgh over a year since.'

As he spoke, Christian Rankeillor felt the blood rush and tumble through her veins, felt herself come alive again, in a way she hadn't been since those weeks in Edinburgh over a year since. She lowered the hand holding her paintbrush, touching her fingertips to her skirts, and glanced down. The brush had left a little spot of paint on the material at the opening which gave access to her pocket.

The sunflower seeds had been planted, bloomed and withered. It had felt like the end of something. The luckenbooth brooch was still in the quilted roll of material in her pocket. She had sewn an extra little pouch for it, to protect it from being scratched by her pins.

Two hearts entwined, surmounted by a crown. Small and dainty and beautifully wrought in silver.

She looked up again: and the grey eyes and the green eyes met.

… to be concluded in
On the Wings of the Storm

Author's Note

John Roy Stuart and Duncan Forbes of Culloden were real people. Although I have imagined and assigned to them specific fictional roles in my *Storm over Scotland* series, including giving John Roy a fictional family, their relative political positions, loyalties and commitment are accurate. Both men played crucial roles in the history of the '45, John Roy passionately in favour of the restoration of the House of Stuart, Duncan Forbes of Culloden passionately opposed. If you would like to read more about the parts they played in those turbulent times, I researched and wrote up their real stories in *Bare-Arsed Banditti: The Men of the '45.*

In the Scottish style, Duncan Forbes of Culloden, Lord President of the Court of Session, was often known simply as *Culloden*, the name of his estate near Inverness, his ancestral acres. This custom continues in farming communities in Scotland to this day.

It's not entirely an accident of history that the Battle of Culloden in April 1746 was fought where it was. It's certainly an irony of history that the name of Duncan Forbes should be forever associated with this mythic and bloody last battle, the last pitched battle fought on British soil, and its brutal aftermath. Forbes could be ruthless in pursuit of his ambitions for Scotland but he believed in showing mercy too. When he protested to the Duke of Cumberland about the cruelties which followed Culloden, Cumberland dismissed him as 'that old woman who spoke to me of humanity.'

Provost John Coutts was also a real person, as was James

Nicholson, the coffee-house keeper in Leith, and Professor Alexander Monro. A banyan was a comfortable and elegant dressing gown, apparently much favoured by intellectual men. If you were relaxing at home wearing one, you might also have called it your dishabilly, pronounced dis-habilly. This comes from the French word *déshabille*, meaning undressed.

There is more information about the perpetual servitude endured by Scotland's coal miners and the position of enslaved African people in Scotland on the websites of the National Records of Scotland and the National Mining Museum.

The library of the Royal College of Surgeons of Edinburgh still has the accounts and receipts relevant to the construction of the bagnio built in the early 18th century. This includes 'a place for the eagle to stand.'

Readers not familiar with the Scots tongue might like to know that gey meaning very is pronounced with a hard g. I think the Scots words I've used are understandable in context. A very useful resource is the Scots Dictionary Online.

Menzies should be pronounced in the Scottish way – Ming-is. Liddell is pronounced Lidl, like the modern supermarket chain, ie NOT with the stress on the second syllable.

My Bible for grammar, punctuation, accepted usage and more is New Hart's Rules: The Handbook of Style for Writers and Editors. (Oxford University Press)

I've used –ize rather than –ise endings, as I was taught at Garscadden Primary School in Glasgow back in the day, because 18th century people favoured those endings – as does the modern Concise Oxford Dictionary – and because I have a penchant for the elegant strokes of the letter z.

Historical Note

Scotland and England waged war with one another for centuries. As an independent sovereign state the ancient kingdom of Scotland always resisted England's attempts to conquer it, referring to her southern neighbours as the Auld Enemy. England found its northern neighbours troublesome in their own right and because of Scotland's long-standing alliance with France, that country and England being equally long-standing rivals in an ongoing European power struggle.

More peaceful ways of resolving the conflict were tried, in inter-marriage between the royal houses of both countries. The resulting family relationships meant that when Elizabeth I of England died childless in 1603, the only possible successor was James VI of Scotland.

He became then also James I of England, bringing the Scottish House of Stuart to the British throne and ushering in the Jacobean age. This term applies also to the style of the period and derives from Jacobus, Latin for James, the name of many of the Stuart kings. From the same root, Jacobite refers to the supporters of the House of Stuart.

James VI and I was succeeded by his son Charles I, whose arguments with parliament led to civil war and his own execution. His son Charles II was restored to the throne in 1666 after the death of Oliver Cromwell. Father of a number of illegitimate children but with no legal heirs, Charles II was succeeded by his brother James.

James VII and II was a devout Catholic, which made him unpopular among many of his overwhelmingly Protestant subjects. Like his father Charles I, he believed in the Divine Right of Kings, that his position was God-given and therefore not to be questioned by mere mortals. His reluctance to rule with parliament as a constitutional monarch proved to be an even more insurmountable obstacle to his continuing to wear the crown of the United Kingdom.

In 1688, in what became known to its supporters as the Glorious Revolution, James was deposed from the British throne and forced to go into exile with his wife Mary of Modena and their young son, also James.

Those who deposed James offered the throne to his daughter Mary and her husband, the Protestant William of Orange. When they died without issue, Mary's sister Anne succeeded, ruling from 1702-14. The last Stuart to wear the British crown gave birth to seventeen children but none survived her.

Anne's death also fulfilled a prophecy made by James V, father of Mary, Queen of Scots. She was born six days before he died after the English defeated the Scots at the Battle of Solway Moss. Told of his daughter's birth, he remarked: 'It cam wi' a lass, and it'll gang wi' a lass.' He meant the Scottish crown, which came to the Stewarts through Marjorie, the daughter of Robert the Bruce. She married Walter, the High Steward of Scotland, and their son was Robert II, the first Stewart monarch of Scotland.

Having spent much of her life in France, it was Mary, Queen of Scots who changed the spelling of Stewart to Stuart, more easily pronounceable in French.

On Anne's death, her younger half-brother – King James VIII and III to his supporters and the Old Pretender to his opponents, might have been invited back. However, James could not bring himself to renounce his Catholic faith or his belief in Divine Right. A German cousin several times removed, safely Protestant and willing to reign with parliament, was offered the throne instead. The Elector of Hanover became George I and founder of today's House of Windsor.

There were several attempts to win the throne back for the Stuarts, most significantly in 1715 and 1745. In 1707, during the reign of Queen Anne, the parliaments of England and Scotland united, putting an end to Scotland's status as an ancient and independent European country.

There was huge opposition to this move within Scotland, rioting in the streets and impassioned speeches within the Scottish parliament. With a few honourable exceptions, English bribes to other members of that parliament ensured they voted in favour of the Act of Union. On the day it came into force the bells of St Giles, the High Kirk of Edinburgh, played a tune called *Why am I so sad on my wedding day?*

This mourning for the loss of nationhood was hugely significant in attracting men and women to the Jacobite Cause. The Stuarts being the old Scottish royal house, there was also a deep-seated personal loyalty to them. While some Scots did well out of Scotland becoming North Britain, others felt themselves over-taxed, over-governed and under-represented.

The '15 ended inconclusively at the Battle of Sherrifmuir, leaving 'German Geordie' once more safe on his throne. Discontent continued to simmer, boiling over in the short-lived rising of 1719, (which saw the blowing-up of Eilean Donan Castle,) Edinburgh's Porteous Riot and Glasgow's malt-tax riots. All of this fed into support for the Jacobite Cause.

In 1588, Philip II of Catholic Spain launched a fleet of warships against Protestant England with the aim of deposing Elizabeth I and restoring Catholicism. The Spanish Armada came to grief because of a storm which blew its 130 ships off course, forcing them up the east coast of Britain and right round the north and west coasts of Scotland. One, the *San Juan de Sicilia,* ended up in Mull in the Hebrides, where it blew up under mysterious circumstances. The wreckage lies at the bottom of Tobermory Bay.

The Protestant Wind blew several more times, including in early 1744. A letter in the National Archives at Kew in west London, in French, mentions the delays to mail and reports two storms scattering the French fleet with debris coming ashore. All the convents close to the coast were full of survivors, being cared for by the nuns. At least ten ships sank, some going down with all hands. Footnotes to history.

About the Author

A born storyteller, Maggie Craig is the acclaimed Scottish author of the ground-breaking *Damn' Rebel Bitches: The Women of the 45* and several page-turning historical novels set in Edinburgh and her hometown of Glasgow. She comes from a family where writing is considered an entirely normal thing to do and numbers among her forbears Robert Tannahill, the weaver-poet of Paisley. She has two grown-up children and a lovely daughter-in-law – the two grown up children are also lovely! She lives in the north of Scotland with her Welsh husband.

When she's not writing, she loves to read, take photographs, listen to music and drink a good, strong cup of Indian tea.

She has served two terms on the committee of the Society of Authors in Scotland and is a regular and popular speaker around Scotland's libraries and book festivals.

Visit her website at www.maggiecraig.co.uk or follow her on Twitter.

All Books by Maggie Craig

Find these titles in online and High Street bookshops
with more information on Maggie's website:

www.maggiecraig.co.uk

Non-fiction

Damn' Rebel Bitches: The Women of the '45
Bare-Arsed Banditti: The Men of the '45
Footsteps on the Stairs: Tales from Duff House
When the Clyde Ran Red
Henrietta Tayler: Scottish Historian and First World War Nurse
One Week in April: The Scottish Radical Rising of 1820

Historical Novels

One Sweet Moment
Gathering Storm (Storm over Scotland Book 1)
Dance to the Storm (Storm over Scotland Book 2)
Storm Tossed Moon (Storm over Scotland Book 3)

Glasgow & Clydebank Novels

The River Flows On
When the Lights Come on Again
The Stationmaster's Daughter
The Bird Flies High
A Star to Steer By
The Dancing Days

Contributor to:

Twisted Sisters: Women, Crime and Deviance in Scotland 1400
&
The Biographical Dictionary of Scottish Women

Printed in Great Britain
by Amazon

54594432R00148